LANDSCAPE WITH CORPSE

When Philipa Lowe and Oliver Simpson attend a week's landscape painting course at an Adult Residential College they feel out of place at first, as the rest of the group are all experienced artists. However, friendly encouragement prevails and there is no more than a hint that past animosities might intrude. When one of the group is killed, suspicion falls on Elise Harcourt, a young woman with whom Philipa has become friendly. The more Philipa tries to help her the more this naïve young lady presents herself to the police as the obvious culprit...

LANDSCAPE WITH CORPSE

LANDSCAPE WITH CORPSE

by
Roger Ormerod

Magna Large Print Books
Long Preston, North Yorkshire,
England.

British Library Cataloguing in Publication Data.

Ormerod, Roger
  Landscape with corpse.

  A catalogue record for this book is
  available from the British Library

  ISBN 0-7505-1218-0

First published in Great Britain by Constable & Company
Ltd., 1996

Cover illustration by arrangement with Last Resort Picture
Library

The right of Roger Ormerod to be identified as the author
of this work has been asserted by him in accordance with
the Copyright, Designs and Patents Act, 1988

Published in Large Print 1998 by arrangement with Constable
Publishers Ltd.

Magna Large Print is an imprint of F
Library Magna Books Ltd.
Printed and bound in Great Britain by
T.J. International Ltd., Cornwall, PL28 8RW.

1

On the Thursday before our special week, the secretary phoned from the college. At once I experienced a fall in spirits, believing that there had been a mistake, and our room was not to be available. But no—it was not that.

'Is that Mrs Simpson?' she asked.

'Well...yes.' I was still getting used to it, still thinking of myself as Philipa Lowe. But Oliver and I were now married.

She went on to say, 'I've been looking at a map, and you're the only ones who wouldn't have to make too much of a detour.'

By this time Oliver was at my right shoulder, and I was holding the phone away from my ear in order to save having to repeat it all, afterwards.

'A detour for what?' I asked.

'Well...it's like this. We have a young lady—one of our regulars on your course—who lives at Leominster, and whose car has broken down. Or rather, she's crashed it, so it's going to be off the road quite a while. And it would be very difficult for her to get here with all her painting stuff.

7

You know how it is—cross-country—and on a Sunday, too.'

'I can imagine,' I assured her. 'Of course we can pick her up, if that's what you mean. If you'll just give me her phone number, I'll contact her.'

This she did. 'Her name's Jennifer Crane. I can't tell you how pleased I am. We'd miss her if she couldn't come.'

I hung up. Oliver and I had a careful look at our map, and it would be more than a small detour from our planned route. But we could leave at what time we wished, and return to Hawthorne Cottage at the end of the week—and that would be it. No trouble at all, really.

I dialled the number, and was somewhat surprised to get a short, impatient 'Yes?' from the woman at the other end.

'I understand,' I said placidly, 'that you're in need of a lift to Bryngowan Manor, on Sunday.'

'Oh yes...yes.' What a change in tone! I wondered what she had been expecting, but she went on brightly, 'I really am stuck. If you *would* be good enough... I hope you'll have room. I've got a great load of stuff.'

'I'm sure we'll cope.' The boot of my BMW is huge. 'And there'll be only the two of us. But I don't know Leominster. Where can we pick you up?'

There was a pause as she thought about it. Then, 'The car park's the best, and as it'll be a Sunday it will be almost empty. I'll be there, with my things at...what time would suit you?'

'How far is it from Leominster to Bryngowan?'

'Oh...around a hundred miles. A hundred and fifteen, to be more exact. I've driven it so often that I know it inside out, and I usually do it in a little under two hours.'

'Hmm!' I said. 'Yes.'

Between Leominster and the Welsh coast there would be a tricky barrier of mountains and winding roads to negotiate. If she'd done that run in 'a little under two hours', and she normally drove like that, it was no wonder she had crashed her car. I didn't say so.

'Shall we give ourselves two and a half hours?' I suggested. 'The car park at three. How's that?'

'That'll be just great,' she told me. 'What direction will you be coming from?'

'What...oh, I see. From the north.'

'That's fine. The car park's that side of town. Next to the fire station. You can't miss it.'

'I'll try not to,' I assured her. 'Three o'clock, then, at the car park. But...if

9

you've got a load of stuff...how'll you get it there?'

'Oh—I expect I can get Paul to give me a lift that far.' And strangely she gave what sounded like a short and bitter laugh. 'See you there. And thank you. 'Bye for now.'

She rang off. I stood looking at Oliver as I replaced the phone. He raised one eyebrow. This was his questioning expression.

'Well?' I asked. 'Something wrong?'

'I don't know.' He shook his head. I could tell he wasn't happy about it.

I said, 'I forgot to tell her how she'll recognize us.'

'No problem there, surely.'

'All the same...'

I dialled the number again. The phone was snatched up at the first ting. 'For Chrissake, Paul—'

'It's me again,' I cut in calmly. 'I forgot to tell you the car's a BMW 525. Blue.'

She was flustered. 'Oh...yes...thank you. Silly of me not to ask. But it'll be almost deserted in the car park. 'Bye. See you there.'

The phone clicked dead. Slowly, I replaced it. 'I hope she's on time.'

'Phil,' he said. 'If you were the one asking for a lift, would you be late?'

'Of course not. But there seemed to be some uncertainty about this Paul person.'

'All the same...' He shrugged.

Two more days to get through, then away, and hopefully to return to a changed approach lane to our cottage. That had been the promise. My solicitor and friend, Harvey Remington, had untangled a number of legal knots, and pulled a few of the resulting strings, in order to get the problem cleared up during our week of absence. He had arranged everything, even, you could say, our wedding.

About three months before, Harvey had asked us to call on him, and then indulged in one of his benevolent lectures. Why, he asked, were we not married? Then he answered it himself. 'Because of Oliver's out-dated scruples about living on your money, Philipa, when he's got only a paltry police disability pension.'

He was not aware that Oliver's hesitation was really based on his fear that, in due course, he was going to lose the use of his right arm. Simply, he was reluctant to become a liability. Ridiculous!

'Go on, Harvey,' I said.

He then explained, mainly aiming his remarks at Oliver, how much more stable and secure we would feel as man and wife, unaware that we were both, already, feeling very comfortably stable.

Nevertheless, we allowed ourselves to be persuaded, and we were married. Register

Office. Harvey gave me away, as he had every right to do, having shared with my father my upbringing, my mother having died when I was very young.

But my father had retired as Chief Superintendent Lowe, and had hoped that I would become a policewoman, whereas Harvey would have liked to see me as a barrister. At the age of ten I could have given arrest warnings and taken statements, and I knew the meaning of *sine die* and *sub judice* long before I tackled Latin at my boarding school. Yes—Harvey had every right to give me away. I never for one moment forget the multitude of debts that I owe to Harvey.

It was on the subject of the approach lane to Hawthorne Cottage that he surpassed himself. The cottage is three quarters of a mile along a side lane off the main road from Penley, the rest of the lane being decrepit, and never used because it goes nowhere. Our three quarters of a mile was, however, becoming almost impossible to negotiate in wet weather.

Yet, the cost of resurfacing such a length of lane was way beyond our resources.

It was here that Harvey demonstrated his abilities. He gave lunch (half a dozen times, I understand) at his club to the Borough Surveyor, and managed to persuade him that the complete lane needed clearing and resurfacing, in fact that there was a legal requirement for that to be done, because it still appeared on the official map. And then—sweetening the pill—he suggested that the sole residents in that lane (Oliver and I) might agree to no more than the first three quarters of a mile being resurfaced. He offered this as a concession, and as such it was eventually agreed.

Thus, we were going to get a new lane (and might then describe it as our drive) without having to trouble my bank manager at all.

Yet there was one snag. There always has to be a snag. This was that the contractors needed a clear run at the job for a full week. We would therefore be firmly shut in, or shut out, for that period.

'Go away for a week,' suggested Harvey, as though that wasn't what he'd been planning all along. A week in June—and the details laid on, too.

It was Oliver's right arm that provided the answer. My own left shoulder, though having been somewhat peppered by shotgun pellets, now hardly gave me any pain. But Oliver's right arm had been much more severely treated, in that it had taken the full blast of a shotgun. Even now—three years after that event—he was often in pain, and though he could drive the BMW, there being an auto gearbox and power-assisted steering, I had to watch his face for signs of strain, and then persuade him to swap seats.

But Harvey had background plans for this aspect, too, fixing up an appointment with our physiotherapist, Lionel Parradine, who had been advising both of us. My arm could be left to sort itself out, but Parradine had ideas for Oliver's right arm.

'Manipulative muscles,' he said. 'Dexterity.'

There were, it seemed, muscles that Oliver had not been using often enough. His fingers, hand and wrist.

'So what do you suggest?' I asked him. We were willing to try anything, Oliver and I.

'What about embroidery?' Parradine suggested to Oliver, with a gentle smile.

'Not on your life.'

'Tapestry?'

Oliver hesitated. Then he shook his head. 'Not for me.'

'Painting?'

'The cottage has only recently been done over,' I told him.

'No, not that. Art. That sort of painting.'

'What!' Oliver glanced at me. 'I couldn't even draw a straight line.'

Harvey beamed. He was not to be thwarted. It was his scheme, and he was

14

determined to carry it through. 'Not many people can,' he said encouragingly. 'And in any event, you just paint what you see, and if it finishes up as something unrecognizable, you call it an abstract.'

So this was why we were taking a week's break at Bryngowan Manor Adult Residential College. Landscape painting. Although Harvey denied it, I knew he had arranged this long before, otherwise it would have been strange that a double room should have been available at such short notice—and for the very same week during which our portion of the lane was to be resurfaced. Such a coincidence! And Harvey showed no sign of shame at his crafty manipulation.

'Painting!' grumbled Oliver, though he could make no complaint that it was a woman's pursuit, there being many more famous male artists than female. Strange, really, that fact, as I understand that there are many more colour-blind men than women—something like six per cent men to one half per cent women.

So...all we needed now was painting equipment. For myself—watercolours. I would have to try to recall the tricks I had once known at school. I might need a little practice, though, before we ventured into the company of no doubt experienced, if amateur, painters. But...

What for Oliver? Watercolours, I felt, would hardly do anything to help his dexterity and manipulation, as there's not much effort required to run a brush across a sheet of paper. The same applied to acrylics and oils.

It was obvious that professional advice should be sought, and accordingly we visited Tom Carter's little shop in Penley. Here, he sold everything you could possibly need in the art line, would mount and frame anything you thought you had done well, and he had experience in every conceivable method of producing a result that could reasonably be designated as art, from etchings to sculpture. And I had been at junior school with Tom.

So that was where we went.

I hadn't spoken to him for years, but he knew me at once. 'Phillie! How splendid to see you. How can I help you?'

He took us into his workroom at the back, where he was engaged in cutting a mask. Not as easy as it sounds. I explained our difficulty, in that I was rather out of touch with available art materials. As to my personal requirements—that question was soon covered. Half a dozen brushes, from a one inch flat to a round number two, a dozen or so tubes of watercolour paint (two blues, two reds, two yellows, a Payne's grey and black, two browns, and two greens) and an earthenware palette in which to do the mixing. And (important, this was) three sheets of Bockingford 250 watercolour paper. This is thick enough not to buckle when it's wet, and would be enough for twelve paintings, ten by fourteen inches, the ideal shape. Now, with memories of my past youth flooding back, I could barely wait to begin covering that pristine surface with colour. I had to drag my mind from this aspect of it, and recall the most important reason for this expedition, Oliver's disability. I explained to Tom that we were going away for a week's landscape painting course, and what had brought it about, and asked him to suggest something for Oliver.

He beamed, having been a little ahead of me. 'Pastels,' he said. 'No question about it. They're like soft chalks, and you can use different pressures for different effects. And there's a certain amount of drag. But no messing about with having to mix the colours before you start. They *are* the colours, but you can't mix 'em too easily, so you have to have a different pastel for each different colour, and all the shades of it. And it's a bit messy. Your fingers get covered with powder. But it's so direct. You see what you're getting straight away.'

Oliver gave me a weak grin. 'I'd better

17

have one of each, then.'

Tom laughed. 'There's over a hundred and eighty in the complete set, and they're a bit pricey. It'd come to around £170. But you don't need all those. Tell you what. You go and have a coffee at Pattie's Caff, and I'll make up a set of around forty. And you'd better have a few hard pastels. They come in pencil form. Those're for fine lines. And I'll throw in a can of fixative spray.'

'What's that for?' Oliver was suspicious. He was beginning to wonder whether he'd committed himself to something way beyond his capabilities.

Tom explained. 'They're only refined chalks, and you do the paintings on special paper—but it smudges easily. So you spray it, when the picture's finished, with a light, clear varnish—to fix it. I'll have some paper ready when you get back, and you have a go—and see how you fancy pastels. Now...you pop along to Pattie's while I get all your stuff together.'

So we went along to Pattie's place, where I was known, and, business being slack at that time of day, she sat with us, to catch up on our news. Pattie was Tom's sister, and she'd been one class ahead of me in junior school. I introduced Oliver.

'My husband, Oliver.'

'Ooh! Lucky you...'

Oliver grinned. He'd encountered this

before. 'Yes,' he said, 'I count myself as lucky.' Very diplomatic, is Oliver.

'I'm Mrs Simpson now,' I told her.

'Simpson? Oliver Simpson? I remember that name. You're a copper.'

'Not now.' Oliver doesn't like to be reminded of that shotgun episode.

'We're going on a week's painting course,' I told her, changing the subject. 'Your brother's fixing us up with the necessary equipment.'

'Ha! You want to watch our Tom. He'll cheat you blind,' she said affectionately.

'We'll watch out for it,' I assured her.

We went for a walk around the little patch of Parkland that Penley boasts, then back to the art shop. Tom had got it all ready for us, my brushes and tubes of colours and the palette, and my sheets of Bockingford 250, which he'd cut into ten by fourteens for me. And Oliver's pastel equipment. There was a flat box, partitioned for the pastels. 'To save 'em nudging each other,' Tom explained. There was a spray-can of fixative and two pads of paper, one dark shades, one lighter, and offering half a dozen tints each. As these pads were backed with heavy cardboard, they could be used on a lap, from a low stool.

Tom had found a cut-off of pastel paper, and handed Oliver a red and a blue pastel.

19

'Just scribble,' he said, and Oliver did. 'That's it,' said Tom.

Oliver stared morosely at the result, then grinned at me.

'Wear an old pair of trousers,' Tom advised, 'because you'll get 'em all covered with pastel powder.'

'Humph!' said Oliver.

We thanked him. I was sure he charged us wholesale prices, and thus made no profit from it, but I wasn't going to argue. You can lose friends like that. Then we walked back to the car, each carrying our own equipment. There had been no need to worry about easels and stools, our information being that these would be supplied by the college.

It now being lunch time, we ate a quick meal and I said we ought to get the feel of our respective media. So why not spend the afternoon having a go with our colours? Oliver's need was greater than mine, as I had at least painted in watercolours, if quite a while back, whereas Oliver's experience ended with his ball-point pen.

I sat him down by the garden hedge, his back to the lane, and said, 'Paint that.'

'Paint what?'

'The cottage.'

'I can't do that.'

'Of course you can. You just put on to paper what you see.'

'Hmph!' he said.

But he tried. His verticals were sloping and his horizontals wandered all over the place. What resulted was a representation of a broken-down garden shed. He got to his feet and we stood and looked at it, face up now on his stool. Then we fell into each other's arms and laughed our heads off.

'It doesn't matter,' I gasped at last. 'It's a picture. Your first picture, Oliver.'

'Hmm!' He was abruptly pensive. 'I'll make a right fool of myself,' he said miserably.

'No you won't. It's a college. They're supposed to teach you. And what the devil does it matter, anyway? It's going to be a very interesting week.'

But he wasn't happy about it.

2

The BMW is an easy car to drive; you can control it with one hand on the wheel, if necessary. Oliver liked to do as much driving as possible, so we decided that he would drive us to Leominster, and I would take over for Jennifer's 115 miles to Bryngowan, as I anticipated a multitude of tight corners over the mountains, which

Oliver would find troublesome. Therefore, after an early lunch, we were on the road at two o'clock, with Oliver at the wheel. There was plenty of time.

The route was straightforward, once we had picked up the road from Shrewsbury. Oliver held the car at a steady fifty, and it was ten minutes to three when we turned into the car park. And clearly, there she was, our Jennifer, decorously standing amongst a scattering of canvas hold-alls, boxes and packages.

Beside her was a white Citroën and a tall, dark man. At the sight of a blue BMW arriving, he gave her a quick peck on the cheek, slipped into the Citroën and drove rapidly past us, with not a sideways glance, his tyres protesting. This, I guessed, would be the Paul she had mentioned.

We drew to a halt. Oliver slid out from behind the wheel, smiling, then we offered formal handshakes, which were no more than the touching of palms.

'So we're both on time,' I remarked. 'Shall we get your stuff inside?'

She shrugged. 'Might as well.' It didn't seem that she was in a good mood.

Her attention was for Oliver. Her smile was for him. I guessed that she would be in her mid-twenties, a slim woman, poised and smart, and wearing an embroidered bolero over a white silk shirt. She was fully aware of the impact she made, casually aware. She shook her head, and a cascade of natural blond hair swung with it, then settled like a swarm of pigeons disturbed from a scattering of bread. Her long and slim legs were clothed in black, tight leggings, which gave the impression, literally, that there was nothing but flesh beneath.

I produced my second best smile. 'I'm Philipa, and this is my husband, Oliver.' It was better to present the set-up right at the beginning, I thought. 'And you'll be Jennifer, no doubt.'

She flashed a look at Oliver that said it all. It was the bright, seeking eye of the predator.

'It's nice to meet you both,' she said. 'And I can't say how grateful I am for helping me out. My friends call me Jennie.'

I had the impression that it was an honour to be included in her list of friends. 'No trouble,' I said, and smiled my own specially empty smile to underline it. 'And we'll call you Jennie.'

By this time Oliver had the boot open. We managed to fit in Jennie's luggage, and there was a spare seat in the rear, which itself soon became piled high.

'I think that's the lot,' she said, nodding.

'You're sure?' I asked, not meaning it in any sarcastic manner.

23

But she darted at me a brisk glance of rejection. 'I've done it often enough not to forget a thing,' she assured me, nodding. 'There are six of these week-long courses every year. I know it inside-out.'

'Such as the route, I assume,' I said. 'So you'll be able to direct us?'

'Oh yes. Of course. So I suppose I'd better sit in the front?' She raised her eyebrows at me, cocking her head.

'It would be better,' I agreed placidly.

She had seen Oliver driving into the car park, and clearly therefore expected him to be driving out. So I held open the front passenger's door, as Oliver slammed his rear one, and she was stuck with me, like it or not.

I fastened my seat belt and started the engine.

'It'll be Brecon, and then on to Llandovery,' she told me, a faint sullen tone in her voice. 'But after that you'll find it a bit tricky.'

She meant, I realized, the barrier presented by the Cambrian Mountains.

I nodded. She told me to turn left out of the car park and pick up the Brecon road at the traffic lights. It was signposted.

I drove. Jennie was restless. She kept giving me instructions just after I had made my own decisions. I simply nodded. After a while, she refrained from telling me

24

that I could have got past some wagon or other, if I'd put my foot down. Blandly, I ignored all such advice. At one time, I had had instruction from a rally driver.

But eventually, she relaxed. 'Is this your first time?' she asked.

'At the college?'

'Well...yes. But I meant on this painting course.'

'Oh yes. To both.'

'What do you do? I mean—what medium?'

I shot her a quick glance. 'Well...Oliver's pastels, and I'm watercolours.'

She gave this some consideration, more than I'd have thought it deserved. Then at last she said, 'I'm acrylics. I used to do watercolours, but I switched over. Now I much prefer acrylics. Very versatile, they are. You can over-paint with acrylics, which can get awfully messy with watercolours.'

'Yes,' I agreed. 'You're right there. But it's the transparency of watercolours that attracts me.'

'Yes,' she conceded. 'I do see that. If you can do it.' She sounded rather doubtful about my abilities.

Then she was silent for a few miles, apart from her odd comments such as, 'Take the right fork here.' Or, 'Second turn-off at the island.' Useful comments, which I appreciated.

I had set the trip indicator on the dash before we left Leominster, and noted the time on the clock, so that when she commented, with forty miles coming up, that we were running a bit late, I was able to say, with a certain amount of confidence, 'We'll make it by five-thirty. That's the clocking-in time, it said in the brochure.'

'But...get there early, and you can grab one of the better parking spaces. Tight corner coming up.'

'In what way better?' I asked, taking it smoothly.

'Oh...closer to Reception. So it's not so far to have to carry all your painting stuff and what not.'

Behind me, Oliver cleared his throat. 'A distinct advantage,' he declared.

She ignored that. 'You're going to enjoy it,' she assured me. 'It's like a top-class hotel.' So she was talking about the place, not the painting. 'The food's very good,' she went on, 'and they've got their own private bar.'

And of course Oliver had to comment again, 'A distinct advantage.'

Jennie ignored that, too. 'Have you got a double room?' she asked me.

'Well...naturally.'

'Lucky you. They're quite swish.'

'Swish?'

26

She touched my arm, making a point. 'Your own bathroom and shower, and loads of room. But you really need a partner, to help fill the bed. Which, of course, you've got.'

I allowed a short time to elapse, dreading that Oliver would put in his comment again. Then, when he remained silent—though I got a glimpse of his grin in the rear-view mirror—I went on, 'So you've tried one yourself?'

She laughed. 'Room or partner?'

'I was,' I told her, 'thinking of both. Together,' I added, in case she'd missed my point.

'Oh yes,' she agreed. 'That.'

I waited while a couple of miles drifted beneath the wheels. We were now climbing, and the corners were becoming more tricky.

'So it's going to be a bit boring for you,' I suggested, referring to her lack of a partner and a double room.

'Oh no. Not at all.' Then she hesitated, deciding how far to take it. 'There're usually eight or so in our group, and a couple of other courses going on at the same time. So you get to meet some very interesting people. You'll see.'

I refrained from mentioning that I'd brought my own interesting person.

Then we took the last of the tricky

bends, and had reached the peak. We came down from the mountains with the sun declining almost directly ahead. The view was breathtaking.

Jennie appeared not to be interested in the view, which was strange for an artist. 'You'll like him,' she said confidently. 'Everybody likes him.'

'Who?' I seemed to have missed something whilst I was admiring the view.

'Geoff Davies. He's our tutor. Oh...he's very good. His tutoring and his own work. A palette knife man, he is. Spreads it on like butter. Tricky, that is. But you'll like him.'

I had the impression, by that time, that Jennie had no difficulty in distributing her affections. Perhaps she had a kindly nature, and felt she ought to spread her favours between all the men surrounding her at any given time. And it was clear that they did surround her. She expected it. Invited it.

'There it is,' she said suddenly. 'Look.'

We had just climbed a tortuous hill and breasted the rise. A magnificent vista confronted us, with Cardigan Bay fading into the misty distance. On a slope, and low in the valley, was an imposing building, copper-red in this lowered sunlight, an isolated mansion.

It looked comfortably placid, and below it, at the foot of a slope that led down to the slim glint of a river, was a small township, which spread its growth to nudge the sea.

'It's lovely,' I said softly, to myself. 'Don't you think it's lovely, Oliver?'

'I can't see it too well from back here,' he complained. 'But you can't deny that there's plenty of landscape just waiting to be painted.'

'And the harbour,' said Jennie with enthusiasm. 'It used to be a fishing village, and the wharfs are still there. Plenty of sailing boats still around, as well. That's where I like to sit myself down—the harbour. Sit there and paint. Where I always go.'

'Ah yes—' I began, but she interrupted.

'There's no need to drive all the way down to the town. If you take the next turn right, you'll find it takes you straight past the college drive.'

I did as she suggested, but I eased the car to a slower speed, as I still had something to ask her, and the asking time was running out. 'Do you mean that we all wander off on our own?'

If that were the case, we might as well have stayed at home, and struggled along as well as we could.

But Jennie dispelled that impression. 'Oh no! It's not like that. Not at all. We all decide where we're going to settle down with our easels and stools and what not, and Geoff—oh, he's lovely—he comes round to all of us, from time to time, and helps, suggests, gives you tips. Take it from me, you'll like him, and you're going to do fine.'

'Ah!' I said, nodding.

'The entrance is on the left.'

'I see it.'

We swept up the long drive between lines of trees, until a bend revealed the building. It was a grand, stone-built house, with stone balconies and balustrades outside the upstairs mullioned windows. We had passed the gravelled area designated Parking. Which Jennie had completely ignored. She was peering ahead, anxiously.

'Keep going,' she said. 'Along the front.'

This had been the terrace in the grand days of the mansion, thirty yards across, and with the stone pillars and balustrades of the balconies repeated at its edge. Fanned steps ran down grandly to a sloping lawn, with trees massed beyond it.

'There!' she cried. 'There's a space.'

I would not have seen it as a space, but she seemed confident. Already, about twenty cars were parked there, and were being unloaded. I stopped the car as Jennie slid out and walked ahead to locate a space, and then, with much gesticulation and a lot of left-hand-downs and easy-nows, she guided me in.

'There,' she said, opening the door again to peer in. 'Didn't I tell you! The office is just round the corner of the main building.'

She was in a flutter of excitement. Clearly, she thoroughly enjoyed these breaks at Bryngowan, though I wasn't certain whether her enjoyment arose entirely from her expectancy of what painting masterpieces she might produce.

She was well known, obviously. Several people called out to her.

'Where's your Porsche, Jennie?' shouted one of the men.

So it was a Porsche she had crashed. She wandered off to explain that two finite objects cannot be in the same place at the same time.

From then onwards we needed no assistance. We took our luggage in, and found the reception desk.

'Ah yes,' said the young woman. 'Mr and Mrs Simpson, isn't it? I see you managed to get our Jennifer here all right.'

'No difficulty,' I assured her. 'The trip has been very pleasant.'

'Well—we've got you in the main house, overlooking the terrace. You go along the corridor, to your left from here, into the hall, and up the stairs. You can't miss it. You're in A4.'

'It's a beautiful place,' I said.

'It is, isn't it. Now...if you'll just look at the notice board behind you, you'll see all you need to know.'

We turned and looked. There were two other courses. Advanced German (Lecture Room 2 at 8.30) and Chinese Brush Painting (Lecture Room 3 at 8.30).

And... Landscape Painting—meet in the Glasshouse at 8.30.

Glasshouse? I hadn't noticed anything deserving that title. Perhaps it had been a greenhouse, when the place was built. Glasshouse now.

We found the hall, graceful and restful. The staircase angled up three walls. And there, facing us across a landing, was A4.

We stopped just inside the door, taking it all in. Carved oak was the motif. The bed could have been a four-poster in its youth, but now lacked its posts and canopy. A pity. That would have been a novel experience. The bathroom (I opened the door and popped my head in) contained both bath and shower—separate. When I went to the windows, to sample the view, I saw that it opened out as french windows, on to one of the balconies.

I ventured outside, and there was my BMW, right opposite, which I'd left unlocked for Jennie. Two cars away was parked a white Citroën.

She was there, reaching out her painting equipment and her luggage. Or at least, that was what she had been doing, but now another woman, somewhat older than Jennie, with touches of grey in her hair and wearing a bright flowered dress, was standing in front of her, looking straight into her eyes and waving a finger angrily beneath her nose. Suddenly, all activity around them was stilled.

Jennie stood still, smiling slightly, though that was obviously forced, as the other woman's voice rose in pitch and in volume.

'I might have guessed you'd be here, Jennie Crane. But I'm telling you something. Are you listening? Just start your funny games again, that's what I'm telling you, and I'll wipe that nasty smile right off your silly face. Do I make myself clear?'

It was not said quietly, nor lightly. There was fury in that voice, and just a hint of despair.

Jennie shrugged, pouted, and then looked round with a grimace of distaste. Then, having captured her audience, she said distinctly into the abrupt silence, 'If you think so much of him, Pam darling, you want to try showing him you do. Shall

I give you a few tips, Pam? Would that help?'

The finger wagged more frantically beneath Jennie's nose. Jennie's expression suddenly hardened. She was clearly fighting to maintain a certain amount of dignity, but an abrupt anger sent her voice into a higher and shriller tone. 'Will you stop waving that damned finger at me!'

'Finger! Finger! You'll get more than a finger...' And the hand closed into a fist.

Jennie's temper flared. 'Stop it!' Her voice was caught on a choke of fury. 'Stop it!'

Then she caught the wrist and flung it aside, twisting it in the same movement. The woman she had called Pam gave a cry of pain, and fell back, to stumble up the first of the steps into the hall. Then, both hands to her face now, she turned and ran up the remaining steps. It seemed she too had a room in the main house. I heard her feet thump up the stairs. Then...silence. No door on the landing opened; no door slammed in frustration and anger.

I looked at Oliver in appeal. He raised his eyebrows and said, 'It's not our affair, Phillie.'

Yet there was a hint of query in his voice; he knows my uncontrollable curiosity. There was silence outside. I shook my head, and quietly opened our door.

34

She was sitting on the top stair, rocking herself, holding her right wrist in her left hand.

'Please,' I said. 'May I help? I saw what happened...'

She turned her head to me. 'Paul went to get our key,' she said miserably. 'He's certainly taking his time.'

She assumed I knew who Paul was, but she couldn't know that I'd thought I had seen him, driving a white Citroën out of the car park at Leominster. Now I saw that her eyes were flooded with tears.

'Your wrist?' I asked.

She whispered, 'It hurts.'

'Then why don't you come into our room,' I said. 'And we'll take a look at it. My husband's got something that might help.'

Her instinct had been to rush to solitude, and then to weep. Already, her face was crumpled with misery, and tears now dripped from her chin.

'Please,' I repeated, and limply she allowed herself to be led inside A4.

Oliver said, 'Oh dear. You know, she could have sprained that wrist. We'd better take a look at it.'

This he delivered in the flat and unemotional voice of a true policeman. His calming voice. The tears became sniffles, and we led her inside the bathroom. Under the cold tap with her hand, and I gently manipulated her wrist. There was no cry of pain. Good. Not too bad, then. She lifted her ravaged face to me.

'Oliver,' I said, 'can you go and collect the rest of our luggage?'

He nodded, and turned to leave, then he paused. 'Ma'am,' he said, 'I've got some cream that'll do wonders to that wrist. Don't go away.' Then he slipped out of the door.

She must have realized that she'd done a very foolish thing, confronting Jennie in that manner, and so publicly. It had in no way eased her situation, whatever that was—though I could make a good guess—and I left her in peace while she washed her face.

When she came wandering into the bedroom, I said, 'I hope this won't affect your painting.' I was assuming she was in the painter's group, as she knew Jennie so well.

She looked morose. 'I'm a damned fool. Never think before I act.' She stared at her hand. 'And I'll feel a worse fool if I can't even hold a pastel.'

'That's what my husband is using. Oliver, his name is, and I'm Philipa. He's going to try his hand at pastels—and he's got a bit of a disability, too.'

'We ought to get together,' she said

36

morosely. But she hadn't missed his smile, and now produced a weak one of her own.

Then Oliver returned, his heavy suitcase under his left arm, my lighter one under his right. He dropped his case on to the bed, and had it open in a second, then fumbled round, and produced his tube of a special analgesic cream.

'This'll help,' he said with confidence. He knew intimately its effect.

I massaged some of it into Pam's wrist. It didn't work immediately, but nevertheless she flexed her fingers and rotated her wrist. It seemed flexible enough to me.

'Better?' I asked.

'A little.'

'It takes a few minutes to get going,' Oliver told her. Then, to me, he said, 'I'll just go and fetch the rest of our stuff.' And I nodded.

'Shall we bind it?' I asked her, as the door closed behind Oliver.

'Oh no! No.' She was adamant about that. 'It would show,' she added, and I understood. 'I think I'll be able to manage.' Her jaw was firm, and her lower lip thrust forward. She wasn't going to let Jennie even so much as guess that she could have inflicted any sort of disablement.

'We'll be seeing you, then,' I said. 'Eight-thirty in the Glasshouse, as they call it. The studio, I suppose?'

'Sort of, though we spend most of our time—weather permitting—outside. It's always left open, so that you can use it any time, if you want to. And you can leave all your painting stuff in there, because nobody'll touch it. Well...' She lifted her shoulders. 'There *was* one time...' She allowed that to tail away, a curious, sour smile on her lips.

'What was that, then?'

'Better left unsaid,' she assured me.

What an infuriating thing to say! 'What is?' I pressed her, but she merely said, evasively, 'They've got special lights in there, supposed to represent daylight.'

I knew then that she was not going to tell me. 'And are the lights as good?' I asked. 'As good as daylight.'

'I've never tried painting in there with them on. I don't think it's a good thing. Colour tones, you know.'

'But if you're painting from a colour photograph, say, the light would affect the painting and the picture in the same way, so it would work out right.'

'Geoff doesn't approve. Says it's sort of cheating, painting from photos.'

'What does cheating matter, as long as you finish with something that gives you pleasure to look at?'

'Geoff's a purist, and he's our tutor.'

38

She was relaxing now. I had deliberately kept her talking in order to calm her down before she had to face her husband again. Already, she presented a less harried face.

'And my husband is, too,' she added. 'A purist.'

'Is he?'

'Oh...yes. Indeed. Paul says—'

'Paul?' I interrupted. 'With the white Citroën?'

My mind was connecting it with the one I had seen in the car park at Leominster.

'Yes. That's our car. But...how did you know?'

I'd talked myself into a difficult situation, and had to fumble my way round it. 'Mrs... I'm sorry, I don't know your name.'

'It's Pam. Pam Wilton.'

'Well, Pam, you tell your husband, if he's such a purist, that Canaletto cheated.' That ought to distract her, I thought.

'*Did* he?' Her eyes were wide with disbelief.

'Oh yes. He used a kind of camera obscura in order to throw an image on to a new canvas, and simply drew in all that lovely perspective, then painted it all in afterwards. Cheated. But does it matter? So long as your finished picture gives someone pleasure to look at, what does cheating matter?'

'You're still talking about painting?' She

said it with a wry twist to her lips. 'But my husband—Paul—he cheats in a different way, and it gives me no pleasure at all. Him, yes. Me, no. One of these days I'm going to lose my temper, and kill him.'

I tried to laugh that off lightly. 'But you won't, you know. I doubt you could do it.'

'I'm strong enough.'

'But you wouldn't be able to screw yourself to the sticking place.'

'I think you could be right, there. Well...I'd better get to our room. We're right next door. I'll have to find out whether my precious spouse saw that nasty scene out there. And appreciated it.'

I followed her out on to the landing. 'As a warning?' I asked.

'Perhaps.' She opened her door—so Paul was back with their key—and went inside. Turned her head. 'And thank you for your help.'

Oliver came in a few seconds later. He had occupied himself by fetching up all our painting stuff, and had it piled outside. 'Is she all right?'

'Oh yes. So it seemed.' Then I told him, as exactly as I could remember, what had passed between Pam and me, so that he wouldn't say the wrong thing at the wrong time. 'She was mainly concerned that she might not be able to handle her pastels,' I explained. 'You two ought to get together, Oliver.'

He raised his eyebrows, thought about it, then nodded. 'Could be a good idea. In the meantime, the bar's open. Dinner's at seven-thirty this evening. Which gives us time—'

'I'd rather not, I think.'

'Oh? Not even a pre-dinner sherry?' He seemed concerned.

'It's not that. It's...oh, you'll only laugh at me.'

He shook his head. 'You know I wouldn't.'

'Well...it's just that I've got an uneasy feeling...disappointed, I suppose. Expecting a quiet and relaxing week, and already it's going all wrong. Oh damn it, Oliver—this Jennie and Pam Wilton business! It's going to get worse, not better. I can feel it.'

'Nonsense.'

'It's not—'

He put his good arm around my shoulder. 'It doesn't have to affect us, Phil. Now...come and have a sherry. We really ought to be sociable...and no, we're not going to cut our week short, just because you've got a feeling.'

'We could—'

'And how would dear Jennie get home?' he asked.

41

'She could always cadge a lift from Pam and Paul.'

He laughed. 'That's more like it, Phil. Your old self again.'

So we went down to look for the bar.

3

We found it simply by seeking out the source of the noise. It was a strange U-shape, with the serving counter at the curved end, and with cosy recesses tucked into corners. The three groups seemed naturally to gather together, former students recognizing each other, and for a few seconds I was at a loss. Then, in the far recesses, I spotted Jennie and Paul and Pam, not exactly together, but involved with a tight group, which seemed to be ours.

We stood there for a few seconds, undecided, until Oliver spotted a spare corner for me, while he edged his way to the counter for our drinks. It was therefore sheer chance that I found myself sitting next to our tutor, Geoff Davies, though I didn't at first realize this.

'Here she is now,' called out Pam, raising her arm and rotating her hand, to demonstrate her wrist's mobility.

The space I had on the settle was small, my companion seeming to loom over me. He half raised himself in a polite gesture, as we shook hands.

'I'm your tutor, Geoff Davies,' he told me, 'and you must be Philipa Simpson. Your husband, Oliver, that's the big chap getting your drinks, I assume?'

'Yes,' I said. 'That's him.'

Oliver was now hovering with full glasses in his hands. I could detect no space for him, and there is a lot of Oliver.

I reached out to take the two glasses from him, for safety's sake, and Geoff called out above the noise, 'Shove along a bit, Philip. And Martin, you don't need two chairs.'

Magically, a space appeared beside me, and Oliver lowered himself into it, making grimacing expressions of apology.

'Welcome to Bryngowan Manor,' said Geoff formally.

He seemed to me to be a cheerful man, somewhat lanky, with bright grey eyes and brown hair. Early thirties, I guessed. I wondered whether this could be a full-time job for him, tutoring art courses, but I wouldn't have thought there could be enough of them, and our group seemed to be quite small, compared with the others. Yet he conveyed all the recognized

43

attributes of an artist, the movements of his hands as he spoke, and the casual but all-over assessment to which he seemed to be treating me. He could go away from there and paint my portrait from memory, no doubt. Or even a nude study.

'We do our introductions after dinner,' he told me. 'In the Glasshouse. That's our studio. But there are only eight of us, nine with me, and the rest of our group are all old-stagers here. It's just like a friendly get-together.'

Friendly? So far I had seen only aggression. But the general atmosphere amongst us was warm, and when the others were now identified to me, they looked friendly enough.

Pam Wilton and her husband, Paul, I already knew, though Paul only by sight, and that distant. And yes, we had met Jennie, I told Geoff, as we had given her a lift to here. But Elise Harcourt I did not know. She was the happy little brunette, whom Geoff indicated by lifting his glass to her and receiving a wide grin in response. Barely out of her teens, it seemed to me, and full of vibrant energy. She had wide brows, across which her hair danced, and beautiful brown eyes, which sparkled in my direction as she waved at me. Which left two men, to make up our eight. They were brothers, Geoff told me.

He pointed them out, slim and placid men, who—and I realized this with a sudden jolt of surprise—were identical twins. Catching my eye, they inclined their heads towards me, smiling hugely at my response, which they must have encountered all their lives. Thirty years, I guessed.

Observing my interest, Geoff said, 'They always come together. Philip and Martin. One's acrylics and the other's watercolours. And they claim they're married to twins.'

'Surely not!'

'So they said, but they both share the same dry sense of humour. Ask either of them if they ever get confused, and take the wrong wife home from the pub, and they'll only say that it wouldn't matter—would it? They take nothing seriously, except their painting. Can I get you another drink?'

'No. No, thank you. It's not worth the struggle to get it.'

'Later, perhaps,' he said. 'The bar's open again at nine.'

'And is it always so noisy?' I asked, raising my voice.

'Well...no. But our group—well, after a full day of peace out in the wilds, with not much sound apart from the birds—then the bar doesn't sound so bad. Welcoming, in fact.' Musingly, he added, 'They're a strange lot, our painters.'

'Strange?'

He smiled. 'Wrong word, perhaps. But all artistic people are a bit strange. It's their lives, you see. They have to excel, reach for something they'll never quite achieve. All the arts, that is. Actors, musicians, writers—and painters. Their own speciality overrides everything. It's a perpetual striving to achieve...well...perfection. And jealous!' He grimaced.

'You're making me uneasy, Mr Davies.'

'No, no. Sorry. But you're new to this—all painting courses, I'd guess. And it's Geoff.'

I nodded.

'I'm just preparing you,' he said. 'Oh yes, you can look round, and they're as matey as anybody could hope for—but each and every one of them strives, every time, to produce something no one else can match. And it *matters* to them. Oh...friendly and chatty now, but oh dear me...they all have to be the best. It's nonsense, really, because it's all in...' He snapped his fingers, lost for a word.

'The eye of the beholder?' I suggested.

He nodded. 'Exactly. And I'm the official beholder. It's the devil of a game, the way I have to watch what I say. Damn it, I don't want to bring on another—' He stopped abruptly. 'I'm talking too much...sorry.'

'Another what?' I asked gently.

'Incident.' He was reluctant to say it.

46

'Do you want to tell me, or not?'

He shrugged. 'You'll no doubt hear about it, anyway, so I might as well get it said. Two years ago, this was. Elise Harcourt, our lovely little brunette—she *is* lovely, isn't she—she'd been concentrating on the harbour, or estuary if you like, the moored boats and the river, and she'd really worked hard at it all day. I could tell that she was producing something very special. The light, you see. The light on the water, and the way it glanced off the boats, and the reflected ripples on their sides. That's a very difficult effect to lay down on canvas. It was lovely, lovely painting. But she ran out of time, and the light was getting poor. The weather forecast for the next day was for cloud and rain, and she was afraid she wouldn't get the same light, and might not get it for the rest of the week. But she had her little camera with her, and she got a few shots, and had them done at one of those fast-service places, and...well...'

He stopped. His face was drawn by the memory.

'And?' I asked, as it seemed he was now regretting he had told me this.

He shrugged, pouting. 'She went on with it, after dinner, working from her photos in the Glasshouse. It's always left unlocked, you know, and we've got special lights in there—5,000K, whatever that means.'

'Like daylight?' I offered.

'Yes. And she went on with it. Into the night. We all knew about it, but we left her to it. I mean...what else could anybody do? And it really had me worried.'

He paused, picked up his empty glass and put it down again.

'I can see you'd be worried,' I told him, prompting him to continue.

'On and on, she went. I couldn't go to bed. I can see the Glasshouse from my cottage, you know. And I waited. Waited. I mean...I wouldn't have dared to interfere.'

'Oh no. Of course not.'

'And at about two o'clock,' he went on, frowning at the memory, 'the lights went off...'

He stopped. I waited. 'So now you could get to bed,' I prompted.

'Yes. I could get to bed.' He sighed. 'In the morning...this painting was in acrylics, you see. On canvas. Did I say that?'

'You mentioned canvas.'

'Yes. Well it was. And the first thing in the morning, I went in to see it. I mean...I wanted to see the finished job. And then...when I went in there...' He drew a deep breath. 'It was slashed across and across. Viciously. A wicked attack.'

'Oh heavens!'

'Jealousy, of course,' he said morosely.

'I suppose,' I replied numbly. 'And poor Elise? When she saw it...'

He tried to smile at me, realizing he should not have told me all this, when it might send me running for my safe home...for all he knew.

'She was in hysterics,' he said flatly. 'We had to get the doctor to her, and she spent the day under sedation. In bed. It was a terrible, terrible thing.'

I couldn't think of anything to add. The sheer black malice of it appalled me. Then I managed to say, 'But she seems cheerful enough now. That's Elise, isn't it? The bright little brunette.'

He tried to smile at me. 'Yes. She thinks that this time she'll do it again—capture the same magic as she did before. But...' He shook his head solemnly.

'But you don't think so?' I asked.

He shook his head stubbornly. 'I think she's beginning to realize that she never will.'

'How sad. But why have you told me this? I can assure you now that neither Oliver nor I will produce anything worth slashing. Probably, not even anything worth looking at twice.'

'There is no point in being too modest,' he said severely. 'We'll see about that, later on, no doubt. But I wanted you to hear it from me, not one of the others. I suppose...what I was trying to get across to you...I simply wanted to persuade you not to allow yourself to get too involved with comparisons and what the others might be able to produce. You're supposed to be here to enjoy a week's painting...'

'Which I'm sure we will.'

'I just want you not to take it too seriously.'

'You can depend on that. We will not.'

'Because,' he pressed on, determined to say it, 'what starts out as a pleasant occupation can easily become an obsession —and possibly it can end in disillusionment.'

'We don't have any illusions about our abilities, I can assure you.'

'We'll see about that.'

So Geoff Davies cared about his work— which, though he obviously didn't realize it, had become his own obsession.

At that point the dinner bell rang, and people began getting to their feet.

'And you're telling me...what?' I asked.

'To enjoy your week here, and if you go home with something that pleases you—something good enough to frame and hang on your wall—then you'll make me very happy.'

I smiled at him. 'And here endeth the first lesson?'

'The most important,' he assured me, sliding back his chair. 'Don't be late. Eight-thirty in the Glasshouse.'

Oliver and I followed the crowd. The dining room was located in an annexe, which also housed the single rooms, built as an extension behind the main house. The tables were rectangular, each seating eight. The meal was really excellent—three courses prepared by a first-class cook.

I found myself sitting between our little, bright Elise and Oliver, who became happily involved with his female partner on the other side, who was trying to converse with him in German. I left him to it, and devoted my attention to Elise, who proceeded to make me welcome.

'Is this your first time?' she asked, passing me the sprouts.

'Yes. First time for Oliver and me.'

'Then you're lucky to be on our course.'

I was eyeing my huge serving of veal, and deciding which of the vegetables to leave out.

'Why lucky?' I asked.

'Because the others have lunch here every day, and *that's* a three-course one as well, and after a full week of it they don't want to see food again, ever.'

'Ah...' I said. 'Yes.'

'Whereas we—out in the wilds and the fresh air all day—we have a packed lunch.

Mind you, it's quite a sizeable lunch, but it does leave you looking forward to dinner back here, while the rest are all groaning by Friday.'

This she said solemnly, then she burst into a little tinkle of laughter.

'I'm beginning to get the idea.'

'Ah!' she said. 'Steamed jam pudding. Lovely.'

'Are we out all day, then?' I asked.

'Depending on the weather. Straight after breakfast we get into the little coach they've got, and they drive us down to the town and the estuary. The locals call it a harbour, but really it's only an estuary.'

'Ah yes.'

'There's a lovely wharf, and boats, and I got a marvellous...it doesn't always click, you know...but this time it did, and...and...'

Then her voice failed her, and she stared helplessly at her steamed pudding.

I said softly, 'I know about it, Elise. Geoff told me. It was a wicked, wicked thing to do.'

'Yes,' she whispered, her eyes now firmly fixed on what she was eating. 'But if the weather's fine tomorrow, and I can set up my easel in exactly the same place...I'll...I'll do it again.'

'Only better?'

She flashed me a sudden, radiant smile.

'Only better—and this time I'll guard it with my life.'

I watched as her lower lip crept forward. She glanced at her watch. 'Ten minutes,' she said. 'Then we have our get-together in the Glasshouse. I'd better rush. See you.'

Then she was off and away, and I found myself praying that she would succeed with her painting. She was too vivacious, and too friendly, to have to face disappointment again. But...the incident had been two years ago. I wondered how she had made out last year.

With Oliver at my shoulder, I walked out. 'The Glasshouse,' I said. 'How do we get to it?'

'Well...that looks like Geoff over there. We follow him.'

Which we did. There was a side door from the annexe, which led almost directly to our objective. By now, the daylight failing, it was already brightly lit.

For a greenhouse—as it must have been at one time—it was huge, and high enough to have housed banana trees. There seemed to be a vast expanse of concrete floor. As a greenhouse, it would have been entirely glass, but now it wore a three-foot skirt of asbestos sheeting, painted white. The light inside was from four overhead reflectors, and could have been genuine daylight. This, no doubt, was what Geoff had called 5000K.

'Ah...here you are,' said Geoff.

The rest were already there, and he explained to them—as though they didn't already know— 'Two new friends. You'll no doubt have met them already, but just in case... Philipa and Oliver Simpson. We shall have to look after them, shan't we!'

There were murmurs of agreement. In turn, they gave their names, but we already knew Pam Wilton and her husband Paul, who tried to smile at us but not very successfully. And of course we knew Jennie, who didn't smile because Paul was carefully not catching her eye. Elise Harcourt I already thought of as a friend. She smiled hugely at me, and, curse her, had a wink for Oliver, then a following grin at me. I felt I could forgive Elise very nearly anything—but not everything.

Now we met the twin brothers, Philip and Martin Graves. And, by heaven, they *were* identical twins, though in fact, in order to help their friends, Martin sported a moustache and Philip smoked a pipe. M for moustache, they explained gravely, and P for pipe.

Then we all seated ourselves on folding

stools, which we would have with us the following day. Oliver would need no more, as he would work with his pad on his lap. I would have to borrow an easel, as watercolours require a slight slope to the paper surface.

Geoff then distributed hand-drawn maps to each of us. The others barely glanced at them; they'd clearly seen them before.

'I ought to explain,' Geoff said, speaking directly to Oliver and me, 'that this is the area we usually cover. It includes the estuary of the river, part of the town, which is on its south bank, and about three quarters of a mile up the coast of Cardigan Bay. We'll be there all day, and probably, with minor changes perhaps, through the week. Unless anybody wants a complete change of venue.'

There was a communal rejection of this likelihood, and he laughed. 'Don't worry. The forecast's set fair. Now,' he said, 'I must explain how we work it, for our new friends. We go there in the coach, to the south end—the estuary. That's to let you all have a look at the harbour, as they call it round here—and see what boats there are, and the state of the tide. Then from there we drive north up the coast, to drop off people where they want to be left. The regulars, mind you, already have their favourite spots, and they disembark where they want to. Then they all stay wherever they settle until about seven. Light permitting. And I stroll round to see how it's progressing—giving everybody time to get going properly, of course. Dinner's back here at eight-thirty. So...a full day tomorrow, folks...'

It was his dismissal. They all knew the arrangements in detail, and they wandered away, chattering and arguing. Geoff made a signal to Oliver and me.

'Stay awhile, and we'll have a little chat,' he said.

We nodded, but didn't speak. We had a lot to learn.

'But first of all,' said Geoff, when the rest had all left, 'I'd like to see what you've brought with you. If there's anything you've forgotten, I can find it for you. Anything. Those cupboards over there are packed.'

There was a whole row of cupboards.

'I'll fetch our stuff along,' said Oliver.

I could see now that we ought to have left it all in the car, which was closer. Too late now. Off he went to our room. I turned to Geoff, who was eyeing me with his head tilted, having noted my concern. He was very quick at noticing things, I realized.

'I'd better explain,' I said. 'While Oliver's away. He had a bad injury

56

to his right arm—the full discharge of a shotgun.'

'Careless,' he murmured, rubbing a palm around his chin. His was a more placid and unadventurous life, into which violence did not normally intrude.

'In the line of duty,' I told him. 'He was a policeman. But it's left him with a rather clumsy right arm, and our tame expert suggested he ought to exercise his dexterity muscles more—his hand and his fingers. And this is what we decided for him. Painting with pastels. I'm sorry, Geoff, but he's no artist—and we're really making the wrong use of your course.'

'Nonsense,' he said, smiling at me—and such a pleasant smile he had. 'Pastels, you say? That sounds ideal for what you need.'

'But he's quite hopeless. He can't even draw a straight line.'

He cocked his head at me. 'Who can? And there're no straight lines in landscapes. Not even the horizon—it's curved. Who suggested this marvellous idea? Your specialist? And...pastels! Just the thing. They need a bit of pressure, and a bit of shoving about.'

'But he's an absolute beginner, and I've about forgotten everything I ever learned at school. Watercolours, that's me. So you can treat us both as beginners.'

57

'I'll treat you both as artists,' he declared, nodding. 'How long since you've handled watercolours?'

'At school. I was seventeen.'

'Then you can't have forgotten already,' he said with grave gallantry. 'It'll all come back. You'll see.'

Then Oliver returned, grinning, and loaded with our equipment.

'What now?' I asked him, knowing that grin.

'There's a great row going on in the next room to us. Pam Wilton and Paul. I got away smart like.'

Geoff looked worried, frowning heavily. 'I was afraid of this,' he said. 'For the life of me, I can't see what either of those two women can see in him. But it's not something new. We've had it before, but I manage to keep them well apart, when it comes to the actual business of sitting down and painting. Jennie usually works from the south side of the river. There's a cliff overlooking the river estuary, and she settles up there. Pam Wilton could hardly be further away—she likes a spot about three quarters of a mile up the coast. She's rather a loner.'

'And Paul?' I asked.

'Oh, he usually settles down on the north side of the estuary, the opposite side to Jennie. He loves wharfs and tethered boats, especially when they're tilted on their sides.'

I thought about this for a moment, before saying, 'From where, I suppose, he can wave to Jennie, the other side of the river?'

He nodded solemnly, but with the corners of his mouth twitching. 'If he so wished.'

'And...could he get across to her side?'

'Well yes...he could. There's a wooden footbridge right beneath Jennie's perch,' He tilted his head, eyeing me with amusement.

'Why aren't you taking this seriously?' I asked.

'Because I'm not a marriage guidance counsellor, for one thing, and their personal lives are none of my business. And because I know he'd not do that. He would not be welcomed, I can assure you. Jennie takes her painting seriously, and it would be wasting good painting time. For both of them.'

I cocked my head at him. 'And painting is what we're here for? Painting being the be all and end all of our lives?'

'For this week, yes. There's no time to waste on other inferior activities.' And at last he released his full grin.

'Painting comes first?'

'For a whole week it does,' he assured me.

4

'Now, Oliver,' said Geoff, 'let's see what you can do with pastels.'

'Hah!' said Oliver. 'Nothing much.'

Geoff set up a folding table and brought forward a canvas-topped stool. Oliver produced his pads of paper and his pastels. Geoff grinned. 'You've certainly got a good set, here. You'll be making Pam jealous.'

'Hmm!' said Oliver, but he was pleased that Tom had set him up well.

'Now...let's see. A vase... Where's that vase gone? Oh—there it is. Sit yourself down, Oliver. This won't take a minute.'

He placed the table about six feet away, and stood the vase on the green baize surface. The vase was brown and glazed. Then he hunted out a duster and tossed it beside the vase. It was yellow.

'Draw that,' said Geoff.

'All of it?' Oliver sounded horrified.

'Just the vase and the duster, and a bit of the table top.'

Oliver looked at him, looked at me, then he hunted through his pastels.

'Vase first?'

'As you wish.'

Oliver chose his pastel, stared fixedly at the vase, at his blank sheet of cream coloured paper, then he drew a curve. 'Side of the vase,' he told us. It could have been anything. Nobody said a word.

At last, Oliver ventured, 'What next?'

'Now—the other side,' Geoff told him.

Oliver concentrated. Another curve emerged, reversed. It bulged a little too much.

'All right,' said Geoff. 'Now a line across the top and the bottom. That's it.'

'It looks lop-sided.'

'All right. So make the other side bulge to match. Roughly.'

Oliver did that.

'That's fine,' Geoff told him. 'A scribble of green around the bottom. It doesn't matter if the green's not quite right. That one'll do. Right? That's just perfect.'

'It doesn't,' Oliver complained, 'look perfect to me.'

'Try the duster. You'll need about three shades of a nice, deep yellow. Right. That's it. Coming along fine. The duster's more difficult, isn't it? Don't worry—it comes with practice.'

'A few years of practice,' Oliver commented.

'Right.' Geoff stood back. 'That's about finished. It's a vase on a table. Not exactly *that* vase, but who, back home, will know that? It's the same with a tree. Your pine might look like an oak. But it doesn't matter. It's a tree. *Your* tree. Nothing has to be an exact copy. That is your painting of a vase on a table, Oliver.'

It looked to me rather like a cardboard box that had been jumped on. I didn't say so.

'Good,' said Geoff. 'It's a cross between impressionism and surrealism, Oliver, you've invented a new style.'

'Are you pulling my leg?' Oliver demanded.

Geoff laughed. 'If you like. But it doesn't matter what you call it. It's yours. You did it. Does it please you?'

'I can't say it does.'

'Why not?'

'It's all scribbly.'

'All right. You can always smooth that with the end of your finger. Tomorrow you'll have all day to experiment. Just look at what's in front of you, and try to get it down on paper. And it'll be *your* style. *Your* picture. Okay?'

Then he turned back to me. I had been keeping diplomatically silent. 'And you're watercolours, Philipa. No painting since you left school?'

I shook my head, my attention still for Oliver.

'Never mind,' he said. 'It'll all come back. What paper have you brought?'

'Some Bockingford 250, cut into fourteen by ten pieces.'

'Good. So it won't need stretching. I'll fix you up with an easel and a drawing board in the morning, and we'll all have a grand time. Now...I'll leave you. Dump your stuff anywhere on the counter along the back. Nobody will touch it. Light switch by the door, and there's no need to lock up after you.'

And he left us.

Oliver and I stood looking at each other. 'I'm going to make a right fool of myself, Phil,' he grumbled miserably.

'No you're not. You're forgetting the reason we came here. To exercise your fingers and hand and wrist muscles. So the more you spoil, the more you do. It all works out the same.'

'Hah!' he said.

'Let's just leave all our stuff here, and we'll go along to the bar. You'll feel more at home there.'

He eyed me quizzically. 'But you're not happy, yourself, love,' he said. 'Come on, what's worrying you?'

'Oh...I don't know. Or rather, I do. That's the trouble. All this talk of finding somewhere to set ourselves down, and the others have already got their sites in mind—and how the devil are we to know what's a good place and what isn't?'

'It'll sort itself out, Phil.'

We left our equipment in neat piles on the counter, and left, switching off the lights. It was now dark outside, an impenetrable black after the brilliance inside. But squat standard lamps along the edge of the terrace were now glowing, and we could easily find our way there. For a few minutes we stood at the head of the shallow steps down to the lawn, enjoying the placid evening. The village sparkled, down there and a little to our right, and a hint of the setting sun was caught by the river, like a red snake lying in wait in the night.

'Well anyway,' said Oliver, 'if we get nothing else from it, we've got this view. Lord, but it's a lovely evening.'

We went inside, and up to our room. Oliver decided to have a bath, so I had a shower, then we dressed ourselves in our casuals. He stood by the windows, open on to the night. From this vantage point the distant village looked all the more romantic.

'Heavens, if I could only get this down on paper,' he whispered, slipping a hand round my waist. And then I knew that he had the mind of an artist.

'Perhaps you can,' I said softly, reaching

for his hand and drawing it a little tighter around me. 'All you need is some black pastel paper, and I bet Geoff's got some, tucked away in one of his store cupboards.'

'Perhaps he has. Perhaps he has,' he mused.

A minor miracle had occurred. Suddenly, Oliver wanted this. He wanted something personal and special on paper—and by heaven he was going to master those pesky pastels somehow or other, if only to capture that sparkling display over the estuary.

'Shall we go down?' I suggested.

My hands were on the two windows, actually about to swing them shut, when a door slammed. The room next door. I was very still. Now Oliver's hand was on my shoulder, his head close to mine.

'Let's get out of here,' he whispered, as Pam's voice snapped out bitterly:

'So there you are. And where the hell have *you* been, may I ask? Down on the terrace—or was it the lawn? Oh...splendid!'

'Don't be a damned fool, Pam.'

'I tell you—I'm warning you—much more of this and I'll be doing something I'll be sorry for.' Pam's voice was breaking. 'They're laughing at me. D'you think I don't know! They turn away when they see me—and whisper together. You're making a fool of me...'

'You're the one who's doing that,' he said. Now his voice held a vicious undertone. 'Act your age, Pam, for God's sake. You're not a silly teenager.'

Gently, silently, I closed our windows. 'Let's get out of here,' I said quietly, echoing Oliver's words, and we hurried down the stairs.

The bar was nowhere near as packed as it had been earlier. Our group had one of the secluded arms of the U-shaped bench to ourselves.

'You're Dubonnet and lemonade?' Oliver asked me, and I nodded. My favourite long drink, that was.

'Right.' He looked around the group. 'Anybody for a refill?'

Apparently not. Much shaking of heads. So I went and sat with the twins, who each had a half of beer.

'Hello,' said the one with the moustache —so he had to be Martin. 'Are you all ready and prepared for tomorrow?'

'Impatient is the word.'

'Ah yes. Well. That'll wear off by Friday. Four solid days of painting, and you've about had enough.'

'Yes, I suppose that's so.'

Then Oliver stood in front of me, a glass in each hand. 'Either of you ready for a refill?' he asked the twins. He was punctilious in this, which was probably a hangover from his days in the police.

As one, the twins placed a hand over their glasses.

Oliver sat beside me. 'Is this true?' he asked the brothers, knowing I was dying to ask. 'What we've been told—that you're married to twins?'

They laughed together, in harmony. 'It's a joke,' Martin told us. 'My wife's a tall, slim blonde, and Philip's is a shorter, stouter redhead. But we don't like to disappoint people, so we invented it.'

'What about painting styles?' I asked. 'Do you paint alike?'

'Oh no. Not at all.' This was Philip. 'I'm watercolours and Martin's acrylics. Different results—so it's easy to tell which is which when we're finished. You'll see, I hope. If the weather holds...'

'Oh, don't say things like that,' I appealed. 'You'll put the mockers on it.'

They both smiled. Philip said, 'I'm watercolours and Martin's acrylics. Much the same, you'd say, but it's easy to tell which is which when they're finished.'

'You've already said that,' Martin pointed out. 'But the point is that you can overpaint with acrylics.'

'But it's the discipline of watercolours that counts.' Philip nodded positively.

'Oh yes,' I agreed warmly. 'That's what I feel.'

At this point, Geoff walked in on us, and looked round. He seemed worried.

'Anybody seen Jennie?' he asked. 'She said she wanted a word with me.'

Then Jennie came walking after him round the corner. 'She's here,' she announced.

She seemed flushed, and her hair was a little untidy, but she was smartly dressed in slacks and a blouse with lace trimmings, a little jacket over it.

'Where've you been hiding yourself?' Geoff asked.

She moved a hand in a dismissive gesture. 'Down in the town.' Then, at his expression, she added, 'It's a free world.'

But Geoff was persistent. 'At this time? The shops must be shut.'

Jennie shook her head in impatience, getting the usual dancing effect from her hair. 'I wanted to have a look at the wharfs. You know...check on them, and see what boats were in. You know. And Geoff—it was really beautiful. From the north side of the estuary—where Paul usually goes—from there, and with the street lights reflected in the water. And just a touch of red in the sky. If only I could get that down on paper...'

I glanced sideways at Oliver, and nudged him. He turned his head to me, smiling.

He and Jennie were of a like mind, it appeared.

But Geoff wasn't satisfied. For the week, we were *his* painters, and he felt responsible for our welfare.

'So—how did you get there, if you haven't got your car?'

'Oh...I walked.'

'On your own? Wasn't that very rash?'

'Oh...come on, Geoff. It's not one of your dirty streets in a city. Nobody was going to touch me. I felt like a walk, that's all there's in it.' And now she seemed annoyed by his concern.

'Well—I think it was a foolish idea,' Geoff said. 'And on your own. Foolish.'

He looked round for support, and suddenly Pam Wilton was there, at his shoulder.

'So what else is she—ever?' she demanded, looking Jennie in the eyes. 'Can't help it—and it's so dangerous, Jennie. Really it is. I'll have a gin and tonic, love,' she said, turning to see how close Paul might be behind her.

'Already got one for you.' His voice was toneless. 'Aren't we going to sit down?'

Not once did he look directly at Jennie, but allowed his eyes to roam restlessly. To Pam, he said. 'Let's go round the other side—shall we?'

It sounded as though he and Pam had

put their dispute firmly in the past. She agreed to his suggestion. 'Yes—round the other side.' My eyes followed Paul.

I couldn't understand what either of the women found attractive in him. He was craggily featured, with deep-set and I thought furtive eyes, a square jaw, and lips that dipped morosely in the corners.

There was an awkward silence. Jennie shook her head; that hair had very little rest. She spoke to Geoff.

'It really was quite splendid, down by the wharfs, Geoff,' she insisted. 'At night, with just the street lights...'

'I'll look at it some other time,' he assured her, but with a complete lack of enthusiasm. 'Just sit yourself down, Jennie. You know you've been foolish...on your own...down there.'

She sat abruptly beside me, and pouted sullenly. Geoff smiled vaguely, and drifted away, leaving me hunting desperately through my mind for something to say, as Oliver settled himself the other side of her.

'You didn't tell me how you came to crash your Porsche,' I told her. Anything to distract her. Her face was expressionless.

'Oh...that. I was overtaking a trailer wagon. A bend coming up, and hidden by a railway bridge over it. Me... I reckoned I could get past, but just as I'd decided

70

that, another wagon came round the corner towards us. So I dropped back, and pulled in behind the trailer. And I suppose the trailer driver didn't know that corner, either—it was really quite deceptive. In any event, he braked hard, and I skidded under his tail, and found myself with a lapful of glass peas and the roof nearly chopped off.'

'Well now...' I said. 'It must have been very horrifying.'

She stared at me, huge eyes vacant. Flatly, she added, 'I think I'm pregnant, Philipa.' She had to tell somebody.

As sometimes happens, the clatter in the bar had suddenly collapsed, leaving a hole of silence, into which Jennie's statement rang out as though she had shouted it. The silence continued for three whole seconds, which seemed like an eternity, then the chatter burst out again—but louder. Nobody looked in our direction. Jennie said, 'I think I'll go to bed.'

'Yes,' I murmured uselessly.

'We'll say goodnight, then,' Oliver said. 'See you in the morning.' And he got to his feet as she stood up. He's very old-fashioned, and I love it.

'Yes,' she replied. 'See you on the coach.' But there was no lively anticipation in her voice.

It was not much later before we decided

to do the same. I was suddenly very tired. Perhaps it was the sea air. In any event, that huge bed beckoned.

But...sitting alone and looking sadly neglected, was Elise, I saw. I touched Oliver's arm, and we moved over to join her.

'What's this, Elise? All on your own?'

'I'm quite all right, thanks.'

'Mind if we sit with you for a few minutes?' I asked, slipping on to the space beside her on the settle. 'I'll have to unwind, or I'll never get to sleep,' I explained.

Oliver asked her whether she would like a drink, but she shook her head. 'No...no, thanks,' she said. 'I'm not much of a drinker. I come here for the painting, not to drink.'

'Yes...well...you'll be painting in the morning,' I reminded her.

'I shall, shan't I!' She seemed to wriggle her way into the idea of it. 'I'm acrylics, you know. What about you?'

'Oh...I'm watercolours,' I told her. 'And Oliver's pastels.'

She pouted. 'Pastels smudge.'

'There's a spray fixative,' I said. 'Oliver— we haven't tried that.'

'True. We haven't. But I've got nothing to preserve, yet. Don't suppose I ever will. Nothing worth the trouble, anyway.'

Elise laughed. 'Is he always so modest?'

'Well...no. But he's an absolute beginner, and with no faith in himself at all. It's just a bit of confidence he needs. We'll have to find a good place to set up, and *then* see what he gets.'

She looked away. 'I've got a good place,' she said softly.

'You *all* seem to seek out your favourite spots, it seems to me. From what I've heard. And we know nothing about the setting, at all. Perhaps you'll be able to advise us, Elise.'

'Well...' She looked down at her hands, then looked up, smiling winningly. 'Why don't you both sit with me?'

I really hadn't paid much attention to Elise. She had been the young woman whose splendid painting had been slashed. She had seemed to be shy and withdrawn, but behind it she was full of life, all bursting to be enjoyed.

'Oh...' I said. 'We couldn't, really. Your special place!' I glanced at Oliver, but he gave me no help, merely lifted his eyebrows.

'Please...' she said. 'It does get awfully lonely, you know.' She looked across at Oliver. 'If your husband doesn't mind.'

That was a strange thing to say. If anybody should mind, surely that had to be me. Oliver winked. At Elise, I felt, rather than at me. I said, 'I'm sure he doesn't.'

This seemed to delight her. 'And I'll feel safe.' She pressed her hands to her cheeks.

I didn't understand that. 'Safe?'

'Safe to leave my painting. If I have to...you know. And the nearest toilet's...you have to cross the bridge. And I'm always worried—leaving things.'

'Hmm!' I said. 'You would be. And we mustn't have that.'

She clapped her hands together. 'Then that's that. I'll sleep better tonight.'

'You can feel extra safe,' I assured her. 'Oliver's an ex-policeman.'

He doesn't usually like me to refer to that. It makes him feel that he's there to keep the peace.

'We appreciate why you're worried,' I told her. 'About leaving things. It was a wicked thing to do.'

'Yes,' she whispered. But now...' She looked at us with a fresh light in her eyes. 'Now I feel much better.'

'Well—we'll see you in the morning, then,' Oliver said, catching my eye. He put out a hand to me.

She smiled. No words. But we left her more relaxed than she had been, though Oliver didn't seem greatly pleased.

'Don't frown,' I told him. 'It saves us having to search around and make a decision. And this is her special spot, which she's going to share.'

'I'm not frowning, Phil,' he said. 'Just thinking.'

I, too, was thinking—that I'd found a special friend in Elise.

We said goodnight to those few left behind in the bar, and made our way to our room.

As I undressed, Oliver stood at the window. Down in the town, lights were flicking off. The magic gradually faded into the darkening sky as I went to stand beside him.

'Better leave the windows open a little,' he said. 'It's going to be a warm night.' Then he gently drew me away from the window.

'What...'

He said quietly, 'Down there. Jennie. Walking up and down the terrace.'

'Then she won't want you to be watching,' I pointed out. 'Let's get some sleep, love. I can hardly keep my eyes open.'

I remember laying my head on the pillow, Oliver's hand resting gently on my waist, then abruptly it was morning.

He fumbled his legs out of the bed. 'You first with the shower?' he asked.

'Are we in a hurry?'

'Well...no. I suppose not. But I'd like to

try that spray stuff for my pastels.'

So we wasted no time, and were down in the Glasshouse at eight o'clock.

Geoff was there already. He looked round. 'You're a bit early. We have breakfast first.' He said it solemnly, to indicate he was ribbing us.

'It's just that Oliver wants to try his fixative spray.'

'Fine. Go ahead. Oliver's already got one masterpiece to try it on.'

'Funny,' said Oliver.

He found his pad, and tore off the used sheet. 'Doesn't look quite so bad now,' he admitted.

A long row of sinks ran along one of the shorter walls. They were liberally splashed with a multitude of colours, from the years of countless artists washing their equipment. Oliver laid his vase painting face up on what was used as a draining board, read the instructions on the can, and squirted a fine cloud of colourless varnish.

'It smells like hairspray,' I said.

'It could well be the same thing. Want to try it?'

'No, thanks.'

My hair doesn't need spraying. It's like a tangle of copper wire, and does what it feels best. I can never do anything about it.

He waved the paper in the air, then put it down on a table. 'Seems to do its job,' he said, running his finger over it as soon as it was dry. 'Last night it smudged as easy as pie. Look at it, and it smudged.'

'So now you know it works.'

'But it's dulled the colours a bit,' he complained.

I stood back and stared at him. 'Not much wrong with your colour sight, Oliver,' I told him. 'Isn't that so, Geoff?'

'Pardon?' He was busy. 'No,' he said, sparing a glance. 'Nothing. But...a tip, Oliver. After you've used the spray you can work over it again. If you want to brighten the highlights, for instance.'

'Right. Thanks.' Oliver was vastly pleased with himself.

'Let's go and get breakfast,' I said. 'Oh...and Geoff...'

'Yes?' He was infinitely patient.

'We're fixed up with a site for painting. We're going to be with Elise.'

'Well now...' He smiled. 'Good. I'm pleased about that. She's terribly shy, and this is the first time...anyway, I'm sure you'll all three get along fine.'

I touched his arm. 'The first time, Geoff?'

'The first time she's trusted anybody, since it happened.'

'Because we're the only ones it couldn't have been?' I asked.

He cocked his head at me. 'Well...not exactly that, I feel.'

5

The college coach was a neat little twenty-seater, driven by the college caretaker, Larry. As there were only eight of us, plus Geoff and Larry, there was plenty of room for everybody's equipment.

Geoff sat Oliver and me in the two front seats, so that he could explain things whilst sitting behind us and leaning forward. The rest chattered away amongst themselves.

'We drive down the road to the junction,' Geoff told us, 'then turn right along the river until we get to the estuary. Everybody seems to want the sea and the boats in their pictures. Look, there's the river, ahead. It's not much of a river, but it's all we've got.'

It ran quietly between trees, the other side of a long run of hawthorn hedge.

The coach turned right at the junction, and the outer reaches of the town now began to appear, backing up from the river, and to our left. To the right there was nothing but trees.

'First stop just by the footbridge,' Geoff told us.

We stopped. Oliver and I got out, and watched as Jennie sorted out her bits and pieces. So much, she seemed to need! Surely, she would never cover the surfaces of what looked like twenty sheets of very stiff watercolour paper.

The bridge over the river was a narrow wooden one, for pedestrians only. From its far end there was a short and steep cobbled lane, heading away, and apparently up into this final reach of the town. A squat building at the top was fronted by a clipped yew hedge, and the hedge by something that seemed to be the flat surface of a sheer sandstone cliff, rising a good fifty feet above the black estuary mud below.

'She paints from up on that flat surface,' said Geoff, pointing. 'There's a grand view from there of the entire estuary and the boats, but I can assure you, it's not every artist's dream. The high viewpoint makes the perspective very complicated.'

'You're not going to let her carry all that stuff and the stool and the easel—all by herself!'

Geoff gave a short laugh. 'Heavens, no. Of course not. Larry and I give her a hand. It's what we're here for.'

We watched as they carried her massive load of equipment across the wooden footbridge, she, with her packed lunch in a plastic carrier bag, strolling along behind them. Then Oliver and I did a bit of strolling of our own, a little further along the route the coach was obviously to take, until the tarmac surface simply seemed to lose heart and melt away, leaving it to the grass expanse ahead. There was a double path, impressed in the grassland with the twin lanes of motor vehicles. This ran away into the distance, parallel to the coastline.

'But how do they get motor vehicles up into the town?' I asked Oliver, as we stood and stared at the estuary and out to the sea, so very far away, it seemed.

'Didn't you notice, Phil?' Oliver asked. 'There's a proper road bridge crossing the river, further back. We passed it on the way here.'

'No—I didn't notice that.'

The estuary was very wide at this point, and it was clear that the mooring of boats depended to a great extent on the tide. It could by no means be called a harbour. At low tide, as it seemed to be at that time, the boats mostly lay on their sides, and no doubt would float free as the tide came in. The underlying surface was in no way sandy, and was very like a black sludge. It would not be attractive, surely, in any painting. So what would Jennie find to be worth painting, faced by a dark and drab grey in her foreground? It was not my problem, though, and no doubt Jennie had faced it before. She could—after all—paint the sludge as bright sand.

As Geoff would have said: it would be *her* estuary.

We turned and looked back. Geoff was waving to us from beside the coach. Jennie was standing, legs apart, on the forward edge of her cliff. Beyond her, even higher than the cliff, there was just visible what could well be the ruins of a very ancient castle.

We waved to Jennie. She didn't wave back. She was wearing her black tight leggings and a bright red T-shirt. It looked as though Geoff had set up her easel for her. Behind her, the yew hedge nicely set off the red shirt.

When we got back to the coach, I asked Geoff, 'Is she all right there, on her own?'

'Oh yes.'

'Isn't she worried about being pestered?'

'Not at all. This isn't one of your crummy cities, you know. The locals come and stand behind her and say nice things. Some of them know her by now.'

'So she won't be too lonely?'

'No. Not lonely.'

The coach got going again, reached the double wheel tracks, and continued along them, following the coastline. This was grassland, speckled with gorse bushes, bracken, and distant sheep, the hills beyond folding and interlinking into the distance. Bryngowan Manor was just visible, but looking like a small outcrop of rock. The coach moved slowly over the poor surface.

Cardigan Bay lay to our left now, as we drove north, but there was little to be seen of it, as massed bushes and trees ran ahead steadily, following the coastline. In places, the greenery thickened and spread itself, so that we ran close beneath and between it, overhanging branches rattling on the roof.

'First stop,' said Geoff, and Larry pulled the coach to a halt. 'This is where Paul likes to work. Come along, and see what it's like.'

'But we've arranged to sit with Elise,' I reminded him.

'Yes. I know. But you're here for a few more days, and there'd be time for a different viewpoint. It's not Paul's secret lair.'

'All right,' I said. 'We'll have a look.' And Oliver nodded agreement.

We helped with Paul's load of stuff.

He didn't seem pleased that we might be intending to trespass on his preserves.

It was at a point where the cliffs curved away north from the estuary. When we reached it, I had to admit that it was ideal, as far as the view was concerned, with the estuary dead ahead of him, and Jennie, beyond it and on top of her cliff, clearly visible in her red T-shirt.

But here—Paul's treasured retreat—there was no more than a patch of scrubby grass, surrounded by towering trees, and there would certainly have been no room for two intruders.

'Very cosy, Paul,' I said. 'You're well located here.'

Indeed, he was, as he had a superb view of the estuary, from the opposite direction to the one enjoyed by Jennie, though it seemed to me that as the sun came round it would be directly in his eyes.

We left him, and climbed back into the coach. The others seemed restless at the delay. Then we moved onwards, heading north.

The twins were next. We put them off, and they carried their own equipment. Both were wearing very battered jeans and linen jackets, all liberally spattered with patches of colour.

'Nothing special where we go,' said Martin. 'And not much room,' added

Philip. It was clear we would not have been welcome, so there was no point in wasting any more time on viewing it.

'Right,' said Geoff, when we moved away. 'Elise's little promontory next. And,' he added quietly, 'where you know you're welcome. Come along, if Elise still agrees.' He glanced at her, but it was to me he winked.

'Oh yes—yes,' she said quickly. 'We've got it all fixed up. Haven't we?' she asked, touching my arm, her eyes big and anxious.

Oliver smiled. 'I'd be disappointed, otherwise.'

So, between us, we carried everything along, following Elise. Two trips. It was by no means an easy access, with the path very narrow between hedges and trees. But we emerged on a flat area twenty feet by ten, with a low cliff down to the water, on three sides of us. The promontory jutted out into the bay, so that there was a flourishing run of greenery to our left, the estuary directly ahead, and the bay to our right, but lapping almost at our feet, there being a ten-foot fall of cliff to the water.

We were, I guessed, about a quarter of a mile from the harbour, with behind it the rise of the town. The castle ruins were now starkly side-lit against a deep blue sky, with delicious white clouds gathered in parade. I could now only just detect the red spot that was Jennie.

'This,' I said, 'is absolutely ideal.'

'Right,' Geoff said, obviously pleased by our reaction. 'There's not much point in taking you to see Pam's spot and bringing you back here. So I'll tell you how I usually do things. We park the coach on a flat patch, about a quarter of a mile from here, after I've seen Pam settled in. Her little spot's a quarter of a mile further on than that. Then, throughout the day, I do a tour. That's to see how you're all managing, answer any queries, and offer any advice you may need. And so on.'

'You walk it?' Oliver asked.

'Oh yes. The coach is parked where everybody knows where to find it. That we *have* to do. You've all got to know where to go if there's any kind of emergency.'

'Emergency?' I asked. 'Sitting here, painting!'

He laughed, then grimaced. 'You never know. We've had some very strange emergencies. One man, stepping back to get his perspective right, fell off the cliff and nearly drowned himself. Pam—our Pam—was sharpening a pastel pencil with a sharp knife, and nearly cut the end off her finger. Oh yes—we get 'em.'

'If they're alone,' I protested, thinking

85

of Pam, 'how can they—'

'That's one of the reasons why I walk the rounds,' he cut in.

'But you must walk miles.'

'Oh, I do, I do. It keeps me fit. For your information, it's nearly half a mile from here to where I'm now going to take Pam Wilton, who'll be getting very impatient if I don't get back to the coach right now. That makes it about a mile between the furthest of you north—that's Pam—and the furthest south —that's Jennie. You get the strategy?' And he winked. 'Right then—see you later.'

Elise sighed when he'd left us. 'He's a bit of a fusspot, and he does rather treat us as children, who have to be guarded with his life.'

'Oh, I wouldn't put it like that,' said Oliver. 'He's just anxious that his little flock should go away at the end of the week, knowing they've achieved something. I think he's just a wee bit too conscientious, that's all. And what about all those miles he must walk! No wonder he's got no flesh on his bones.'

Elise sighed. 'I'm always telling myself I ought to walk more. Oh...but never mind that. Shall we set up our easels side by side,' she suggested to me, 'then we can make catty remarks to each other.'

'That sounds ideal,' I agreed, to the

sitting together, anyway.

'Ye Gods!' said Oliver. 'What have I got myself into?'

Then, after a bit of arguing and discussion, Elise and I got down to some serious work. Or at least, we got light pencil outlines of the general perspective on our paper, whilst Oliver grumbled to himself, with his pad on his knees.

He was sitting beside me on his stool, pastels displayed in their box at his feet, and Elise the other side of me. Oliver didn't seem to be getting anywhere.

'I don't know how to start,' he moaned.

'You draw a general layout, like this,' I told him, showing him what I had done. 'Use a grey pastel pencil. But Oliver, I've never done pastel work, so I might be advising you all wrong. Do as Geoff said—put down on the paper what you see.'

Elise was on her feet at once. 'Oh, I've done pastels. I'll just show you.'

And then she was hanging over his shoulder, one arm resting on it, peering at his pad, leaning her face close to his and saying, 'Like this, look: row of trees, distant castle, edge of cliffs, water, sky.'

That grey pastel pencil was racing over the paper, and they were considering the result with their heads so close that I expected a spark to fly between them.

Oliver was pleased with her assistance. Then I realized that I could have done that for him, all of it, and I understood now why she had offered to share her cosy little nook. Not, really, with us, but with Oliver. Suddenly, I was surplus to requirements.

But this was Elise, I reminded myself. Elise, the flimsy flirt, not Jennie, the wildly possessive and practised lover. Elise—who would run a mile if Oliver responded with the slightest gesture that suggested blatant sex. But I ought to have known. He had the situation under control.

'Well now!' he said. 'If that's not a clever girl! I've got my outline, Phillie. In a flash she did it. Now, let's see if I can get some green in those trees.'

He grabbed up three greens in three shades, and scribbled and cross-hatched and rubbed with his finger, and said, 'There! Trees.'

'But they're not a *bit* like I drew them!' Elise complained.

'But they're *my* trees,' he said. 'Just as Geoff said. Mine. Isn't that grand, Phil?'

I agreed that it was. 'Thank the lady, Oliver.'

'Thank you, Elise,' he said. 'But you mustn't waste your time on me. Your precious time.'

She returned to her stool, pouting a little.

Ten minutes later we were each locked in our private enclosure of concentration. Little was said. Elise, with acrylics, was painting her fluffy white clouds. With watercolours, I couldn't do that, but had to float-in a flat wash of blue, and use a fistful of tissues to pick out the clouds, then, while the white patches were still damp, carefully edge in a touch of Payne's grey, to add an impression of bulk. The difficulty was that I had forgotten to bring my box of tissues.

'I've got some,' said Elise. 'Help yourself.' Bless her.

Beside me, Oliver was now working silently and intently. More and more sheets of Ingres pastel paper were scattered around his feet. He had dispensed with an opening sketch of outlines and positioning and now simply plunged in and scribbled hard, and was making splendid and positive passes with his pastels, steady curves and bold masses, apparently carelessly but now at last with a certain amount of confidence. He was producing rather splendid pictures, with the sunlight blasting through the trees, his clouds rubbed in with a finger, and a darned sight fluffier than mine.

It was coming up to time for our lunch, when Elise suddenly spoke into what had been an extended silence. 'I'll have to ask you to excuse me for a few minutes.'

'Something you've left...'

'No. Oh no.' She turned her head away. 'I'll have to pop along to the Ladies.'

'What!' I said. 'Where's this Ladies you're talking about?'

'It's over the bridge and up that cobbled bit of lane—and it's on the right. Behind where Jennie's doing her painting. Are you coming with me?'

I couldn't help laughing. 'Heavens no! With all these acres of trees and hedges around?'

'Oh...I couldn't...' She was unable to look at Oliver.

What a delicately nurtured young lady she was! Oliver said, 'If you like, *I'll* walk along there. Have a word with Jennie, perhaps, and take my time.'

'No, no. Really.' She got to her feet and smoothed her slacks. 'I need to stretch my legs, anyway.'

'The trees,' Oliver said, in that flat and solemn voice he uses when he's about to produce one of his funnies, 'would surely be sweeter and fresher than the Ladies. If they're anything like the Gents, anyway.'

She blushed. 'I'll have to rush.'

'We'll stop for lunch,' I told her.

And off she went. We stopped for lunch, as I'd said, after indulging in a bit of a laugh over our dear Elise.

The packed lunch was splendid, sandwiches of a chopped filling that I couldn't identify, but which were delicious, an apple, a chunk of fruit cake, and a carton of fruit juice.

'You know, Oliver,' I said, 'you're a natural artist. I mean—just look at some of those...' They were scattered on the grass around him. They were closer to being sketches than actual completed paintings, but he'd naturally been more interested in getting as much done as possible. By the end of the week, he would, I thought, be concentrating more on detail and overall effect. In that event, I could see him taking half a day on one painting, even a full day.

'I didn't know, Phil. I just can't believe it. And Phil, by the end of the week, I'll have a painting from our window at night. I swear it. It's just as Geoff said: you put down on paper what you see.'

'That's the general idea,' I said.

'Hmm!' He glanced at his watch. 'She's certainly taking her time.'

'It is not necessary,' I pointed out, 'to time her, Oliver. It's quite a distance, you know.'

'Yes—but getting on for twenty minutes... It's nearly one o'clock.'

'Would you like me to go and check?' I asked, a little ashamed of my laboured tone. 'But I mean—'

I didn't get to tell him what I meant, because suddenly I could hear screaming, coming closer, and which surely must have been our Elise.

Oliver knocked over his stool, jumping to his feet.

The screams ceased, being replaced by the crashing of undergrowth, then Elise burst into sight, panting and half-weeping, and appearing about to collapse as she caught sight of Oliver.

Then she stood, swaying before us, her face puffed and red with exertion and her eyes wild.

'Oh Phillie,' she whimpered. 'It's Jennie. Back there.' She made a wild and sweeping gesture. 'And she's d...dead. I'm sure she must be dead.'

'Now...Elise...' I was trying to use a calming voice, but she burst out, 'It's true! I've seen her. Dead. Oh...what are we going to do?'

'We are going to stay here, until somebody comes and tells us what's happened.' I nodded, to emphasize it. Whatever had occurred, we would be doing no good by going to investigate.

She stared at me numbly.

'I could go and find out,' suggested Oliver, his authoritative voice working full time.

'No, no,' appealed Elise, her hands against her face, eyes wild behind her fingers. 'I couldn't. Not back there.' Then she waved her arms around frantically.

'I didn't say we,' said Oliver. 'Me. On my own. And I didn't mean back there. I meant to the coach. To see if Geoff knows about it—whatever it is. You just sit down, Elise. Come along now, and be a good girl.' He offered her his hand. 'Just sit yourself down, lass, and take a deep breath, then you can tell us what it's all about.'

She did not sit down, but clung to Oliver's hand even more fiercely. Then she drew in a deep, shuddering breath, and said, in a reasonably controlled voice, 'It's definitely Jennie. The red shirt and the hair. Jennie. And she's lying there—her easel knocked over—and Phillie,' she whispered, 'she's dead. I *know* it. Lying there.'

'You've said that Elise,' I reminded her, trying to erase the image from her mind, trying to remain cool and calm, myself.

Then she released Oliver's hand, and clawed at my arm. 'It's Jennie...'

'Now Elise,' I said, 'you just sit yourself down on this stool, and tell us exactly what's happened. Exactly.' I eased her down on to the stool.

She drew in another deep, shuddering breath.

93

'Take it from when you arrived there,' I told her.

'I just w...went there. Across the foot-bridge.'

'Yes. Of course. And straight to the Ladies?'

'Yes,' she whispered.

'And did you see anybody the other side of the bridge—either coming towards you or going away, before you reached the Ladies?'

It was quite irrelevant at that time, but it helped to drag her mind away from the basic, appalling fact—that she had seen Jennie dead—and lead her slowly towards the fact that she must actually have seen Jennie.

She frowned heavily, and began to pad at her face with a handful of tissues. 'It depends...I don't know why you're... Coming towards me? No. Oh no. Nobody.' She looked agitatedly around her, as though she was being stifled by distress.

'But going away?' I asked. 'Is there anywhere anybody could be going away to?'

'Of course. Of course there is. Oh, Phillie, don't you *know?* There's the market-place, up there. Don't you know?'

'How could I, Elise? You mean—up the cobbled lane and past the Ladies?'

'Yes, yes. Oh...why are we wasting time?'

94

'It's because there's nothing else we *can* do. Only wait. And while we wait, we're just talking. Getting things straight. Now...you saw somebody walking away?'

'Yes, yes!' She bit her lower lip. 'Well...I think so.'

'Think...'

'The sun was in my eyes, Philipa. So how could I see anything much?'

'Yes. Of course. But can you tell me...a man or a woman?'

'As though I could tell!'

'Skirt or slacks?'

'Oh...I don't know! Oh—all right—slacks, I suppose.' She dismissed the validity of this with a flick of her hand. 'What does it matter, anyway?'

'I don't know, Elise. I don't know. Then you went into the Ladies?'

'I've *said* that. How many more times...'

'You haven't, Elise. Anybody else in there?'

She shook her head frantically. 'Not as far as I know.' She was impatient now, jabbering the words. 'What on earth does *that* matter? Jennie's lying there dead, and you're talking about who was where and who wasn't.' She looked wildly around her for assistance. 'We ought to be *doing* something.'

'If there was anything we *could* do,' I said gently, 'then we'd do it. But we're here, not there. I thought I heard a siren, which means that the police are on the job, so there's nothing *we* can do. In any event, they wouldn't allow us to get anywhere near.'

'Yes.' She pouted. 'I suppose you're right.' Her tone was of relief, a vast load of responsibility suddenly sliding from her shoulders. 'I suppose you're right,' she conceded.

'I am, I assure you. Now...did you, from inside, *hear* anything going on outside?'

'Oh yes.' She sighed. My persistence was wearying her. 'Somebody running. Across the bridge. I could hear the planks. Yes. I'm pretty sure of that. Then—I think—round to where Jennie... Jennie...where she was painting. Then straight back. Back to the bridge.'

She stopped, biting her lower lip to stimulate her memory. 'And?' I prompted.

'Then I came out myself...and got down as far as the bridge, and there was somebody—behind me—I glanced back. A woman came, from the market-place. Came and walked round to where Jennie was... Jennie was...and then back. But running—and then there was a lot of noise and shouting and screaming, from the market-place...screaming...'

'So you went back to have a quick peep—to see what all the fuss was about?'

96

I asked, that being what I could not have resisted. Then, at her blank stare, and her eyes bright and wild in her ashen face, I prompted, 'Did you walk round to Jennie's spot—and actually see—'

'Oh, yes, yes! Philipa...' The fingers clawed at my arm again. 'And she was lying there, blood in her lovely hair. She *must* have been dead. Easel knocked over. Must have been dead.'

'That need not actually be so,' I told her. 'Then what did you do?'

She was becoming impatient. 'How do you mean, Phillie? For heaven's sake...'

'What did you do then?' I persisted.

'I ran back here.'

'Over the bridge, then. Did you see anybody ahead of you, on the bridge, or even over the other side of it.'

'No—yes—I don't know. You're just confusing me...'

I could see she was close to collapse. 'Have a drink of your fruit juice, Elise. And a bite of your sandwich. There's nothing any of us can do except sit and wait.'

She did as she was told, nibbling cautiously at a sandwich. Gradually, the shaking eased and the eyes shed their bright desperation. She drank her fruit juice.

'We'll have to tell Geoff,' she whispered eventually, producing a fact that I had not considered. Of course we would.

'I'll go and see to that,' said Oliver. 'The rest of the group will have to be told, too.'

'Oh...don't go,' Elise whispered, too late though, because he'd already disappeared into the greenery.

'I'll stay here with you,' I assured her. 'And we'll just have to wait.'

There seemed to be no point in doing otherwise. But restraining Elise was difficult, as she wanted to be with the rest of our group, with Geoff. So I suggested that we should move out into the open, where at least we might detect movement of one sort or another.

This we did, leaving all our belongings behind, and picked our way through the trees, just in time to see Oliver hurrying back.

We stopped. We waited.

6

He had been running, and was short of breath, but eventually he managed to say, 'It's worse than we thought, Phil. It's Pam, love. She's dead, too. Geoff's just found her.'

Elise clutched frantically at my arm.

'Oliver...you're sure?' I asked.

'I got a peep, Phil. A quick look. It's Pam, and she's dead, and it looks like a blow to the back of her head. There's a length of old post...' He shrugged. 'Let's get back to the coach.'

Elise clung heavily to my arm, mumbling and sobbing, and Oliver had to help me with her. She was instantly brighter.

We reached the coach. Larry sat stolidly behind the wheel. Geoff stood stiffly by the steps.

'How long since you found her?' Oliver asked.

'What? Pam? You mean Pam?'

'How long?'

'But you said, Jennie.' Geoff looked round wildly, as though searching for Jennie. Elise was now clinging to my arm, her fingers digging into the flesh.

'Jennie's dead, Geoff,' Oliver said quietly. 'Poor Elise has seen her. But—about Pam. You haven't answered.'

'What...what?'

'How long since you found her, Geoff?'

'Oh...just before you came. Ten minutes, say. You *did* say Jennie? Jennie as well? It can't be...' And he watched while Oliver nodded.

Geoff didn't know where to look, at the trees in desperation, or at Oliver with some kind of hope that he could take it all off his hands.

'I saw Pam earlier,' Geoff went on. 'She was all right, then. Sketching an outline. Oh God!' Frantically, he rubbed his hands over his face.

'Show me again, Geoff,' said Oliver. 'But keep behind me. You too, Phil, if you want to come.'

'Of course I want to come.'

Geoff led the way with confidence, though I could not detect any break in the trees, until we came close. 'This way,' he said.

'I remember now,' Oliver said, and Geoff fell back. Thankfully.

The path was quite long, and eventually opened out on to a fair-sized flat area. Oliver paused, then stood and stared at what was there to see. I was at his shoulder.

Pam was lying face down beside her overturned stool. Pastels were scattered around her. The easel had been knocked over when she had fallen, and her painting, dog-clipped to a thin board, lay face upwards beside her. Above and slightly behind her right ear the skin was broken, and blood had run down beneath her chin. Her right hand was palm down on the grass, and a white pastel pencil peeped out from between her fingers.

A two-foot length of wood, two inches square and rotted at one end, lay beside her. There was blood on the solid end.

Oliver crouched. Cautiously he fingered through her hair and felt the neck beneath the curve of her chin. Tried again, then turned his head up to face me.

'She's dead, Phil,' he said quietly. 'I can see broken bone in the laceration. It was a vicious blow. Vicious.'

He made a move as though about to get to his feet, then changed his mind and reached over to touch the surface of the painting, and looked at his fingertip. When he rose to his feet he said, 'She'd finished her painting, Phil, and she'd spray-fixed it.'

I just nodded. I couldn't understand what he wished to imply. He gave the scene a last, comprehensive appraisal, and turned to leave.

Geoff was close behind me. 'Is she...' he whispered.

'She's dead,' Oliver said flatly. He led the way back to the coach, and when he got there he asked, 'Has this thing got a radio-phone?'

Geoff was bemused, and stared numbly. Then he understood. 'Oh yes.'

'Have you called the police?' Oliver raised his eyebrows. 'No? Then you'd better do it. Just tell them Pam's dead and that it looks like violence.'

But Larry, still sitting quietly behind the wheel, was already using the phone. Geoff managed to get himself up the steps, and clambered past Larry, hunting for somewhere he could sit. He had glanced emptily at Elise, who was sitting just at the foot of the steps on one of the folding stools. She tried to smile at him, but it was a poor effort.

I followed Geoff into the coach. He allowed himself to slump into one one of the seats. I sat beside him.

'Geoff,' I said gently, 'I'm afraid you haven't heard it all. There's more. It's Jennie. Surely Oliver told you. Poor Elise went along there, to the Ladies, and saw her. Jennie's dead, too. No... it's no good shaking your head like that. It's a fact. Elise saw Jennie lying there. And—the way she told it—there's a good reason to believe she died in much the same way as Pam. A blow to the head.'

'Oh God...no!' He stared wildly at me. 'And Elise actually *saw* her?' This seemed to be the fact that really shocked him.

'Yes. And lying much as Pam is, from what Elise told us.'

'Oh hell. Poor Elise!'

'I'll have to go to her,' I said. 'We can't leave her sitting out there alone...and brooding.'

He nodded numbly. I edged my way back into the open air.

She was sitting still where I'd seen her last, on a stool, head hanging low, with Oliver standing beside her.

'It's true, then?' she whispered.

I nodded. 'Yes, Elise. It's all horribly true. Both Pam and Jennie dead. It's a terrible fact, but it's happened.'

'Yes.' Her voice was toneless. 'I suppose.'

I looked round for Geoff. He was right behind me. 'Can you find her a drink, Geoff?' I asked. 'Something alcoholic.' But Geoff simply stared at me emptily.

'I've got a drop of brandy,' Larry said. 'For emergencies,' he added, catching Geoff's eye. He produced a quarter bottle with an inch left in it, and poured a little into a plastic cup. He handed it to me, and I crouched to hold it to Elise's lips. She spluttered as I heard Oliver say, 'Is there any way to get down that cliff, Geoff? Without having to go through Pam's place, I mean. Just for a quick look round, and before the police get here.'

Geoff shrugged. 'Any space you can find to get through the trees. But why—'

'Something I want to look for.'

Oliver can be very annoying sometimes, going all secretive. He caught my eye. 'There's something missing from Pam's site,' he told me, 'something that should be there, and isn't.'

'Then leave it for now, Oliver,' I said.

He simply smiled at me. 'Give me a pip on your horn the moment you get a sight of a police car, Larry,' he said.

Then he hurried away towards the tree barrier, choosing a gap twenty yards from Pam's entry point. How very annoying of him!

'They're a hell of a time getting here,' grumbled Geoff.

Now Oliver's words echoed in my mind. Something missing that ought to be there. If he thought he was going to play guessing games with me, he was shortly to be hearing a few things about his character that a wife, however new, might feel free to express.

They came from the direction of the estuary, bumping up the track we had used, a single police patrol vehicle, with its flasher working, but no siren.

'Larry!' I said, and he gave the horn a single pip. Half a minute later, Oliver appeared from beneath the trees. He was a little short of breath.

'You cut that a bit fine,' I told him, but he simply shrugged.

'And where have you been,' I asked, 'and why?'

He made no answer at once, and

instead had a question for Geoff. How very infuriating!

'Did you get a good look at that painting of Pam's, Geoff?' he asked.

'I looked.' Geoff seemed ashamed to admit it.

'And did it seem that she'd finished it?' Oliver persisted stolidly.

'What? I don't know. Well, yes. Finished. Pam's usual attention to detail—the light slanting through the trees. Her speciality.'

Oliver considered that for a moment, then he went on, 'So you'd say she managed to do such a perfect job of it—'

Geoff cut in sharply. It was clear that he hadn't really been listening. 'They're here, Oliver. Talk about something else.'

Oliver gave him a wry look, probably wondering why it should matter what they were talking about.

We watched as the police car drew up, a few yards away. Two uniformed men got out, one a sergeant.

'What's all this, then?'

He would have been well aware that there was already a murder in the town. A second violent death would seem to be an unlikely coincidence. But nevertheless, it had to be investigated.

'Where?' the sergeant asked.

'I'll show you,' Oliver offered, as Geoff obviously didn't wish to.

'Stay with the car.' The sergeant shot a glance at the driver. 'I'll be right back. Now...' To Oliver. 'Show me.'

By this time, I was beginning to feel a little left out of things, what with Oliver's something missing, and now the sergeant's complete ignoring of me. But...

'My wife had better come along,' said Oliver, detecting the light in my eye.

'We don't need...' The sergeant was dismissive.

Oliver cut in quickly. 'To observe things that we men might miss,' he explained. 'Feminine things. It's a woman who's dead.'

The sergeant glanced at me doubtfully. 'Come if you want to. And watch where you put your feet.' But he clearly wasn't happy about it.

Oliver led the way, followed by the sergeant, then me. The scene had not changed, but now I paid more attention to the painting, as something about it seemed to have attracted Oliver's attention. And it really was a splendid piece of work, full of the detail that one didn't expect from pastels. But she had pencil pastels, a white one still clutched in her hand, and it was with these that she had managed to catch the sunlight rippling on the water and slanting through the trees, which ran unbroken from here to the estuary.

'Chalks?' said the sergeant. 'She'd been drawing with chalks?'

'Pastels,' Oliver corrected stiffly. 'And it's painting, not drawing.'

The sergeant took no notice of that.

I cast my gaze around, but I couldn't imagine what it was that Oliver had said should have been there, and was not.

'You know her name?' The sergeant glanced at me as he got to his feet.

'Yes,' I said. 'It's Pamela Wilton.'

'Mrs Pamela Wilton?' He had noted her ring.

'Yes,' I said. Oh Lord—and we ought to have let Paul know. Nobody had thought about that.

'Her husband—where?' he asked.

'He's busy painting.' I pointed back towards the estuary. 'Back there.'

'And nobody's told him...'

I shook my head. 'It's been a great shock. Nobody thought to.'

He drew himself up to his full height. 'Let's get out of here.'

We threaded our way through the trees and back to the patrol car. The sergeant went to use its radio.

'Well?' Oliver asked me.

'Well what?'

'Did you spot what ought to be there, and isn't?'

I suddenly felt very tired. 'Let's not play

107

games, Oliver, please.'

'She'd finished her painting and she'd spray-fixed it. So—where's her spray-can?'

I shrugged. He could be so very irritating. 'She threw it away. Perhaps over the edge of the cliff.'

'No. I had a good search, and the tide's far enough out not to have floated it away. Quite simply, it's been taken away.'

'But why?' I demanded. 'Are you saying that the person who killed her took her spray-can away? There's no sense in that.'

He shrugged. 'There has to be a reason.'

I now understood what was worrying him—and was now worrying me. To have taken it away would have been a deliberate action, and therefore it mattered.

'Somebody's coming,' said Geoff suddenly. A red Rover was approaching, and drew up twenty yards away. A door opened, and from it came a man in a smart charcoal-grey suit. He was a slim six foot two. He approached the sergeant.

'You're sure about this, Sergeant?'

'It's obvious, sir. Head bashed in with what looks like a fence post. It's lying beside her.'

'Have you got on to the SOCO?'

'No sir. Left the decision to you.'

'Then I've decided. Contact him, and let's have the team here, and on the job. Who can show me?' he asked, looking round at our, no doubt, set faces.

'This chap here,' said the sergeant, indicating Oliver. 'He was the one who found her.'

I nudged Oliver, who cleared his throat. 'That's not quite correct. Mr Davies, here, he found her. We're a group from the college, a painting group, and Mr Davies is our tutor. On a routine check of how his students were doing, he found the dead woman. Pamela Wilton, her name is. He fetched me, and I checked she was dead.'

'I hope to God you know what you're doing. I'm Superintendent Llewellyn. D. S. You know what that is?'

'I do,' Oliver assured him. 'I'm ex-police. That's why—'

'I know, I know,' said Llewellyn. 'Show me.'

His eyes were grey, and rather deep-set and penetrating, yet with lines from them that suggested a sense of humour. His eyes now scanned the scene before him, the coach, Larry and Geoff, Elise sitting on her stool, her face still swollen and flushed—and me. 'Hmm!' he said. 'Let's go and have a quick look.' His eyes swept over our group, and centred on me. 'And this is?'

'My wife, Philipa. I'm Oliver Simpson. And that's Geoff Davies, our tutor.'

'Show me then.' His head jerked to Oliver. He knew whom he wanted.

I allowed them to get on with it without me. I'd seen enough of poor, dead Pam.

They threaded their way out of sight through the trees. I didn't expect a long visit, as the superintendent, at this stage, would require nothing more than a quick look round, to get a general impression.

They spent only a few minutes on it, and emerged in close conference. Llewellyn was saying, 'So the dead woman, here, has a husband who chooses to do his painting elsewhere?'

He seemed to be addressing this to me, but I said no more than a simple 'yes', and gave him a sad smile.

'In solitude,' he suggested, 'she could concentrate, and clearly she was able to take advantage of her seclusion, because she was obviously good at it—and I'm no expert. What was I saying?'

He would never, never lose touch with the trend of his own thoughts, but he clearly derived a dry amusement at his own expense.

'You were saying,' I supplied, 'that Pam Wilton—the dead woman—has a husband somewhere in the vicinity. Yes—and he is. Not far away,' I clarified. 'By the estuary.'

'Then I propose that you and I—and

110

your husband if he wishes—should walk to where he's hiding himself—'

'Not hiding,' I said positively, although Paul had not shown himself, and he must have heard the activity, and might even have caught glimpses of the flashing blue lights shining through the trees. Yet he seemed not to have investigated. Too involved with his own work, no doubt. 'Shall we say that he cherishes his solitude?' I pointed back towards the town. 'You passed him on your way here.'

'Then I suggest that you show me where.'

He began to walk away, shepherding me along with a gesture. Oliver fell into step, and Llewellyn glanced at him, but made no comment. 'Let's hear what he's got to say for himself, and why he wasn't sitting with his wife.'

'I don't think they ever did work together,' I told him, then realized that it was a reflection on their marital relationship. Trying to mend fences, I went on, 'I understand that this is usual. All the other painters, they like to paint, and don't usually care for company.'

He looked down at me benevolently. 'But you...were sharing?'

Oliver was now at my other shoulder. They were both much taller than me, and could exchange glances over my head.

'Yes,' I said. 'My husband and I were sharing with the young lady you saw, in considerable distress, sitting on a folding stool. Elise Harcourt is her name.'

'So that all three of you were together when you heard that this woman, Pamela Wilton, was dead? Have I got that right?'

'You have,' I assured him. 'Except for the fact that we didn't know she was actually dead.'

'And how did you hear that there'd been something...well, distressing, shall we say...that *had* happened?'

It was Oliver who answered that one. 'I met Geoff Davies, coming along to find me, all upset, and he asked me to come quickly—so I did.'

'Yes. Are we nearly there?'

'I'm not sure,' I had to admit. 'About here, I think.'

'Another hundred yards,' Oliver said. He sounded quite certain.

'Are you sure, Oliver?' I asked.

'I made a mental note. The shape of the gap—those two firs together. Habit.'

'Clever you.' I patted his arm. 'Don't you think that's clever, Mr Llewellyn?'

'Not for an ex-policeman. It becomes instinctive. Now—here?'

'Yes,' said Oliver.

Llewellyn glanced at his watch. 'Twelve minutes,' he said. 'From the site of his wife's death to the husband's painting den. Walking a steady pace.'

'Is that relevant?' I asked.

He smiled at me. I'd swear one eyelid flickered in Oliver's direction. 'It might be. It might not. Call it a building block. Would you care to lead the way?' he asked me.

'Certainly,' I agreed. I led the way, until Paul was revealed, still industriously working away with his acrylics, a brush in his hand.

He clearly heard us, but didn't glance round.

'Haven't you got settled yet?' he asked. His peripheral vision must have been excellent, in that he saw us as Oliver and Philipa. But it hadn't recorded the superintendent's presence.

'What the devil's going on over there?' Paul went on. 'I saw Jennie settling in. No mistaking her, in that red shirt. Who else could it have been? But now...look for yourself...there's quite a crowd.'

Then he did look round, his hand stilled. 'Who the hell're you?' he demanded. Slowly, he raised himself from his stool.

'Detective Superintendent Llewellyn, sir.' He said it gently, quietly.

'Why the devil should we need a...' Paul's voice faded away, and he turned back abruptly, to stare fixedly over the estuary. 'Here...you don't mean... Something's happened, hasn't it? Over there. I knew... I just knew it! One minute, Jennie was there—you couldn't miss that red shirt of hers. What *is* this? What?'

Llewellyn was smiling thinly, I saw, standing beside him. It wasn't a smile of pleasure, and I could only assume it was to disarm Paul.

'I'm sorry, sir, but I have some bad news for you. The young lady with the red T-shirt is dead.'

Paul stared blankly at him, then blinked. 'It can't be...can't. Look, I've got her in the picture. See, That red spot. That's Jennie.'

'No doubt you painted that when she was alive, Mr... Mr Wilton, would it be?'

'Yes. Look—what's going on? Why're you here, instead of over there?' He gestured with the brush he was holding. 'Jennie's dead? That's what you said. So why aren't you over there?'

'Miss Jennifer Crane is dead, sir,' said Llewellyn, his voice as flat and toneless as he could make it. 'But I didn't come here to speak to you about that. I came to speak to you about your wife. Pamela, is it?'

'Everybody calls her Pam,' Paul told him, hopelessly and uselessly, his voice now empty of emotion. At last he was registering the fact that he was personally involved with somebody even closer to him than Jennie. Pam. His wife. 'What about Pam?' he asked, his throat dry.

'I'm sorry to have to inform you that your wife is dead, too.' Llewellyn was bleak, his voice painfully polite.

'No!' said Paul. It was a flat rejection. 'I'm sorry...'

'You said Jennie,' Paul shouted. 'You're just trying to be funny. Jennie! She's dead, you say. Isn't that enough for you?'

'Enough for me, sir,' said Llewellyn. 'Apparently not, for the person who killed her. The evidence at this stage is that the same person killed both of them. The site of the wound and the method of attack are very similar. The basic fact is that the two women *are* dead. I'd like you to come along with me now, Mr Wilton. I would like you to confirm that the dead woman whom I've just been looking at is in fact your wife.'

Slowly, Paul subsided on to the folding stool he had been using. He seemed to realize he was still holding a paintbrush in his fingers, and threw it, in anger, to the ground.

'Yes, yes,' he said hollowly, though he made no move to comply. He half turned, and gestured to the painting he'd been working on. 'She's on there,' he said hoarsely. 'Jennie's on there—alive. I just don't believe...and Pam! No, no! Oh Christ, no!'

Then he put his hands over his face, and we stared down at his shaking shoulders.

'You'd better come along with me, sir,' said Llewellyn. 'The walk will help. Walking always helps.'

But, I thought, only when you're walking away from horror, but not walking towards it. Llewellyn put a hand on his shoulder and his voice abruptly contained more authority than compassion. 'Come along, sir.'

Paul got to his feet and stared Oliver in the eyes. 'You've seen this, Oliver? Is it true?'

'It's true, Paul. Sorry.'

Numbly, Paul now moved to obey. He cast one look at his painting, and at his equipment spread around, another glance at the scene across the estuary, then he moved obediently, but stumbling, to the tree barrier.

I bent and picked up the brush he had thrown to the ground, automatically noting that it was a round number three, loaded still with red paint, the black handle indicating that it was a sable. He had a small bottle of water standing beside his tubes of acrylic paint, so I popped it in there, to preserve it. Something to preserve from the double tragedy. There was no time to wash it properly.

Llewellyn walked shoulder-to-shoulder with Paul, but not speaking to him, Oliver and me following. I wondered why Llewellyn had asked us to come along with him. Geoff could have done it. But the obvious authority of Oliver helped to add reality and truth to the fact that both Paul's wife and his mistress had died within the past hour.

Yet Llewellyn could not have known of this connection between Pam and Jennie. Paul had stood between them, both physically and emotionally.

'Are there any more of your group scattered around?' asked Llewellyn.

'Well...' said Oliver. 'Somewhere along here—I can't exactly remember where—there are two brothers. They'll have to be told.'

'Where—exactly?'

'I told you, I can't be sure.' Oliver looked around for a guiding sign. 'Ah...look... There they are now.'

Philip and Martin were standing clear of the trees, waiting for us. 'What's going on?' called out one of them. I couldn't tell which, at that distance.

'There's trouble,' I said, hurrying on ahead to break the news as gently as possible.

'We guessed something was wrong,' said

117

Martin, I was now close enough to see. 'Police cars...'

'I'm afraid this is real trouble,' I told them. 'Two sudden deaths. Pam and Jennie. Violent deaths. Can you leave your stuff—I don't know what the police will want us to do.'

Llewellyn was then at my elbow. 'What I want,' he said, 'is for everybody to stay up by the coach, until we've sorted out a few things. D'you think that'll serve, Mr Simpson?'

He had nominated Oliver as the one to play shepherd. Oliver made no objection.

Llewellyn had now got his first clear look at the brothers. I introduced them.

'Martin and Philip Graves, Superintendent.'

'Oh my God, twins,' he said. 'Just what I needed.'

7

I thought I was beginning to understand the superintendent's very dry sense of humour, and this seemed to confirm it. Tradition had it that twins might alibi each other, though no policeman could quote an instance. In this particular case, alibis were not on the agenda, so his joke was, quietly, at himself.

Nevertheless, the twins stared at him blankly.

'What've you got against twins?' demanded Martin. 'We can't go back and start again, and it was Mother's fault in the first place.'

Philip nodded. 'Yes,' he agreed. 'And who the hell are you?'

'All right, all right!' Llewellyn held up a conciliatory hand. 'I was not being serious, anyway, and I am Detective Superintendent Llewellyn. But there *is* something very serious involved here. In the past hour, two members of your group have died violently. And I'm sorry to tell you that it's going to upset your plans seriously.'

'Died?' asked Martin blankly.

'It's Pam Wilton,' I told them. 'Killed while she was working at her painting. And also...Jennie killed while *she* was working. And well... I don't know what's going to happen now.'

I turned to face Llewellyn. 'What *is* next? It seems that you're in charge.'

'I am, indeed,' he declared. 'And for now, let's all get back to your coach. I'll have to be there...ah, you see, they're coming now. The Scenes of Crime team. I'll have to brief them.'

And he marched away towards the coach, we trailing behind him. A van was bumping along the twin tracks from the direction of the estuary. We walked on, leaving the twins staring after us, then, realizing that they were not going to be given the time to tidy up their working place, following us with reluctance.

The van drew level with us as we reached the coach. Elise must have gone inside, as Geoff was now sitting on the stool, knees apart, his head hanging low. Hearing us, he got to his feet.

'What now?' he asked, in a dead and defeated voice.

Llewellyn smiled reassuringly at him. 'I'm going to ask you all to climb into that coach, and then leave everything to us. Go back to Bryngowan Manor. That's right, is it? That's where you're from? Good. The personal property you've had to leave behind you will be looked after, and you'll get it all back. Shortly.'

'Shortly...' said Geoff hollowly.

'Yes sir.' Llewellyn looked round. The team was disembarking from the police van. 'Later on—this evening—I'll be along to the Manor, and we'll have a little introductory meeting. But I'll need a map indicating where you were all—'

'I've got one you can use,' Geoff interrupted shortly. Now, he seemed

120

anxious to get away from there. 'I drew it up myself, so it's not really accurate. But it indicates where everybody was. All right?'

'Thank you.' Llewellyn made an enveloping gesture. 'I'm not used to getting this much help.'

'I want it over,' said Geoff, gesturing to embrace the whole vista. 'Over and done with. And leave us in peace. For heaven's sake, we're just artists. It's a peaceful pursuit.'

Llewellyn beamed at him. 'This time, sir, not quite so peaceful. So...if you'd all like to get aboard—and I'll ask for you up at the Manor, Mr...er...er...'

'My name's on the map,' said Geoff, handing one over to him. 'Now...can we please get away from here?'

'Any time you like.' Llewellyn examined our various gloomy expressions. 'And I don't suppose I need to tell you all that I don't expect everybody to go diving into their cars and rushing off home. As a favour to me.'

He flashed us an empty smile, and turned away.

We climbed into the coach, silently, miserably. It seemed to be nearly empty with two of the group missing, and none of our equipment aboard. Larry sat quietly behind his steering wheel. Then, the moment the coach started moving, the complaints were expressed.

'My brushes are going to set solid.'

'The light'll never be the same again.'

'I bet there'll be dirty fingerprints all over everything.'

And so on.

'They'll be very careful,' Oliver said reassuringly. 'Don't worry.'

But this was received with scepticism. By now they all knew that Oliver had been in the police, and they were wondering, darkly, on whose side he might be. Which was saddening, really.

I was aroused from my thoughts by the abrupt turn into the gateway, and raised my head. The coach drew to a halt on the terrace, and Geoff said, trying to lessen the gloom, perhaps, 'All change.'

Larry had clearly phoned ahead, because they were all there waiting for us, strained and ghoulish expressions focused on us as we alighted. The full collection of the two other groups had come out to welcome us, along with the staff. But it was not a joyous welcome.

In silence, they drew aside from the coach door, so that we filed between a double row of set faces, Oliver leading, with me just behind him, and Elise, at my heels, whispering, 'wait for me, wait for me,' then Paul, stiff and unresponsive, the

122

twins trailing behind, Geoff as rearguard at their heels. Larry did not stir from his driver's seat.

The principal, Donald McHugh, was waiting for us in the reception hall, full of anxiety and solicitous in the extreme. 'Have you eaten? Does anyone care for a drink? We could fix you up with a hot meal.' And so on. Concerned and fussy, he was. But all we wanted to do was get to our rooms, to collapse on the bed in tears or to head towards a hot bath to wash away the tarnish of death. Or simply to mope in solitude and distress. Nobody expressed any desire for food.

Paul was ahead of us up the stairs, almost running, and we reached the landing as he slammed his door violently behind him. I did not dare to allow myself to wonder how I would be feeling should Oliver be dead. And as I was about to open our own door, a voice whispered from behind me, 'Please!'

I turned. Elise was at my heels, Oliver smiling behind her, She turned up her harried face to me and almost sobbed, 'I'll go mad in my room—all on my own.'

'Then come along in,' I offered. What else could I have said? Oliver raised his eyebrows at me.

I closed the door behind them, and Elise stood just inside it, looking about her.

'Ooh!' she said. 'This is nice. Swish.'
That had been Jennie's word for it.

I sat her down on the edge of our bed.
'I intend to have a bath,' I told her. 'Or
a shower.'

'D'you mean you've got a choice?'

I nodded.

'How lovely! There's only one bathroom
to each corridor, in the annexe. And you
can bet they'll be queuing for them.'
She left that hanging, the actual request
remaining unexpressed.

'So all right,' I told her. 'You can use
our bathroom. A shower or a bath. Two
of us together, because they're separate.
It's a matter of choice. Oliver and me, or
you and me, or Oliver and you.'

I'd said this with deliberate gravity, as a
small levity designed to distract her from
her morbid thoughts. She blushed, and put
her hand to her lips. 'Oh...I couldn't.'

Oliver grinned at her.

'You two girls carry on,' he said. 'I'm
going down to see if they've opened the
bar. Mr McHugh said something about
that, and I could certainly do with a drink.
Shall I bring something—'

'No, Oliver, I think not,' I told him.
'You run along. Give us twenty minutes.
There's a lot to be said.'

He raised his eyebrows.

'Is there?' Elise looked quickly from one

face to the other, huntedly.

'I rather think so,' I assured her, using my reassuring voice, and I heard Oliver close the door behind him.

Elise pouted at me. 'There's only one thing on my mind, and I can assure you I don't want to talk about *that*. Not even think about it.'

'I'm sure you don't, Elise.' I smiled at her, trying to relax some of the tension in her expression. 'But I do.'

She tossed her head. 'Why do you want to?' she demanded. 'It's not a nice thing to think about, let alone say out loud.'

'I've been talking about not very nice things since I was in my early teens, Elise. My father was a senior officer in the police force, and he used to like to have somebody to discuss his cases with him. Get it out of his system, as he put it. But my mother died when I was very young, so there was only me. And we talked together, my father and I. It means that I'm rather immune to all the horrors that human beings can inflict on each other. And I'm interested. I can't help that, either. Aren't you interested in finding out the exact truth? It's a fairly rare thing, is absolute truth. It hides itself away, sometimes with a bit of help.'

She had wandered over to the window, and was staring out towards the scene of

Jennie's and Pam's deaths.

'It doesn't sound very nice to me,' she said, lifting her chin. 'Not at all ladylike. Can't we talk about something else?'

'It's not a ladylike thing to do—murder.'

She turned, staring at me, wide eyes startled. 'Are you saying that I...that I could have... Jennie...oh, you couldn't be saying *that*.'

'Of course not, Elise. All I was trying to do was explain that I might be able to help our group if I can get enough information. You know what I mean. Enough background. And the social niceties—ladylike and things like that—are at the moment very irrelevant. Do you get what I mean, Elise?'

'Well, *I've* got nothing to tell you.'

I eyed her, my head cocked sideways. 'I'm sure you know something, Elise. It's just that you don't care to say it. Or you don't even realize that you know it. Everybody's the same.'

She tried to go all regal on me, lifting her chin. But it didn't work very well with the face she had. I grinned at her.

'Want to go and get your shower?' I asked, nodding towards the bathroom door.

'Ooh—yes. I can't wait...' Anything to change the subject.

'Then we'll do that.'

'We?'

'Yes. You use the shower while I have a bath. Or the other way round, if you like. They're separate. Shower stall and bath.'

'Oh...I couldn't. Can't I just go and have a shower—on my own?'

'And me wait?'

'It wouldn't take long,' she assured me.

I smiled at her. 'But I don't want to wait, either.'

'Then you're wasting time just talking,' she pointed out briskly.

There are women so shy that they don't want even other women to see them stripped. Perhaps it's the same with men. Yet I was equally eager for my bath or shower—and it was our room, after all.

'Very well,' I said, 'I'll go first, and with a bit of luck Oliver will be back in time.'

'In time for what?' she asked suspiciously.

'I could ask him to sponge your back,' I offered her. 'If, as I said, he returns in time.'

That did it. At least, I had got something moving. She was in the bathroom inside five seconds, and I heard the latch thrown over.

The difficulty now was that I might lose her confidence, and I had so much to ask her. But, if my understanding of

127

her was correct, she craved company, and I wanted to get to know her better, to a point where she would be willing to offer me confidences she would normally cherish to herself. In the first instance, I wanted to know whom she suspected of having slashed her precious painting. She had hinted that she had a good idea as to who had done it—that it was a woman's work. But the only women in our group (and presumably in the group at the time of the slashing) had been Jennie and Pam.

Both of whom were now dead.

It was impossible that Elise could have killed Pam. She could not have found the opportunity in order to have done that. But she *had* found such an opportunity to kill Jennie; in fact, she had contrived the opportunity. I found it difficult to accept that, even with her extreme delicacy, she would elect to walk all the way to that ladies' toilet, and reject the privacy of umpteen acres of woodland. Elise had (if Jennie had been the one to slash her painting) an excellent motive. She had provided herself with the opportunity. And she might have found it quite easy to come across a weapon. Anything handy and hard would have sufficed.

I realized that the shower had been turned off. 'There's a bathrobe over the rail,' I called out.

'It's all right. I'm dressing again.' Too modest to walk the corridors to her room in a bathrobe! Oh dear me. Yet I would have expected her, after a shower, to have wanted clean underwear next to her skin. But there was no point in arguing about it.

There was a knock at the door—or rather, a thump—and Oliver's voice. 'Are you decent?'

He must have meant Elise, because he would not have troubled about me.

'Come in,' I called out. 'We're decent.'

'I can't open the door.'

I did so, and found him with a glass of what looked like pale sherry in each hand. He had had to kick the door.

'Where is she? Has she left us?'

'She's in the bathroom.'

'I've brought you a drink, Elise,' he called out, his head close to the bathroom door. 'D'you want it in there?'

'Oh no...no!'

'She's a delicately brought-up young lady,' I told him. 'We have to treat her with extreme care. Like porcelain.'

'Ah yes.' He put one glass on the bedside table and handed me the other. 'Will that do you, my pet?' he asked.

I wished he wouldn't call me that. It was only recently that he had been doing it.

'Thank you. And now tell me what you've found out.'

He shook his head. Nothing relevant.

The bathroom door opened, and Elise appeared. Her colour was even higher than before, and she looked startled. There had been no shower cap in there, because I had no need of one. Towel-dry my hair, and it springs back into place. Hers was still damp, and hung about her face in a tangled, auburn mass.

'Oh!' she said, abruptly aware of this as she caught sight of Oliver.

'There's a sherry for you, Elise,' Oliver said. 'Buck you up. It's on the bedside table.'

'Oh...oh, thank you, but really...at this time of day...' She gave him a shy smile. 'Thank you for the thought, Oliver.'

He caught my eye, and I inclined my head. We were at the stage where we were very nearly able to converse without words.

'I'll leave you two girls together, then,' he said, 'and I'll go and give myself a good old soak.'

Elise smiled weakly.

Oliver sings in his bath. At home, it is more often than not something a little risqué, but in deference to company he ventured into: 'On Mother Kelly's Doorstep', which, he had told me, his

130

father used to sing. Randolph Sutton's song, surely!

It did occur to me that singing, at this time of loss and distress, was not exactly appropriate. But actually, neither of us had known the dead women with any intimacy, and we could not be expected to mourn for them. To do so might even have been considered as cynicism. And Oliver was ex-police, after all. He was trained to consider murder in a dispassionate manner.

Yet Elise frowned her disapproval.

'Do you always come here alone?' I asked her.

She walked over to stare out of the window again. 'Well...yes,' she said. 'I don't know any other painters, back home.'

'Aren't you a member of an artists' group?' I asked casually, sitting myself on the edge of the bed.

'Well...Sort of. Evening classes.'

'And no particular friend you could bring with you?'

She discovered she would like a little sherry, after all. She used it to blur her response. It was difficult for her to shake her head with the glass to her lips, and I had to guess that she meant no.

'No young gentleman friend?'

'Oh—my father wouldn't approve of that.'

'Approve? How do you mean?'

'Going away for a week with a man!' Her eyes were huge. 'Of course.'

It sounded as though she approved of this attitude.

'But you're surely old enough to make your own decisions on things like that,' I said. 'How old *are* you, Elise?'

'I'm twenty-two, if it's any of your business.' She lifted her head. I was supposed to flinch, but refrained.

'I was just chatting,' I told her. 'If we're to be friends...' I shrugged, letting it go at that.

'Oh...are we?'

'Surely. You have my complete sympathy, you know, in regard to your slashed painting.'

'I don't want your pity, thank you.' She was trying to maintain her dignified front, but the cracks were showing. She needed somebody, desperately needed a woman friend, but was too proud to admit it.

'I said sympathy,' I reminded her. 'Not pity. Pity's shallow. Sympathy is supportive. For instance...you'll have realized by now that I'm a very nosy person, and can't prevent myself from trying to dig out facts. Well—as an example—I'd like to help you to discover who slashed your painting.'

I had an uneasy feeling that this slashing

episode might be linked with the present violent deaths. Two people were most certainly not involved, but if it had been Jennie, and Elise had discovered that, she was, though she might not have realized it, in a very delicate situation.

She stared at me, then turned away to look out of the window and murmured something to the glass. Oliver was now on: 'My Old Man Said Follow The Van'. Marie Lloyd?

'Pardon?' I said, having missed something she'd said.

She turned. Her expression was empty of emotion. 'I don't need your help.'

'Surely you need somebody's.' Then I realized what she'd meant. 'You mean you've already got somebody helping you?'

She tossed her head, as though about to deny that, with dignity of course. Then she whispered, 'Yes.'

My mind did a rapid run through the possibilities. A man, certainly. Her rejection of me suggested that she didn't wish to confide in another woman. So...who? Not the twins. She had implied *a* person, whereas the twins were never singular. Not Paul, either. His interests were—or had been—centred on Jennie. So...who else was there? Geoff?

'Geoff?' I asked gently.

I could hear the bath water running

away. Oliver, in a very short while, would be sweeping out, wrapped—no doubt inadequately in the bathrobe. Then I would have lost her.

She tucked her lower lip between her teeth, and nodded.

'So it's Geoff who's your friend? Geoff you come here to meet?'

'Yes,' she whispered.

'He's not married, then?'

'No.' Then it registered. 'Oh—no! Of course not.'

'Otherwise you wouldn't for one moment...'

'I don't want to talk about it.'

'Because he doesn't respond?'

'I don't know what you mean by that.' She was all dignity again.

'Oh...come on, Elise. You're in love with him. Don't deny it.'

She made no attempt to, but her eyes told me everything.

'And he?' I asked. 'Does he reciprocate your feelings?'

She tossed her head, and the hair flopped about heavily. 'You don't have to wrap it up in fancy words, Philipa. Yes—we want to get married. I come here as often as I can, and he's got a cottage, round the back of the Glasshouse. He does other courses, you know. Oh...he's ever so clever. There's a ramblers' group he does, and a photography one. He's got his own darkroom in his cottage. I book a single room here, and just untidy the bed each morning. There! I've shocked you.'

I very nearly laughed, and would thereby have lost her for ever. But I managed to remain quiet and involved.

'Not shocked, Elise,' I assured her. 'Don't be foolish. It's your life. So why not marry him, and move in with him?'

'Oh...I couldn't do that. It would upset my father.'

'Oh dear.'

'He thinks artists are drunken louts.'

'Does he? That hardly describes our lot.'

'But look at the Impressionists, he'd say. Spent all their time in bars and nightclubs. Look at their pictures, if you don't believe it. And always painting women having baths or sitting naked on the grass with men friends. How *could* I take Geoff to him?'

'Offhand,' I told her, 'I can't think of anybody more respectable than Geoff. Except Oliver, of course. You ought to try throwing a few more artists' names at your father. Reynolds, Turner, Gainsborough. Surely they were respectable enough for anybody. Don't you think you're being...but it's not my business. Now—tell me—has Geoff got anywhere

with discovering who slashed your wonderful painting?'

She shook her head. I didn't believe her.
Yes, he had, her eyes told me.

'And he told you who?'

She nodded, lower hp between her teeth.

'When did he tell you, Elise?'

She turned her head away.

'Last night, for instance?'

I thought then that I had lost her. She
put a hand to her untidy and damp
hair.

'I've brought along a hair-dryer,' I
offered.

'It's all right. I'd better get along...'

'Did he tell you last night, Elise?' I had
to be very gentle with her.

She stared at me numbly. She had
revealed a sacred confidence. I put a
hand to her arm. 'Who?'

'Jennie,' she whispered.

I released her, and she was out of
the door in a flash. I closed it after
her.

Oliver came up behind me, the bathrobe
wrapped around him. 'And that,' he said,
obviously not having missed a word of
it, with the bathroom door opened just
a crack, 'really puts the cat amongst the
pigeons.'

I said nothing, but headed for the
bathroom. My turn at last.

8

We were in the otherwise empty and silent bar, what was left of our group. It was four o'clock, and we were gathered in one corner, with Geoff as the chairman. It was he who had arranged this meeting.

I assumed that Geoff had accepted that he was still our leader, and thus carried a load of responsibility on his shoulders, not simply in regard to the continuity of our painting programme, but even for the deaths. If he had been earlier and more alert with his routine tour of our sites, he might have prevented, or in some way averted, the double tragedy.

The twins seemed to have adopted a detached attitude, as though they were there merely because their presence had been requested, yet they plainly felt it was none of their affair, at all. They wished to be no more than spectators.

Paul was repressed, pale and morose, there because he had been requested to attend. In one short period he had been deprived of both a wife and a mistress. He seemed bemused, his brain paralysed by the double impact.

And Elise was there—now for some reason unable to look me in the face. Perhaps she was resenting the fact that I had drawn from her more information than she had really intended to confide.

'What's all this about, Geoff?' I asked, to get things moving.

He was leaning forward, elbows on his knees, and now looked up at me from beneath his brows. 'Oh...it's something that's been mentioned to me by one or two.' He didn't indicate by whom. 'They want to go home. The policeman said he'd be round, this evening, and it's all going to be very unpleasant. We want to know how we stand. He said he didn't want any of us to leave, but...' He lifted his shoulders in an expressive shrug. 'I mean...*can* he prevent people from leaving, if they feel like it? That's what they all want to know. I mean...the whole set-up's ruined now. They haven't even got their painting equipment.'

'All right,' said Oliver. 'The position at this stage is that he's only at the beginning of his investigation, and of course he needs to have everybody available. So he's asked us to stay, to be here when he wants us. And after all, we're booked in for the week, and there's really no reason for us to sit around being miserable, and staring at each other. I expect Geoff can find us something to do...' He turned his attention to Geoff, raising his eyebrows in interrogation.

I noticed that Oliver had simply dismissed any consideration of leaving, and was taking the practical angle of deciding what we would actually have to entertain us, and fill the empty hours.

'Well...yes,' said Geoff. He looked round at all our faces, trying to discover any sign of enthusiasm—and seeing none.

'But can he *make* us stay here?' asked Philip. 'That's the point.'

'He can only ask,' Oliver told him. 'At this stage.'

Then everybody started talking at once, to offer their individual grievances. Oliver had to hold up a palm to silence them.

'Shall we just wait and see what Mr Llewellyn's got to say about it,' he suggested. 'I expect he'll make everything clear.' He seemed very confident about that.

They all nodded, though a little reluctantly. It was sensible and valid, but they were not comforted.

Then Paul drew himself up, sitting stiffly, and looked around the group. 'Shouldn't we get a solicitor in on this?' he asked.

I had expected some such suggestion, but hadn't decided from whom we might get it.

'A solicitor?' Oliver made rejection gestures. 'What on earth for?'

'To protect our interests,' Paul explained politely. There were half-hearted mutters of agreement.

Oliver held up his hand, again putting a halt to the sudden flow of 'yes's and 'no's. 'Surely it hasn't come to that. By no means. If you're actually taken in for serious questioning at the station, then you could ask for a solicitor to be present. But...shall I tell you something? When I was in the force, we always took a request for a solicitor as an indication that we had our man—or woman. If we had any doubts about the arrest, that is. I mean, looking at it psychologically, why would they need a solicitor if they're innocent? There'd only be the truth to tell, and that doesn't need outside help. Having a solicitor beside you implies that you've got something to hide. No. No solicitor—at this stage, anyway.'

They stared at him, as though he had refused them a glass of water when they were parched.

'I'm a solicitor,' put in Philip politely, gesturing with his pipe.

There was silence. They looked at each other, and shook their heads. Philip was too close to us, too involved.

'And I'm an accountant,' Martin put in. 'I do Phil's accounts, and I can tell you, he charges the earth.'

'And I'm civil. I've never done any criminal work.' Philip nodded, dismissing the idea finally and positively.

Oliver sighed. 'Let's leave the question of solicitors for now,' he suggested. 'Let's just wait and see what the superintendent's got to say for himself.'

That seemed to put an end to our little conference. They got to their feet and moved around aimlessly.

And as Geoff stood and stretched, I said quietly, 'Could we just have a word, Geoff?'

'Why not?' He looked from Oliver's face to mine. 'What's this about?'

I suggested that we should go outside and do a little walking. Geoff nodded. 'There's something I wanted to do in the Glasshouse, anyway,' he said. 'Shall we go there, and talk if you want to?'

He led the way through a rear door, which proved to provide a short cut to the Glasshouse, and held open the door for us to precede him.

Once we were inside, I asked, 'What was it you wanted to do?' All was neat and tidy.

He shrugged. 'I'm trying to keep ahead of things, so I'm wondering what painting we can do, without going out of the grounds. Two choices—work in here from photographs that I've taken in the district, over the years. It would be something to do. Or I could set up a still life, or a number of them. The grounds are packed with flowers. Or...of course...' he went on gravely, inserting a third idea, 'we could do some nude studies, if one of our two ladies cared to oblige.'

'Over my dead body,' said Oliver.

'Yes. That too,' Geoff went on placidly. 'Nude With Corpse. It would at least be original.'

'Suggest it to Elise,' I told him, 'and she'd pass out on the spot.'

He smiled to himself. 'That she would.'

'And her father would bring a hatchet and carve you to pieces,' Oliver told him.

'You know about her father?' Geoff asked. He was leading us the length of the Glasshouse, to the counter than ran the full width of the far wall. He didn't look round. 'She's never told me anything about him.'

'Yes.' I spoke to his back. 'We know. Elise came to our room, when we got back. She didn't want to be alone, and I'm not surprised. We let her use the bathroom, and she and I had a little chat.'

He turned, leaning back against the counter. 'Little?' he asked casually. He obviously knew Elise very well. 'She's a right chatterbox.'

'Well—she confided. So naturally I can't repeat what she said. Except to you, Geoff, of course.'

'She told you about us?'

'Yes,' I said. 'A little.'

'She must have taken a liking to you, then.'

'I think perhaps she did. We got along together very well indeed. I mean...in a situation such as this, and the rather tricky position she has in the overall picture... Tell me, Geoff—how did you discover who had slashed her painting?'

He stared at me blankly. He was not pleased with this. 'What do you...she told you that?'

'Oh yes.'

'The silly child.' He said it with affection, smiling softly.

'Not silly, Geoff. Naïve, yes. Immature, perhaps. But not silly. You see, she's in a situation that could make her life very difficult, and when the superintendent gets going he'll be sure to pounce on it.'

He stared blankly at me. Some of the colour had flowed from his face, leaving spots of red high on his cheeks. Beyond him, Oliver was wandering the length of the counter, opening each of the drawers and peering into them.

'What situation?' Geoff asked. 'Nobody's told me anything.'

'I don't think she realizes, herself.'

'Then tell *me*, for God's sake.'

I took a deep breath. 'You know she was sharing her special spot with Oliver and me? What happened was that she wanted to go to the toilet, and in spite of the acres of trees all around, she insisted on going to the Ladies—and you know where that is, I expect.'

He groaned. 'Yes—I know.'

'So she placed herself at the scene of Jennie's death, and at about the time that it happened, and later—up in our room—she told me what she had heard from you, that it had been Jennie who'd slashed her lovely painting. Is *that* true?'

For a moment he looked hunted, then he whispered, 'Yes.'

'So that puts Elise in a very tricky situation, Geoff. She had a positive motive for doing Jennie harm, and she was ideally placed for doing it. And she realizes that, and she could very likely go into a panic, if pressed, and say anything. Literally anything. *Then* what?'

'But you can't really believe that Elise could do such a thing.' He rubbed his hands over his face, and stared round at Oliver for assistance. But Oliver simply smiled, and said nothing.

144

I shook Geoff's arm. 'She's a woman, Geoff. A grown woman, and she'd been deeply wounded when her painting was slashed. That was two years ago, and she still feels it. A woman, hurt in that way, is capable of anything, and don't delude yourself about that. Anything! And Mr Llewellyn has probably come across dozens of cases where they have. So...he'll give special attention to Elise, and we'll need to look out for her welfare, Geoff.'

'D'you think I shan't?' He looked keenly at me. 'We?'

'Yes. Include Oliver and myself as supporters. Do you think she would have confided as much as she did, and to a woman she barely knows, unless she was completely innocent?'

'What did she confide?' He was wary.

'What's between you and Elise. I got it all—including her father's attitude to artists.'

He rubbed his hands through his hair. 'I'm completely beyond the pale,' he admitted. 'A pariah.'

'So...tell me. How did you discover who had slashed her painting?'

He drew a deep breath, then relaxed, his shoulders slumping again.

'It happened two years ago,' he said. 'There've been a lot of painting courses between then and now, because we have weekend ones as well as full week ones. And although there's a tight little circle we've got here, who never seem to miss one, there are others of course. Semi-regulars, if you like. So...there were three women here on the night the painting was slashed—and who're not very regular students. It's been a long and tiresome business. You see, it's not easy to slash a canvas. It needs a sharp knife, such as a Stanley knife. Razor sharp, those blades are. And I have one here, in one of the drawers.'

'Third one along,' said Oliver, and Geoff flashed him a brief smile.

'Right,' he said. 'So I had to wait and wait, for the times when I was alone in here with one of our past artists. I wasn't certain it had to be a woman, but it seemed like a woman's work. Anyway...I'd have a sheet of watercolour paper, say, on my cutting surface—which is on this counter. And, with just one person here, and me with my steel straight-edge in position, I'd say, "Reach me out the Stanley knife, will you," in a casual voice. And usually they'd have to ask, "Where is it?" And I'd say, "Third drawer along." So *that* person hadn't known. And...oh, it took ages.'

'Two years,' I said emptily. Two years! 'But you eventually succeeded?'

'Oh yes. In the end, there was just one

person who didn't ask, and just went straight to it.'

'That person being Jennie?'

'That's right.'

'So then you knew?'

'Yes. Then I knew.' He nodded sagely.

I groaned, but internally. 'That was very clever of you, Geoff,' I said. 'But it's not valid, you know.'

'What? Of course it is.'

'It's not positive thinking. For one thing, the picture-slasher could be very quick-witted, and have spotted the trap. And for another, Jennie could have known where you kept it, simply because she'd seen you put it there, at one time or another. And so...your slasher might be anywhere, not necessarily here at this time. But...and you must see this, Geoff...we're left with the fact that Elise *believed* it to be Jennie, and she went within a few yards of her at the time when Jennie was killed, and when she really had no valid reason for going there, with acres of woodland in all directions.'

'Elise wouldn't—'

'I know. It wouldn't be ladylike to resort to a barrier of trees. And I'm sure she's sincere in that. Her father—'

'Her father!' he interrupted, groaning.

'Who isn't going to allow his delicate little girl to become embroiled...he would use that word, I'd bet. Wouldn't allow his

147

girl to find herself in a nasty situation such as a double murder. If he gets to hear of this business—'

'Don't even *think* it!'

The door was flung open, and Elise rushed in. 'Geoff!' she cried. 'It's going to be all right! And when he meets you, and gets to know you...'

'What the devil!' Geoff said. 'Easy now, easy.'

'I've phoned Daddy. He's going to get right in his car, and come along to see that everything's sorted out. And Geoff—he's going to meet you at last.'

'I can't wait,' Geoff whispered.

She linked her arm in his. 'You'll like him, Geoff.' Then she looked round at Oliver and me. 'I told him I've got friends here, and he said he'd give me eight to five that I couldn't trust them.' She managed a little tinkle of a laugh. 'But I never did understand odds. Who gets what if it is or isn't! So complicated.'

'I'm sure I can't help you,' I told her. 'It's all a great mystery to me, too. The best thing is to keep away from betting. You never win.'

Oliver laughed. 'Unless you're the bookie.'

'That's true,' Elise agreed, jutting her lower lip. 'He never seems to lose.'

We stared at her.

'Are you telling us that your father's a

bookmaker?' Geoff asked.

'Well...yes. Didn't I tell you that?' She pouted. 'I was sure you knew.'

'Not until now, my sweet. And he's got the utter nerve to criticize me for being an artist!'

'It didn't seem worth mentioning. And it's ever so legal.'

'Oh, I'm sure it is. But so's painting pictures.'

'Ah yes.' She linked her arm in his, drawing herself closer. 'But you can't earn a decent living by painting pictures and tutoring courses.'

Geoff looked down into her flushed face. 'How very true,' he admitted, sighing.

'But if Daddy taught you about odds, you could start your own book, Geoff love, and earn lots and lots of money.'

'Thank you for the advice.'

'Oh now...don't be silly, Geoff. I *know* you could do it.'

'Would you rather marry a bookmaker—or an artist?' Geoff was keeping a tight control on his voice.

'I just want to marry *you*, Geoff, and you know it.'

'As an artist or a bookmaker?' His voice was toneless.

I was becoming disturbed. A few seconds before, Elise had simply been teasing him, but now a fresh tone had entered into it.

She wanted Geoff, and she was staring at him now, abruptly aware that she had to make a decision.

'As you are, Geoff,' she said softly. 'Of course.'

I caught Oliver's eye. Silently he was asking the question: can we get out of here?

Quietly, we left them to work it out between themselves. We stood outside. 'What now?' I asked.

'Walk,' he suggested. 'We've done no exploring at all. It's about five o'clock, and dinner's not until seven-thirty. What about a walk down into the town?'

'It's the best part of a mile,' I pointed out. 'And all uphill coming back.'

'Since when can't you walk that distance?' he asked.

'Give me five minutes to change into slacks and my walking shoes.'

Oliver, I knew, wanted to see the site of Jennie's death. That suited me fine, because I wanted to see it too.

So I changed, rejoined him, and we walked down to the town.

9

It was still rather warm for walking, but this portion was downhill, and hopefully, when we plodded back and upwards, the sun would at least be nudging the horizon.

'There's something you want to look at, isn't there?' I asked him.

'Naturally. The scene of Jennie's death, of course.'

'There'll be nothing left to interest you, there.'

He paced a further hundred yards before answering. 'All right. Just to look at it, then. To see what Elise would have seen.'

'That's not going to be any help, Oliver, and anyway it's officially a police case, and they won't want us poking about.'

'True,' he said. 'But they'll have cleared off long before this, and it always helps to see for yourself. At any other time, you'd be the one to suggest it, Phil. What's got into you, so suddenly?'

'Oh...I don't know. Perhaps it's because I'm wondering if it wouldn't have been better to stay around, back at the Manor.'

He was silent. We walked two hundred yards, with not a sound from him. Then at last he said, 'Why better?'

I found it difficult to put into words. 'A feeling.'

'Hmm! Let me guess. You're interested in that Elise lass, and you don't know how far away her father lives, so you can't guess how long it'll take him to get here, and—'

'All right, all right! Yes, yes, and yes. I'm worrying about Elise. To phone her father...well, it was a mistake. I can see trouble coming from that.'

'True,' he agreed. 'Very true, in fact.'

'Heavens,' I said. 'If he comes here, he's certainly going to be heading into trouble, one way or another.'

He paced ahead, not glancing sideways at me. We were nearing the river now. At last he commented, as though he had given it deep thought, 'I think Elise could have been exaggerating a little, about her father. Didn't you think so, Phil? Perhaps it's she who's a little tentative, and not absolutely certain that it's Geoff she wants.'

'Her father,' I said, 'would call that hedging her bets.'

'So you know that much about betting.' He nudged my elbow. 'You can bet, then, that her father wouldn't do a thing, or come to any decision, before he weighed up the odds, for and against.'

'Then it's possibly a good thing that he's

going to meet Geoff,' I said hopefully.

'Or a bad one.' He turned his head and grinned at me. 'Want a bet?'

'I never bet.'

'And a good thing, too.' He was silent for a few moments, then he went on, 'And what would you bet that our drive isn't finished when we get back to Penley—and no access?'

'What!' I stopped in mid-stride.

'Just a thought, my love. But do contractors *ever* finish anything by the promised time? Think about it, Phillie.'

'But—if it wasn't—what would we do?'

He turned back to face me. 'We'd phone our friend and benefactor, Harvey Remington, and demand accommodation from him. As compensation for a consideration that has failed. He'll know that phrase.'

I thought it best not to comment, and we walked on.

We had now reached the river, and the turn-off to our right along the road to the footbridge. There was no traffic. We saw nobody, and no cars passed us.

Then we reached the footbridge, and Oliver paused, looking round.

'Things I want to check,' he explained, and he moved on to the bridge.

'Let me guess.' I wanted to do a little checking, myself. 'You want to see whether

153

any of our group could have approached in this direction, and not been noticed by Jennie. Deny it.'

We were now standing in the middle of the bridge, which, designed for pedestrians only, was a mere six feet wide. It was a strongly built wooden erection, with hefty railings each side, though the planks under our feet seemed loose. From its centre we were looking directly down the estuary.

In the intervening time since we had last seen the sea, the tide had turned, the water flowing back, though moving sluggishly.

'I don't see that it would be possible,' Oliver said.

'What? What have you got in mind?'

'I'm looking for some way that a member of our group could have approached this bridge, and walked over it, without being seen by Jennie. From up there. As you said yourself, Phil.'

We both turned and looked up to the top of the cliff, at the far end of the bridge. The sandstone face rose vertically, and on the near edge of its flat top surface, we knew, Jennie had set up her easel. The only apparent access to that site, at the far end of the footbridge, was the steep, cobbled lane. A pedestrian way, this was, clearly.

'Would it matter?' I asked softly. 'About being observed, I mean. Jennie would have seen anybody from our group as a friend, and not, surely, as someone aggressive.'

'Pam Wilton?' he suggested. 'Jennie would've seen Pam as anything but a friend.' He nodded his head decisively. 'Especially if she was carrying something weighty and lethal.'

'You're surely not suggesting that Pam could have walked the best part of a mile here, *and* back, *and* managed to finish her painting. You're getting to know pastel work now, Oliver, and even I—from just a glimpse—could tell that the sort of work she's been doing is far from being sketches. They're detailed paintings. In fact, from the view I got of it, I'm surprised she'd managed to finish it in just one morning. You saw it, Oliver, and you ought to know. *Could* she have done it—all that beautiful detail—*and* walked all the way here, *and* back—'

'All right. All right. I agree. She couldn't have finished that painting *and* finished off Jennie, in the time.'

'That,' I said positively, 'was a joke in the poorest taste, Oliver.'

'Yes—it was. Sorry.'

'Let's go and look at Jennie's site,' I said, smiling at him.

We reached the other end of the bridge, and the steep, cobbled walkway faced us. I found that my walking shoes had soles that slipped on the highly polished cobbles. Oliver had no such difficulty, his soles being rubber.

The path mounted, gently curving to our right, until we came to the side of a modern brick building. There was, on its wall, a white signboard, with an arrow pointing to our right, towards Jennie's chosen painting position. Next to this sign was fastened a brass plaque, with information engraved on its surface. It was, however, in Welsh. The only words that made any sense to me were Owain and Glyndwr. I gathered from this that Owen Glendower had done something of historical interest on this cliff top. Perhaps he had stood there, looking out to sea and waiting for reinforcements that were due to arrive in ships. Or enemies, of course. Or Irishmen, always keen for a good fight, on either side.

We followed the direction of the arrow, walking through a narrow gap in the high yew hedge, and found ourselves on the wide rock platform on which Jennie had chosen to paint—and had died.

This would clearly have been a most advantageous situation for an artist interested in the harbour. Apart from that, the bay was widely visible to the left, so that beyond the estuary and directly ahead was the gentle curve of the headland, on the outside edge of which Paul Wilton, we were given to understand, always chose to settle himself. He would have been clearly visible to Jennie, as she would have been to him. Yet he had not seen her attacked—or so he claimed.

From our position on the platform of rock it was possible to look directly north along the route the coach had taken, and we could detect the indented parallel tracks in the grass. But the grassland seemed more narrow than when we had driven northwards along it. The trees—those hugging the cliffs—now appeared to be more tightly massed. The greenery on the other side reached across and appeared almost to intertwine. It *would* have been possible to walk to the bridge from along there, hugging the woodland, and not be observed from this site. Only for the last hundred yards before reaching the bridge, and across the bridge itself, would anyone approaching be seen clearly.

We looked round the area of naked rock where Jennie had died, but now there was no sign of such violence. Any traces of blood, all Jennie's equipment, and the stool and easel had been meticulously removed.

'Have we seen enough?' I asked, there being nothing to see. Its very nakedness was eerie.

'Enough for me,' Oliver agreed.

So we turned back to those slippy and dreaded cobbles.

It was not until we turned the corner of the building that I saw the sign, which we had missed on the way in. It was a white board, with the single word LADIES in black, fastened to the brickwork above the door. This had been Elise's objective.

Beneath it, fastened to the door itself, was a smaller notice on somewhat weathered cardboard, and intended, one hoped, to be temporary.

'Closed', it read 'for Alterations. Nearest Convenience in Town Square.' Well now... I stood and stared at it.

'So she lied, Phil,' said Oliver, his voice toneless.

'Wait. Oliver, wait. Let's not jump to conclusions. Let's just see if we can find somebody.'

I walked and slipped the last few yards up the steep slope of cobbles, to discover that this narrow lane led to the end of a wide and extensive expanse. Here, too, the surface was cobbled, but now there were also pavements. This was their marketplace. And there were shops and people.

I looked round for a woman, and one walked out from a milliner's shop, which was displaying a deplorable collection of hats.

'Excuse me.'

She stopped, half smiling. 'Yes?'

'Can you tell me how long the ladies' convenience has been closed?' I waved in its general direction.

'Oh...weeks,' she said. 'These councils! They promise, but they don't deliver. Weeks, but I've not seen a soul working there. But the other one's not far. Look...' She turned and pointed to the far end of the nearly deserted market-place. 'The narrow lane on the left. Twenty yards up there.'

'Thank you. I'm much obliged.' And I stood and watched her walk away in that direction herself.

Then Oliver was at my elbow. 'So Elise lied to us,' he said softly. It was the second time he had said it.

Elise! I shook my head stubbornly, but couldn't speak. I would have wagered literally anything (and let her father hold the money) that Elise could not tell a flat lie—not looking directly into my eyes.

'I don't know, Oliver. Let me think... think.'

'You're not her guardian and protector, you know.'

'But I like her, Oliver. I really do.'

'All right. Me too.' He smiled encouragingly, but he rubbed a hand up the back of his neck, and looked worried. 'So look it

159

straight in the face, and try to forget that she's a naïve and delicate young lady—and that you like her—and then what do you see, Phil?'

I had to clear my throat. 'I suppose...I see that she could have come to Jennie's site intending to do her harm...damn it, Oliver, I can't say it.'

'To kill her,' he said gently.

'All right. To kill her. That she found a chunk of wood on the way, and simply walked up behind her and...well...did it. And that she invented the alibi of being inside the toilet, which she didn't realize is closed, and of hearing this and seeing that and the other, and getting vague sights of somebody coming or going, all to make it sound valid—whereas in fact she can't have given one glance at the toilet door, otherwise she'd have known the place is closed and out of order.'

He put his arm round my waist. 'Let's get back. There's nothing more to be seen.'

But he seemed hesitant, and when we reached the footbridge he moved more and more slowly, finally coming to a halt.

'What is it?' I asked.

'Well...if I were a member of the group—'

'Which you are.'

'Who had an overwhelming desire to kill

160

Jennie—and that excludes me.'

'Yes, Oliver,' I said patiently.

'Such as Pam Wilton,' he suggested.

'Yes—but she was very busy painting.'

'She'd finished it, and she'd sprayed it.'

'All right, Oliver. Leave her in for now. Though how she could have—'

'Yes,' he agreed, having made his point. 'We'll have to leave her in for now. Or...the twins? No? No motive, I suppose.'

'None that we've even heard a whisper about,' I said. 'We'll have to have a chat with them, Oliver.'

'All right. When we get the chance.'

'So you can take Philip, and I'll tackle Martin. That moustache really sends me...'

He frowned. 'If you're not going to take this seriously—'

'Sorry. Go on,' I said, a little worried, because he usually sees through my jokes.

'Or Paul.'

'Paul! Good heavens, Oliver, he was crazy about Jennie. He wasn't seeing straight.'

'Nevertheless, let's leave him in for now. Or—who else is there? Oh yes...Geoff.'

'Geoff! Good Lord that's stretching it a bit.'

He had been leaning over the top rail of the bridge, staring down at the trickling water. 'Well...he did have a free run of the territory, you must admit that.' He straightened, and turned to face me again. 'And he loves Elise, and would do anything for her.'

'Anything?' I stood back from him, trying to decide how serious he might be. 'Such as murder?' I demanded. 'For Elise? Oh...come on! Her slashed painting might well have been traumatic to Elise—but to Geoff? Oh, do talk sense.'

'He might think of it as more personal than that. *His* studio, that Glasshouse is. *His* students. Probably *his* paintings. And he's right over the top about Elise.'

'What a way of putting it, Oliver.'

He shrugged. 'It's how it is. In any event, he'd do pretty well anything for her.'

'All right—all right. But I still say...not murder...not for her slashed painting.'

'All right, Phil. But, whoever it was—you tell me...how could he or she have crossed this bridge, with a two-foot length of post in his or her hands, and not been observed by Jennie? And if she *did* see that—'

'Wait a second. Wait.' I put up a hand to halt him. 'You're rushing on, Oliver, and assuming that Jennie was killed by the same piece of post as was used to kill Pam. There's no evidence of that—'

'But...the same sort of blow, to the head.' He was smiling. 'And the same

162

result. Didn't Elise say, in respect of Jennie, something about blood in her lovely hair. As there was with Pam—I had a damned good close look at Pam's head. Phillie—it *sounds* like the same weapon.'

'Sounds, sounds. You ought to be ashamed, you an ex-copper, talking about sounds. It's not yet a *fact*—as far as we know.'

He held up a palm, almost in surrender. 'All right! But it doesn't alter the fact that Jennie was assaulted with a heavy object to the head, and so was Pam.'

There was a short silence. Then I said, 'As we know next to nothing about the weapon and the blows, can't we change the subject?'

'By all means,' he agreed. 'Not exactly change it, perhaps, but there's something that I haven't been allowed to say, Phil—and do stop grinning at me like that—which is that I wouldn't, if I was intent on killing Jennie—approach her by way of this bridge, in full sight of her. Not with a heavy object in my hand. Damn it, she'd be waiting for me.'

'I suppose she would,' I had to agree.

'Exactly.' He sighed. I could have killed him. 'But now we know that there's access to that site by way of the market-place. And *all* these strange artists of ours have been here often enough to know that they wouldn't *have* to come over this bridge.'

'All right, Oliver.' I reached up and touched the tip of his nose with my finger. 'So come along, you great sniffer dog you, and show me what you're getting at.'

He sighed. 'I thought we were never going to get to it.'

So we walked on to the far side of the footbridge, and began to walk back along the road, the way we had arrived.

'You're looking for the motor-traffic bridge, aren't you?' I asked.

'Exactly.'

We walked quietly side by side for a while. 'And here it is,' he said. 'Just ahead.'

There was a car turning into it. When we reached the entrance I could see how small the hump-backed bridge was. Geoff had said that the river was a meagre thing, and the bridge was certainly narrow. There was barely room for two vehicles to pass each other. Half the cars in the town probably had scratches along their near sides.

'And *there* you are,' said Oliver.

But it wasn't the bridge he had come to show me. He turned me, so that we faced across the road to the massed woodland opposite. 'I thought I remembered it,' he said.

It was not necessary for him to explain. There was a stile set in the hedgerow facing us, and beyond it a clear walkway disappearing into the trees. Nevertheless, he did explain.

He pointed. 'You see. Facilities for walking through the trees. You can bet there're paths wandering away in all directions, leading to picnic spots. People who live all their lives within sight of the sea tend to go away from it for a picnic. Phil, from the other side of all this greenery, from where our group was staked out, it would surely be easy to make your way to here, cross this road and the bridge, and walk up through the town centre, and to the cobbles just behind Jennie's site, without allowing her to get a single glimpse of you.'

I pouted. I was dubious. 'That would be all right for the locals, but one of our lot would get hopelessly lost in all this woodland.'

'Oh...I don't think so. They're artists. The position of the sun is very important to them. I think any one of us—possibly excluding ourselves, as we're new here—but any of the others would be able to orientate themselves by the way the sun was striking through the trees. And...have you thought of this? They'd probably be able to pick up a useful length of wood on the way.'

'Oh, let's get back,' I said. 'I don't like the sound of any of it.'

'And Elise *was* quite a long while away.'

'Nonsense,' I said.

I was suddenly very tired, and it was mostly uphill, back to the college. Oliver noticed, slid his good arm round my waist, and tried to help me. But I think my exhaustion was mainly emotional, because I found myself strangely reluctant, when it came to it, to turn in at the drive entrance.

We had reached the point where the terrace began when a blast from a car horn alerted us. We stopped, and stood aside, as a sleek, black Jaguar XJ6 saloon slid past us, to stop right opposite the main door to the house.

It was being driven by a small, sharp-featured man, who could not be described as a chauffeur, because he wore no uniform and he made no move to get out and go round to open the passenger's door. He sat there, staring ahead.

Then the passenger's door was flung open, and a burly, red-faced man, neatly dressed in a rather sharply tailored suit, got out. As he straightened and assessed the frontage, he noticed our approach.

'Heh!' he said, not very politely, 'Where'll I find Elise Harcourt?' He was staring at me.

'I couldn't tell you.'

'Well...' He was impatient. 'Who can?'

'I don't know if there are any of the office staff around, but we could look for her. If you like.' I was being specially polite, resenting his overbearing attitude.

'Wasn't that what I said!'

I felt Oliver stir beside me, and touched his arm. Leave it to me.

'If you'd care to come inside, we can take you to the bar,' I said. 'You'll be Elise's father...' He made no response, so I went on, 'The bar's probably empty, so you could wait there while we ask around. I don't even know her room number.'

'A lot of good that'll be, then,' he grumbled.

'Shall we try at the office first?' I asked. 'If you'd prefer that. And if anybody's there, of course.'

'Anything. What you like.' He was impatient. Then, for the first time he turned and actually looked at us. 'Are you in this blasted painting lot?'

'We are.'

'Then you ought to know.'

'Well...we don't,' put in Oliver, using his flat voice. 'And can I give you some advice...' They stared at each other. Harcourt said nothing. Nevertheless, Oliver offered his advice. 'If you'd try being a bit more civil, you might get somewhere. Or don't you know how?'

'Who the hell...'

'My name is Oliver Simpson, and this is my wife, Philipa. We're friends of Elise. Now...I suggest...'

He was unable to complete his suggestion. There was a clatter of running feet, and Elise ran in from the side corridor. 'Daddee!' she screamed, and she threw herself into his arms.

Then he held her away from him, saw whatever he wanted to see in her face, and said, 'Pack your bags, my love. I'm taking you home.'

He could not have been concentrating on her expression, or he could not have understood it. But most certainly, this was not what Elise desired.

'I wouldn't do that,' I said quietly. 'If I were you.'

He thrust her aside, so that she was hidden by his shoulder. 'What's it got to do with you?' he asked—not graciously.

I kept my voice low and carefully controlled. 'Just a bit of advice,' I assured him. 'There's a superintendent of police going to be here this evening to explain the situation, and how we stand. He might be in a position at that time—'

'To the devil with your superintendents!'

I glanced at Oliver. His eyebrows were lifted, and I could have sworn there was

168

amusement in his eyes. I shrugged, and turned back to Harcourt.

'I'll give you some advice—shall I?'

'To hell with your advice, too.'

'Free advice. Take Elise home now, and it'll look bad. The police will want to see her and talk to her, and they'd have to ask your local police to do it.'

'To hell—'

'And it would look awfully guilty, as though Elise was running away.'

'Pack your stuff,' he said to Elise, then he turned back, in order to glare at me. 'Running away? What the hell does that mean? Running away from what?'

I shrugged. 'She's a suspect—the same as the rest of us—for the killing of a young woman named Jennie Crane, and Elise can be placed on the scene of the murder at the correct time—'

'Now just you bloody well listen.' He poked a finger in my general direction. 'It's nothin' to do with you, anyway.'

'Oh...but it is,' I assured him. 'We're her friends. Isn't that so, Elise?'

With her lower lip tucked between her teeth, and her eyes wide with distress, she nodded.

'And if, Elise,' I ploughed on, ignoring Harcourt's rumbling antagonism, 'you tell the same lie to the police as you told to me—then you'll be in great trouble.'

'Lie...lie?' She looked round her frantically. 'What lie? I haven't told you any lies.'

'That you used the ladies' toilet—the one right behind the yew hedge.'

'But I did. I *did!*' She actually stamped a foot, like a child in a temper.

I shook my head again, and turned to face Harcourt.

'Do you see? The police will be very suspicious. Even more so if you take her away from here. She'd do much better to stay here. It's got to be sorted out. You must understand that.'

'I *did!*' squealed Elise.

I shrugged. 'So all right. But tell it to the police *here,* Elise. Please. It's much more sensible.'

She looked frantically from my face to her father's. He turned on me, his face dark with anger and suspicion. 'If you're making this up...' His voice was now a barely controlled growl.

'Of course I'm not. Take her away and it'll mean trouble, I can assure you, Mr Harcourt. You *do* understand that, I hope?'

He mumbled something indistinct.

'I don't want to go home, Daddy.' She looked desperately up into his face.

'You see,' I explained to her, 'if you tell the same lie to the police as you have to me, about using that specific ladies' toilet—'

She didn't allow me to finish. 'It wasn't a lie. It wasn't! I've *told* you that.'

'All right, Elise. Now...why don't you go and see if there's anybody in the office, and if so, maybe they can find your father a room.'

He now seemed to have accepted that what I'd told him had a certain validity, and he was prepared to stay, if with reluctance.

'And one for my driver,' said Harcourt.

'Oh...you haven't brought Len!'

'You know I never drive, my lass. Of course I've brought him.'

And Elise stared at me almost in apology, before she turned away. Was she ashamed of another little lie she had told? I couldn't even guess.

10

Dinner was to be at the early time of seven-thirty, as we hadn't completed the normal painting period—when it would have been at eight-thirty. And it definitely hadn't been a normal painting period. I would want to tidy myself, and change out

171

of my walking slacks and blouse. But we had plenty of time, so that whilst Oliver was taking Harcourt along to the office, to see if anything could be done for him, I wandered into the bar, to see what might be happening.

Nothing was happening. Paul was alone in there, sitting morosely in a corner and cuddling an empty glass. The bar grill was down, and due to the location and the surrounding buildings, no setting sun enlivened the scene. It was all very depressing.

I sat beside him, and told him, 'I was hoping to get a drink.'

'I've been waiting for hours,' he complained. 'Hours—and nothing. I found an empty glass, but I can't find any way of filling it.' This, from Paul, was verging on humour.

'You'd have done better to get outside,' I advised him. 'Get some exercise and fresh air.'

He gave a bark of joyless laughter. 'And walk away from it all? Not a chance. Not a bloody chance. It'd be out there, too.'

I knew exactly what he meant. 'You shouldn't be alone.'

'Hah! With Pam dead, and Jennie dead—I can't be more alone than that.'

There was no response I could make. Paul gave the distinct impression that the life had been pummelled out of him, leaving just emptiness.

'Suppose we go outside and stretch our legs a bit, then. Put it like that. We've both been sitting all morning on our painting-stools.'

He gave the same little laugh. 'Hah! But you just wait and see. They'll say I haven't been doing much sitting. That I can't have been if I've been running up and down that bay, waving a lump of wood in my hand. You see—they'll say I was clearing the decks...getting rid of Jennie and Pam. To give me a fresh start.'

There could be no response to that. So I remained silent, waiting. It seemed that he was brooding on what he had said.

'Come on, then,' I said, getting to my feet, and having to fight an instinct to offer him a helping hand. He stared up at me emptily, then tried a smile that turned itself into a grimace.

'Why not?' he said, making an abrupt decision. Then, on his feet, he dredged from somewhere a hint of dry humour. 'As long as that big husband of yours doesn't get the idea that I'm already looking round for a new partner.'

'I don't think he will—and I certainly am not.'

We used the emergency door, which opened close to the Glasshouse, then strolled round the house to the terrace. The Jaguar was no longer there, but was neatly parked on the proper parking patch. There was now no sign of the driver, Len. So Harcourt and Len had managed to acquire rooms, and were staying. The thought was quite depressing.

'Do you want to take a look in the Glasshouse?' I asked.

'No. Not really. The police have been around, and all our stuff's neatly laid out. Or so they say. I can't claim I'm in any hurry to see it.'

'Yes. Llewellyn promised that.'

'Llewellyn?' Paul asked dully, not really interested but making an effort to respond.

'The police superintendent. He did promise that we'd get all our stuff back.'

He was silent. We stood on the terrace, looking down the sloping lawn to the woodland beyond.

'Shall we walk down and see what it's like, down there?' I asked.

He shrugged. 'Please yourself.'

We strolled down, leisurely and, in his case, without enthusiasm. A squirrel scrambled from a tree to have a look at us, then up again to tell his mates. A red squirrel? I'd thought they were about extinct.

I said, 'You must surely have seen

174

Jennie being attacked, from where you were painting.'

He didn't reply.

'Surely you must,' I repeated patiently.

'I don't want to talk about it.'

We walked in beneath the trees, and suddenly it was cool. A gentle breeze was rustling the leaves. There was a pathway worn in a winding lane through the trees. Paul kicked a fallen branch out of the way.

'You'll have to talk about it to Mr Llewellyn,' I told him.

'I suppose.'

'So why not to me?'

He was silent. Then he stopped abruptly, and turned to face me.

'Why would you want to know?' he asked quietly. It was a polite request for information.

I could not walk round him, but had to stand and face him, looking up into his harried face, his hair untidily falling over his forehead.

'Just accept that I'm nosy, if you like. But I *have* got a personal interest.'

I waited. He stared at me, then he turned, and we continued with our walk, the path becoming less and less accommodating with every step.

'Such as?' he said at last.

'Elise. I like her. We—my husband and

I—want to help her.'

'Help? Why would she need any help?'

'Because she's going to be the prime suspect in this business.'

He stopped again, viewed the unentrancing prospect ahead of us, and turned to retrace our steps. The male of the species automatically making the decisions.

'I don't see that,' he said, after a long pause for consideration. 'I'd have said that Elise wouldn't swat a fly.'

'But...' I let it hang for a few seconds. 'But you must...you surely must have seen *something* happening, up on the top of that cliff. Must have.'

'Well—I didn't.'

'You painted Jennie in. A spot of red. So you must have been able to see her.'

'Ah...yes.'

'And...whatever happened, you'd have seen it. Damn it, Paul, you'd got your eyes focused on the scene in front of you, and she was bang in the centre of it.'

'Ah!' He seemed suddenly to become mentally animated. 'It all depends on how you operate, as a painter—as an artist. Some artists have long visual memories, some short. Some people have to keep looking at what they're painting, then to their canvas—or whatever—then up again. But I'm not like that. I can memorize quite a lot, and not have to look up from my

176

painting for a little while. Two or three minutes, say. It must have happened in one of those gaps. I didn't *see* it happen.'

'A pity.'

'Yes. I realize that, now.'

We were silent for some considerable time, during which he kept his gaze on his feet.

'The police will question you about it, you know,' I told him.

'I can't tell them anything different.' He lifted his shoulders. 'I'd have liked to help, but I can't.'

'Of course. Tell the truth and shame the devil.'

'What?'

'A saying.'

He grunted. 'There's a devil in this, anyway. But I reckon you won't see any sign of shame.' He looked down into my face and gave a strange grimace.

'No,' I said. 'The devil would hide it.'

He made no reply to that. We emerged from the protection of the trees, and the hot, sultry air pressed down on us again.

'And why would Elise be suspect number one?' he asked. 'I mean—it's ridiculous. She'd got nothing against Jennie, and she was very friendly towards Pam. The whole suggestion's just plain stupid. What motive could Elise possibly have had?'

'I'm talking here, Paul, about the killing

of Jennie. Not Pam. From what we know so far, I can't see it would've been possible for the same person to have killed both of them.'

'Don't you?' he asked, in a tone suggesting that he didn't care a damn what I thought.

'No, I don't. Let's talk about Jennie. Just Jennie.'

'All right,' he conceded. 'Just Jennie. What possible reason could Elise have had for killing Jennie? It's plain stupid.'

'Hmm!' I wondered how much he knew about the slashed painting. Had he and Pam been here at that time? Perhaps they had not.

We were now taking a circular route, around the borders of the lawn, as this would reduce the angle of the slope we would have to mount. And, in this heat, any fractional lessening of the energy we put into it was of paramount importance.

The thing to do was ask, I realized. So I did. 'Don't you know about the slashed painting?' I asked him. 'Elise's masterpiece.'

'Oh yes. That. We were here at that time, Pam and I.'

'Well—Geoff did a lot of research on it. Experiments. Seeing whom he could trick into knowing where his Stanley knife was kept. Or revealing that they knew. Which

178

drawer along the counter. I thought, that was quite clever. It had to be something like a Stanley knife, Geoff said. Something that sharp.'

'Hmph!' He was plainly disgusted. 'In what way clever?'

I went through it in detail, Geoff's assumption that it had to be a woman—with which I did not agree, though I hadn't argued about it—and so on. When I got to the end, Paul made another sound of disgust.

'And that came up with a thumbs-down for poor Jennie?' he asked.

'So he told me.'

'Rubbish. Nonsense. Jennie could've had a dozen reasons for knowing where it was kept. The real slasher would never have fallen for a corny old trick like that.' He gave a short, cynical laugh. 'In fact, the real slasher had her own Stanley knife.'

I stopped dead, and turned to face him. 'What? What're you saying, Paul?'

'I know who slashed Elise's canvas. I woke when Pam slipped out of the bed, that night. My wife—Pam—had her own Stanley knife. She said it was the only thing she could find that would sharpen her pastel pencils, without breaking the points off. It was Pam. She reckoned she was the best—and had to be *seen* as the best. That wasn't my opinion, mind you,

179

but I kept my mouth shut. Too much like photographs, her work's always been. As long as I can remember. No imagination. But she had to be tops. Had to be accepted as tops. And that painting Elise produced...now *that* was really something. It glowed. It was alive. And Pam hated it, hated it. Bitterly.'

I released a breath, which I seemed to have been holding for several minutes.

'But Elise *thought* it was Jennie,' I said, clearing my throat. 'And Elise can be placed on the scene of Jennie's death at about the correct time—the time when Jennie died.'

'She headed in the wrong direction, then. Didn't she?'

'Oh Lord! And you're *sure* you saw nothing happening up there, at Jennie's site?'

'Nothing.'

'You realize you'll have to tell the superintendent all this?' I asked him anxiously.

He shrugged. 'Oh, sure. If he raises the question.' He looked at me with his head tilted, a sardonic smile on his lips. 'Or you can tell him, if you like.'

'I think I'd have to, if you don't.'

'Oh—I'll tell him. Don't worry.'

'I'm not exactly worrying,' I assured him. 'But I *am* concerned.'

'Yes. I can understand that. Shall we go and see if the bar's open? I'm dying for something long and cool.' He could be charming when he tried.

'Me too,' I said.

It was open, and business was brisk. Oliver was there, sitting with the twins, all three with glasses in front of them. He was on his feet at once, demanding to know what we were having. Paul's was a lager, mine a Dubonnet and lemonade.

Paul headed to sit with the twins, and this seemed to suit Oliver. 'Got to have a talk,' he said to me, drawing me aside.

'Yes,' I agreed. 'Round the corner? It might be less packed, there.'

We tried round the corner, and there proved to be plenty of space around us. We settled in. I then told him what Paul had said, about Pam and the slashed painting. It was vitally important, I thought.

Oliver shook his head. He got up to open the door that Paul and I had used earlier, to let in a little fresh air. But it was warm air, and didn't help at all.

'The important thing is not who actually slashed Elise's painting,' he said, taking his seat again. 'It's what Elise believed. And she thought it was Jennie.'

'Yes. Of course.' Then there didn't seem to be anything more to say on that subject.

'I take it,' I said at last, 'that Harcourt and his driver are fixed up with rooms?'

'Yes. And a bit of a laugh, this is.' But I noticed that he didn't seem to be amused. 'There was one of the office staff still on duty, and they had two rooms available. But she couldn't let them have them unless they were students. It's a rule. It *is* a college, after all. So they've gone down as individual-study pupils. Hah! I suppose they can always study the odds on something or other. Harcourt and his stooge, Len Farmer, who's his chief clerk, and, incidentally, the one Harcourt's chosen as the best person for his daughter's husband. Brainy, though, these bookmakers' clerks. They need to be—though I suppose they use computers, these days. I've been getting some instruction. They have to know, at any moment, how much they stand to gain or lose, should any specific horse win a race, or is placed, and either raise or lower the odds, or lay off bets to other bookies in the district—or the other way round. I can't remember it all. It all has to work out that the bookmaker can't lose, whatever happens. He's not doing any betting. It's his livelihood. If he gets it wrong—and he relies completely on what his clerk says—then they could drop a packet on any one race. So this Len Farmer's been

182

telling me. It's positively fascinating. Don't you think so, Phil? And it all depends on the clerk...'

'You said so.'

He ignored that. 'Actually, Farmer's the head clerk. Sort of boss over six betting shops that Harcourt runs.'

'He must be clever, then.'

'A walking computer. And...as I said... it's Len Farmer that Harcourt wants his Elise to marry. Can you imagine two men more contrasted than Geoff Davies and Len Farmer?'

'Oh dear,' I said. 'Poor Elise. What a choice to have to make.'

'You don't have to worry about Elise having to make a choice. It's done for her. How simple life can be, when your choices are settled for you.'

'Philosophy, Oliver?'

'Cynicism, love.'

'And you...' I said. 'You were with the twins when Paul and I got back. I suppose it wasn't just idle chat?'

He grinned. 'You see right through me. No—not idle chat. I was probing for motives.'

'Oh...come on, Oliver. It's one thing to pull their legs a bit, but...motives? What sort of motive could they have to kill either Jennie or Pam, singly or as a team?'

He tried to smile at me, but this time

it came out all distorted. 'It's Jennie I was asking them about. And there *is* some sort of motive there. And it's the alibi theme, but twisted backwards. In respect of Jennie anyway. She tried to use it against them. It seems that she was a terrible trouble-maker, Phil. And rather vicious with it. You see...those two, they have a special relationship with each other's wives. They're a very tight foursome. And that doesn't work unless all four are absolutely trustworthy. And Jennie understood that. Maybe she tried her sex appeal on both of them, at one time or another. But if so, she'd have got a very brisk brush-off. So she tried a variation on that theme. Pure evil, it was. One morning...it was the previous time they were here, just for a weekend. She met one of them in the corridor, and walked past, saying, "You were wonderful last night, darling." Then she met the other, and said exactly the same. The idea was simply to cause each one to lose trust in the other.'

'What a vicious trick!' I said in disgust.

'But it didn't work,' Oliver went on. 'They're too close, those two. They know each other too well. But since then they've hated Jennie. There you are, Phil. Motives for two.'

He was now treating it as a poor joke, but I didn't like the sound of it at

184

all. Those two twins might have sworn revenge.

'Heavens—look at the time,' I said. 'Ten minutes to the dinner bell. I'll have to rush. Keep me a seat, Oliver, if I'm late.'

I hurried out and bounded up the stairs, unbuttoning and unzipping as I went. Paul, emerging from his room as I reached the landing, stared at me as though I'd gone mad.

'Shower,' I said breathlessly, and I rushed into our room.

I was out of my clothes, in and out of the shower, into fresh underwear and my cheerful flowered dress, all in three minutes. A belt for it...I chose a black one as a hint of mourning for both Pam and Jennie, and pounded down the stairs as the bell went.

As I had requested, Oliver had reserved me a seat, between himself and Elise. On her far side was Geoff.

Elise said, 'Daddy's going to take me home.' Her voice was empty and emotionless. It was fate, and she had to accept it—had been trained into accepting it.

I shook my head. 'That doesn't sound like a very good idea, Elise.'

'Oh...don't you think so?'

'Wouldn't it be best to wait until we've

heard what the police have got to say,' I suggested.

'Daddy says, after dinner we'll go home.'

'But he's already booked rooms for himself and Len Farmer. That doesn't sound as though he intends to turn round and drive back home, with or without you, Elise.'

'I didn't know he'd booked rooms.' She didn't sound as though she cared what happened.

I persisted. 'I got the impression he was going to stay on until it was all settled.'

'Oh! He couldn't do that.'

'Couldn't he?'

'There's sure to be races on somewhere. Races all the time. How could he bear to be away from it? And Len...they need him at head office. Oh no—they couldn't stay.'

And did I hear more than a hint of dejection—that they might?

'Perhaps,' I suggested, 'there's a phone in the car. They could keep in touch with that.'

She turned to me, her face shining with admiration. 'Oh yes. How clever to think of that! I can't really imagine Len without a phone to his ear. Sometimes two.'

'There you are, then. Problem solved. Your father can stay here and look after you, and at the same time Len can control his little empire of betting shops. How splendid! What a boon this modern technology is.'

Oliver said quietly, 'Don't tease the girl, Phil.'

'But really,' I said, 'I can't help an image lifting its head and leering at me.'

'And that is?'

'Len Farmer in bed with her, and with a phone at each ear,' I whispered.

'Hmm!' he said.

We finished the main course, and I'd about had enough. But—pudding and coffee yet! I realized, now, what discomfort the members of the other groups would suffer by the end of the week, whereas we... Ah yes—what about us? To where had this splendid set-up of days spent out in the open air disappeared? Packed lunches on the hillsides, with a paintbrush in one hand and a sandwich in the other...was this all lost?

Towards the end of the meal, at the coffee stage, Geoff got to his feet and tapped on the table with the handle of a knife. The room rustled to silence.

'Sorry to interrupt, folks,' he said. 'This is just for the painting group. There's to be a meeting in Lecture Room number one, immediately after this meal. That's just off the main hall, for anybody who doesn't know. And I'm informed that all our painting equipment has been brought along and taken into the Glasshouse. But...meeting first in Lecture Room one, and the Glasshouse afterwards. Okay?'

He sat down. Our group was a very small portion of those present, but it was clear that our situation, and the two deaths, were proving to be much more interesting than Advanced German and Chinese Brush Painting. We might have difficulty in excluding them from the meeting.

Lecture Room number one proved to be a small room in the main house. I reckoned it was directly beneath our bedroom, but in this house the definition of small was only relative. It still retained much of its original elegance, but our little group seemed lost in it. We spread ourselves around, as though any close contact might be with a murderer. But nevertheless we still gave the impression of a tight group of inoffensive artists.

Harcourt and Farmer rather blurred the image. Harcourt was poised like a bulky predator, prepared to launch himself at any moment to the defence of his brood, which numbered only one. Elise. Who, I was quite certain, had told me a lie. Farmer sat in the seat beyond him, and looked quite lost and bewildered. Elise was beside me, with Oliver on her far side.

Geoff was arranging a table, putting three chairs behind it. When he had done this satisfactorily, he came to rejoin his team, and we waited.

Nothing happened. We waited. After five minutes or so, Geoff became restless, and went out to see where the expected police had got to. He must have met them in the hall, because almost at once he returned with Superintendent Llewellyn and a smart woman in slacks and a white silk blouse, a bulky bag hanging from one shoulder.

They took their seats behind the table. Geoff seemed to think we needed an MC, and elected himself, taking a seat beside the superintendent.

'You'll all have met Superintendent Llewellyn,' he said. 'He's come along now to clue us in on what's going on—so I'll leave it to him.'

Llewellyn shot him a glance, in which I detected a grimace of amusement, possibly at the 'clue us in' bit, then he concentrated on us.

'Now...' he said. 'Let me first introduce Detective Inspector Perry, who'll remind me if I miss anything, and make notes if we need them. Is that clear? Right.' He looked round our meagre group, frowned, and asked Harcourt, 'And who are you, sir, and the gentleman sitting next to you?'

Harcourt stirred in his seat. 'I'm the

189

father of Elise, here. My name's Harcourt. I've come along to take her home.' Right to the nub of it, went Harcourt.

'I suggest that we discuss that later.' Llewellyn smiled thinly. 'And your friend?'

'My head clerk. Len Farmer.'

No doubt Llewellyn was wondering what a head clerk had to do with it. But he inclined his head. 'Then I'll ask both of you to sit there quietly, and listen. These remarks are addressed to the painting group. Right?'

There was nothing but politeness in his voice. He even managed another smile, but the warning was there: keep out of this.

He went on to address the rest of us.

'Now...you all know what has happened. Mrs Pamela Wilton is dead, and Miss Jennifer Crane is dead. The obvious connection between these two deaths is that they were both members of your group. That they were physically the furthest apart is not, I think, significant.'

He was perhaps incorrect there. They were that far apart because they sincerely disliked each other.

He went on. 'My information is that, during former painting weeks, they always chose the same sites from which to paint. We have no positive information on which to work at this time. But what has emerged

190

may be of interest to you all, and that is that the two women were killed in the same manner: a vicious blow to the back of the head. And it seems that the same weapon was used in both instances—a length of wood, apparently from a fence somewhere, because it's of squared section, two inches each side, and rotted badly at one end. Where it had been in the ground, no doubt. But...' He grimaced. 'But, unfortunately, it would not take finger prints. There is very meagre evidence at this stage. Any questions?'

The evidence was, indeed, very meagre, otherwise he would not have told us. I stirred. Oliver whispered, 'Leave it, Phil.'

I muttered, 'No. Let me say this.' Then I raised my voice. 'One question, Superintendent. Is there any evidence that this lump of wood *was* used on both women? Or is it too early for blood analysis?'

He beamed at me. 'Yes—too early for positive forensic evidence. But our own doctor has said that two blood groups are involved.'

'Thank you.'

'Anything else?' His eyes were on me. He was smiling slightly, almost challengingly.

'Well...' I said, taking up the invitation.

'Pam Wilton. She had finished her pastel painting, and she'd sprayed it with a fixative. My husband checked that, by touching the surface with a fingertip. But we didn't see any spray-can at her site, so I'm wondering...did your team find a spray-can?'

'Well now...' He looked round at our unresponsive faces. 'It's for me to worry about clues and the like, and I haven't had time to go through the lists of what was found where. But I can say—from my own observation at the site—that I didn't see one. You can confirm that yourself, as everything that was recovered has been brought here—for all of you—and it's spread out on the long counter in your studio—what you call the Glasshouse—and marked with each owner's name.'

'Thank you,' I said. He had been more informative than I had expected.

'Anything else?' he asked, scanning our faces.

'Yes, there is,' said Harcourt. 'And I'm not doing any asking. I'm taking my lass home. First thing in the morning.'

He had already paid for two rooms, so he wouldn't want to waste money.

'Are you, sir?' asked Llewellyn, as though it was no more than a matter of minor interest. 'Are you indeed?'

Harcourt was silent.

11

'Now,' said Llewellyn. 'I just want to put you all in the picture and explain what's going to happen. You're all closely involved, if only because you're all members of the same painting group, and as the two deaths are those of two of your friends. I think I could put it that you're intimately involved. At this stage, I haven't got much to tell you, because I'm not in possession of all the facts, myself. Your names and addresses I can get from the college records, and your various painting sites I already know, from the map given to me by your tutor, Mr Davies. Thank you for that, sir.'

Geoff murmured something, and looked at his feet.

'Now...' went on Llewellyn, 'just to get the background information. I would like to speak to you all, individually, in order to get some idea of what went on this morning, where you were, what you did, and so on. When I have the technical officers' reports, I shall be able to get a clearer picture. And it's then that I'll be prepared to take proper witness statements from you all.'

He paused, smiling around at us, as though we were all chums, and preparing to launch into an agreeable outing, one that should be both entertaining and pleasurable to all.

'And to you, sir...' He indicated Harcourt. 'Let me explain that I'm not yet in a position to prevent you from taking your daughter home. It would simply make my job a little more difficult, but unless and until I have evidence implicating one or more of your group in these deaths, I can do nothing to prevent any of you from packing your bags and leaving.'

He swept a benign look around at our set faces. Nobody spoke.

'But...' And now he waved a finger at us. 'But there will come a time when I shall need positive witness statements from you, as I said, and if at that time you've returned home I shall have to ask the local police to call on you, and take those statements. Or drive there myself and do it. You can see, it would be more convenient if you were all to stay here, where you're more easily available.'

He looked round attentively, waiting. He didn't have to wait long. Harcourt spoke up.

'I'm taking my lass home in the morning, and that's that.'

'As you wish, sir. As you wish. I'll ask your local police to call on you at your home.'

'You can't do that. I don't want damned police cars—'

'Of course I can. I would have to. You'd have forced my hand. And if evidence arises that seems to implicate your daughter, I would have to send a car to fetch her back to my office, for serious questioning, because, of course, though I try not to allow these thoughts to influence me, I would naturally wonder—and have to bear in mind—why there's such a hurry to get her away from here. You get my point, sir?' He took a deep breath. The inspector looked down at her hands in her lap.

It was done so smoothly, so affably, that he almost robbed it of any unpleasant implications.

Harcourt was left with nothing to say. Llewellyn smiled at him. 'So...' he went on. 'I suggest that we now have little informal chats as to the basic facts, one of you at a time, in surname alphabetical order, which means...' He glanced down at a piece of paper in his hand. 'Mr Davies first.' He looked sideways at Geoff. 'If you'll just stay behind, then the rest can retire to...shall we say...what you call the Glasshouse. And you'll be able to check out your belongings while I have my little individual chats. Thank you all for your co-operation.'

He got to his feet.

So we went into the Glasshouse, where the lights were now on, and, as was natural, went first to find our own bundles of equipment, as rescued for us by the police officers.

They had laid them all out, neatly separated, on the long counter at the rear, with name labels derived from Geoff's plan. Philipa Simpson. And I'd looked for Philipa Lowe! How long would it take to get used to it? I wondered.

They had made a thorough and careful job of it. Even the folding stools and easels were allocated to us, though in fact these were the property of the college. The brushes had been cleaned, though some of them had lain there in the heat for quite a while before they'd been collected. But they had done what they could. Give them praise where it was deserved.

Oliver, of course, had no such concern. His pastels were dry from the start of their lives. But his paintings had become smudged a little, as he hadn't had time to spray-fix them. His aerosol can was there, but he seemed not to care what happened to his efforts, now.

We moved on. The others, the acrylicists, were complaining that some of their brushes were ruined, because they hadn't had time, or had not given the matter a thought, and had left their brushes out in the open air, and not in the water bottles they all used. And acrylic paint, when set, cannot be removed.

And Pam Wilton's... There it all was, along with her superb pastel painting, still dog-clipped to her board, her highlights and her back-lit trees in all their glory. It had been spray-fixed, but Oliver now with a certain amount of expertise in pastels, touched the highlights, which were so delightfully alive, with the tip of his finger. It picked up a little white.

'You see what she'd done?' he asked. 'Painted the complete picture, sprayed it, and therefore lost the brilliance of the highlights, and touched them in again, probably with pastel pencils. And...'

He was very still.

'Yes, Oliver,' I said. 'I've noticed.'

For there was her aerosol, along with the rest, the spray-can that we had not been able to see at the site, and which the superintendent had not seen there.

'There you are then, Oliver,' I said. 'You missed it, and Mr Llewellyn missed it. But it must have been there all the time, and his searchers found it. Never mind. Maybe she'd tossed it over her shoulder, and it'd got hidden in the long grass.'

He reached over and picked it up. He shook it close to his ear, then close to mine.

'It's got plenty in it,' he said. 'So why would she toss it anywhere? She might have had need of it again, and—'

'All right, Oliver, all right,' I said. 'But don't make an issue of it. It can't really matter.'

'No,' he agreed, but pursing his lips. 'No?' He raised his eyebrows at me.

'Surely not.' But though I spoke with confidence I had a feeling that it did, and I hate to have to face anything that I can't understand.

Then Geoff came in from his little chat with Llewellyn, and sent in the twins. They left without comment, but they each looked anxiously at Geoff, for a hint as to how rigorous the questioning might have been. But no such hint was obvious. Geoff was cool, and wrapped in thought.

I thought to tell him about the spray-can, but he seemed so self-absorbed that I decided to give him a rest. So—a nod to Oliver did it—we went out to the terrace, so that I could see whether fresh air might clear my brain. Oliver was concerned that it should need clearing. We walked to and fro, until we saw Philip and Martin coming down the steps from the house, both frowning heavily.

'I haven't seen Elise,' I told them, knowing she was to be the next, but Martin said they had just met her, and she was now with Llewellyn.

'And her father?' I asked.

Martin laughed. 'He went in with her, loud-mouthing, as you can imagine. But Llewellyn turned him out, after a minute or two. He came out shouting.'

'Nothing physical, I hope?'

'Oh no.' Philip picked it up. 'He threatened to arrest him for impeding the course of justice—whatever that means. But it shook Harcourt, and he's mooching round the hall like a caged lion.'

'Hmm!' I said, and we resumed our placid strolling.

Then Elise came bursting out from the hall, clattered down the front steps, and went dashing towards the Glasshouse, sobbing. Oliver put a hand to my arm. 'Leave her,' he advised. 'It's our turn next.'

We met Harcourt in the hall, but I didn't dare to speak to him. He was still prowling, and looking completely lost. I guessed that Elise had probably rushed past him, not even acknowledging his presence.

'He wants you,' he said flatly.

'We know. We're on our way in.'

'The man's a fool.'

'Never mind,' I said, patting his arm. Then Oliver and I went in to see Llewellyn. There would be only Paul to follow us.

They had made it cosy and informal, no longer using the table, but with four easy chairs, which had been standing at the back of the room, now encircling a smaller round table. The superintendent made a gesture. We took the two free chairs.

'Now,' said Llewellyn, sighing. 'Now, perhaps, we can hear a little common sense. Why are there people like that Harcourt? You'd have thought I was going to snatch his baby away and hide her in a dungeon. And he didn't, for one moment, realize that he was making things worse for her. "Don't answer that, Elise." That sort of thing. And telling me he wanted a copy of my report. Report! Who the hell does he think he is, the DCC? Oh...never mind...forget it. I'm just trying to discover where everybody was, whether they moved around, and what they might have seen.' He sat back, relaxed. 'It's a pleasure to speak to an ex-copper, who understands what it's all about, and to you, young lady, who also seem to know what I'm trying to get at.'

I could appreciate the 'young lady' bit, but it was all flannel, intended to enlist my sympathies on his side. This was disturbing, as he must have been given the impression that we had got together as a solid group, and sworn to oppose all Llewellyn's activities and reject his persuasions.

'We understand,' I assured him. 'And there's really not much we can tell you. We didn't go anywhere, just sat there, painting. And we saw nothing.'

He smiled. 'The "we" in that statement being you and your husband?'

'Yes. That's so.'

'But it does not include the young lady, Elise Harcourt?' he asked, producing what he thought to be a persuasive smile.

'We can't speak for her, now can we?' Oliver put in. 'What did she tell you?'

Llewellyn leaned forward. Nothing had changed in his expression of calm patience. 'She told me the truth, and I was hoping you'd be able to confirm it.'

'How can we do that,' I asked, 'when we don't know what she said?'

'You're edging round it, aren't you? You know the truth.'

'No, Superintendent. Or yes—I suppose yes would be more correct. We're edging because she's a friend, and we know her rather well now, and I'd swear she couldn't have—'

He cut in sharply, his patience running a little thin. 'Nobody can say such a thing. Nobody knows what other people are capable of doing.' And now he was no longer smiling. 'Ask your husband,' he said flatly. 'I have seen things that're well nigh unbelievable.'

'And have you any reason to suppose that Elise did do something?' I asked him quietly, trying to leaven it with a smile.

'I think I have a reason, yes. From what has been said. Not simply by Elise Harcourt, but by others. Snatches of detail, which fit together. Hints at the background. Implications. She left you. At one stage she left your painting site, I gather.'

Oliver and I were silent, then he touched my arm. Leave it to him, that was supposed to mean. He had detected that I was becoming angry. For Elise. In anger, mistakes are made.

'Who told you that?' Oliver asked casually, as though it could be no more than a matter of mild interest. 'That she left us, I mean.'

'She did.' Llewellyn nodded. 'I must say that I don't think she would have told me, if it hadn't been for her father. "Don't say a word, my lass!" Things like that. And, "Don't admit to anything." The great idiot. She clearly resented being told what to say, and what not to say. I had to ask him to go outside.' He allowed himself a thin smile. 'Persuade is perhaps the more accurate description. So...she left you, and, as she herself put it, went to answer a call of nature. But not, it seems, to the security of about twenty thousand trees, within a few yards of her, but across the footbridge to a ladies' toilet right next to the scene of Jennifer Crane's death. Which toilet, she tells us, she used. Strange, that is. Very strange. Inspector Perry, here, tells me it's had a "Closed for Alterations" sign on its door for weeks. Isn't that so, Inspector?'

'Indeed it is,' she said, nodding in emphasis. 'I noticed the sign was still there, only a couple of days ago.' She gave me a tight little smile. 'I had to go to the other end of the market-place. But all the same, she stubbornly claims that she went inside the closed one, and heard things from inside there that may or may not relate to the death of Jennifer Crane. Very graphic. Sounds she would have heard, of course, if she had been the one making them. When we asked her about it, she said she didn't notice any sign on the door. What a very artless young lady she is. You *do* see what the superintendent is getting at, I'm sure.'

Very serious now, Llewellyn looked fixedly at us and waited for a response. And yes—we did see what they were getting at.

'Yes, we understand it very clearly,' I admitted. 'She placed herself at the scene of Jennie Crane's death, at about the right time, and using a reason that doesn't sound very valid to less delicate people—such as you and me, Superintendent. She had a valid motive for killing Jennie. Has she told you all about that? Knowing Elise, I'd guess she did.'

He inclined his head. 'Yes, she told me. In spite of her father shouting his head off. As she put it, we were going to find out, anyway. So she told us that Jennifer Crane had been the one who'd upset her so severely by slashing her lovely painting to pieces—and that she had hated her. Completely open about it, she was. Her father didn't seem to appreciate that what she was telling me, and how openly, was all in her favour. And of course—the question of a weapon...she would surely have been able to pick up something suitable on the way there. Such as a stake of wood from somebody's fence, somewhere. You can see, all the basic elements are present: means, motive and opportunity.'

And yet, if he had what he seemed to consider to be a perfect case against Elise, why had he not already taken her along to the station for some serious interrogation?

'We're aware of all you've said,' Oliver told him. 'So isn't it a pity that Geoff Davies—in all sincerity, and eager to help his precious Elise—produced for her the wrong picture slasher?'

The Inspector looked up from her notebook and gave Oliver a sharp and interrogative stare. Then she lowered her eyes again. The superintendent merely gave him a somewhat cynical smile.

'It wasn't Jennifer Crane who slashed the painting, then?' he asked me.

I shook my head. 'No, it was not.'

'But,' he said placidly, 'that can't be very relevant, because Elise Harcourt was convinced it *was* Jennifer Crane. That's the point. She believed that, right or wrong. Which means that the motive is still there, and intact. Don't you think?'

I nodded. I didn't notice Oliver's reaction. There was a hint of a headache behind my eyes.

'And are you,' Llewellyn asked, 'going to tell me who it really was, and how you found out?'

'If you feel it's relevant?' I asked, and he nodded, smiling faintly.

'All right. It was Pam Wilton. And I'm convinced that it's the truth. Her husband, Paul—who, I think, hasn't been in to see you yet—would be prepared to tell you, I'm sure. He told me that she woke him, sliding out of their bed, on the night of the slashing. Of course, there can have been a number of reasons for her getting out of bed, but Paul might have seen or heard her searching out her Stanley knife, and the period she was away might fit the time necessary to do the job. You'll have to check that, Mr Llewellyn.'

'Yes,' he said gravely. 'I'll bear it in mind.'

I glanced down at my hands.

'And why would she have had such a thing as a Stanley knife in her kit?' he asked. 'It seems to be a rather strange thing for a lady to carry around.'

'Paul told me it was the only thing she'd found that would sharpen her pastel pencils without breaking the ends off. Oliver...' I suddenly thought. '*Do* they break off?'

He frowned. 'With my penknife they do. That's a bit of expertise I really needed to know. A Stanley knife.'

Llewellyn smiled at me. 'There you are then. And tell me...I rather had the idea that painting and such other artistic pursuits were gentle and quiet pastimes. I'm beginning to think they're deadly, and quite dangerous to get involved in. Or is this incident unusual?'

I sighed, deciding that he might as well get the lot. 'You need to know about this painting group, Mr Llewellyn. Oliver and I are new to it, but I understand that the same people—give or take one or two, from time to time—keep coming.

And the competition is hot. Of course, it's supposed to be an interest, a gentle session of art. But every one of them strives to be the best, and to surpass their own earlier efforts at previous courses. And Pam Wilton felt she *had* to be the best. Never satisfied, always driving herself. Or so I gathered from Paul. Damn it, you know what I mean. And you haven't seen Paul Wilton yet. Ask him about it. He'll tell you what he told me—that Pam Wilton slashed Elise's lovely painting because she couldn't bear to see a painting better than she herself could produce.'

'But,' he said gently, 'did Elise Harcourt know this? It seems that she did not—so we're back where we were.'

'I don't think she did.' I smiled at him. 'But if she did, and she had revenge on her mind, she would have aimed it at Pam Wilton. And then, where would your lovely theory go, Superintendent? Because Elise could not have possibly killed Pam.'

'I see that. There was never any such suggestion. Indeed, the evidence points to both women having been killed by the same person.'

And if he believed that, I thought, he was going to tie himself into some very tight knots. 'But that can't be,' I told him.

He raised his eyebrows at my certainty.

'The same weapon—we're sure about that now—and I have an interim medical calculation that Jennifer Crane was killed first, Pam Wilton later. Perhaps half an hour later. So I think your friend Elise Harcourt can be eliminated from any list of suspects relative to Pam Wilton's death. One or the other—possibly. Both...no.'

I turned and smiled at Oliver. He grimaced. Perhaps he was seeing beyond my thoughts on it.

'And the spray-can?' I asked.

'What spray-can?' The superintendent glanced at his inspector. She pouted, and shook her head.

'Pastel paintings,' I explained, 'need spraying with a fixative varnish, to prevent smudging when they're handled. Pam had finished her painting, and sprayed it—it's there in the Glasshouse for you to see—and she'd touched-up her highlights after she'd sprayed it. But there wasn't any spray-can in sight where she was painting. You didn't see one, Oliver didn't see one, and I didn't. So—where was it hiding itself? Oliver suggests it was tossed over her shoulder, and was lying hidden in the long grass. But it's half full, and she wouldn't have tossed it anywhere; she would've simply put it down beside her stool. Yet apparently, she didn't. You could check where it was found—ask whoever it was who searched

Pam's site. It's now on the counter, along with the rest of her stuff.'

'I think I can make my own decisions, Mrs Simpson, as to what action to take. If any. Now...let me hear about *your* morning's painting.'

We told him what we knew—information that he already had from Elise. He seemed satisfied. These interviews he was undertaking were no more than preliminary outlines of the situation in general. Serious witness statements would come later.

'Perhaps you'll ask Mr Wilton to come in and have a little chat,' he said. Which we did, on our way to the Glasshouse.

'He wants you now, Paul,' I told him.

He nodded. 'I guessed.' Then he gave me a thin grimace of a smile, and walked briskly towards Mr Llewellyn's last talk. Last, for now.

12

'Fingerprints,' I said.

Oliver and I were standing on the terrace, at the head of the flow of steps down to the lawn. The terrace lights were now on, thus diminishing the view of the twinkling town below.

'What about fingerprints?' he asked suspiciously.

'On that spray-can. It might be worth—'

'Oh no,' Oliver cut in. 'No chance there, surely. No murderer is going to handle an item of evidence with bare hands. And anyway, Llewellyn would have to be persuaded that there was any point in it, and then justify taking a set of prints from every one of us. Oh no. When the net result would be: Pam Wilton's. You can imagine what an uproar that would cause, and probably for no results.'

'Yes,' I had to agree. It was unpractical, and probably unrewarding, in any event. 'I want to talk to Elise, anyway, and without her father around.'

'Must you?'

'Well...somebody's got to get through to her. It's simply foolish to persist that she used that particular ladies' toilet. She would be in exactly the same position, anyway, if she'd gone to the other one.'

'Or neither,' he said gloomily.

'What!'

'If she's lied about one thing, she wouldn't hesitate to lie about another.'

I turned to face him. His features were heavily shadowed, so that I couldn't read his expression.

'Lied about what other thing, Oliver? Come on—don't keep it to yourself.'

He shrugged, one-sidedly. 'About the whole background to it,' he said moodily. 'This ridiculous business about being reluctant to use all that available greenery— even if she *did* need to use a toilet. Which, itself, could have been untrue. Her intention could have been purely and simply to find herself something hard and handy, and repay Jennie for the slashed canvas. That—pure and simple. Her whole story could be a complete lie. Simply, she went there, did what she intended, and left in a hurry.'

I shook my head. I couldn't go along with that at all. 'She was in great distress, Oliver.'

He shrugged heavily, the right shoulder not lifting. 'As she would be,' he said moodily. 'As anybody would be, having killed somebody. And she found she had to substantiate her story by claiming to have used the ladies' convenience, which she could have known all about from previous courses here, when she probably never even glanced at it this time. If she had—'

'I know—I know!' I seized his arm. 'But what you're saying...that it was a deliberately planned murder! Not Elise. Never.'

He sighed. I could have kicked him, but instead took a deep breath.

'For somebody,' he said, 'it would have to have been carefully planned. Whoever did it...did them.' He sounded morose, depressed at the very thought.

'Them?' I demanded. 'But the two deaths were nearly a mile apart. The same person couldn't have done both.' I thought about it, and added, 'Surely?'

'It was so, whoever did it, or both.' He sounded morose, depressed by the thought of it. 'Shall we head for the bar?' he asked. Clearly, he didn't want to continue talking about it.

'I'm not sure I want to,' I said, not feeling too bright myself. 'Our friend Harcourt might be there, with that mathematical genius of his. It could be awkward.'

'I don't think so. I'm sure I saw Farmer heading for their car. He probably wanted to use the car-phone, if it's a private call. They're sure to have an in-car-phone.'

I turned, to see if there was or was not a person in the Jaguar. It was at first difficult to detect, because I was trying to see beyond the terrace lamps, so I moved sideways, and at once I saw that the Jaguar's interior light was on. And the impression was that the door was wide open. But nothing was moving. Nobody was getting in or out of the car, and there was no shadow seated behind the wheel.

Oliver, too, had noted it. 'Shall we go

and have a look?' he asked.

I was already moving. He caught my arm. 'Take it easy, Phil. It's a bit strange...' Nevertheless, he lengthened his stride.

Before we reached it, I heard the groans. We both broke into a run.

'Easy now, easy,' said Oliver.

The last few yards of our approach were therefore taken with more caution. I saw him then, lying just outside the open car door, Len Farmer, trying to get himself to his feet, but with his head hanging low.

I went down on one knee. His face was twisted with pain, angles carved into it by the weak side-lighting from inside the car.

'What is it?' I asked him. 'What's happened?'

Oliver was already helping him with his good arm, and managed to get him sitting on the gravel instead of kneeling painfully.

Now Farmer had both hands free, and could handle his chin gently.

'That idiot,' he mumbled. 'That big lout who's running this painting lark.'

'Geoff Davies?' I asked.

'Mmm!' he mumbled in agreement. 'God...I thought he'd busted my jaw.' He fondled it tentatively.

'He attacked you here?' I asked. It sounded so unlikely.

'Yes, yes. The bastard. Yanked open the car door and dragged me out. I didn't stand a bloody chance. Didn't even get to stand up straight. He just hit me—and I was out. Like that...out.'

'Didn't he say anything?'

'Nowt.'

'I'll go and get Mr Harcourt,' I said. 'You just stay there—'

'No! Oh Christ—he'll kill me.'

'Here...' Oliver put in, reaching past me. 'Let's see if you can stand on your own two feet.'

He could, awkwardly and with uncertainty, Oliver having only one good arm to use in assistance. Farmer stood, swaying.

'I've gotta find the boss,' he mumbled, contradicting himself.

'No,' I said. 'You ought to take it easy. Sit inside the car,' I instructed him.

'No.' Stubborn, he was. 'Gotta find the boss.' His speech was somewhat hampered.

'It'll wait.' I glanced at Oliver. He smiled thinly—no help at all.

'No.' Farmer was becoming agitated. 'He's gotta know. The bastard's nicked the car keys.'

'The keys...' I looked to Oliver for assistance. 'Can you get him inside, Oliver? The bar—that's the nearest. Get him a drink. And then I'll know where to find you.'

Oliver cocked his head, and viewed me with suspicion. 'What have you got in mind?'

'I'm going to get those keys back, Oliver. Please do what I'm asking.'

He gave me one weighty and considered look. 'Then be careful, Phillie, please.'

'Don't be ridiculous, Oliver. Careful indeed! Geoff's not going to hurt me.'

'Of course not. But all the same...'

'You're wasting time, Oliver.'

He grunted, and turned to Len Farmer. 'Come on, then. The bar it is. It's not far, the back way. I can lend you an arm, but only one.'

Feeling his jaw tentatively with one hand, the other clutching Oliver's left arm fiercely, Len Farmer took one or two hesitant steps.

I turned away.

The Glasshouse was the obvious place to investigate first. The lights were still on, but Geoff wasn't in there. Paul was alone, wandering around uselessly with his hands thrust into his pockets, his face drawn and white.

'You're doing yourself no good, you know,' I told him. 'And you shouldn't be on your own like this. Company...'

'I'm all right. Leave me alone.' But he wouldn't look directly at me.

'You don't look it. You look terrible.'

For one flash of a second he glanced at me, and at first I thought I detected anger in his expression, anger and rejection. Then it was gone, and only anxiety remained.

'It shows, does it?' he asked.

'It most certainly does. I'm sorry, Paul. Really I am. Why don't you head for the bar? You could do with a stiff drink...and company. Believe me.'

'Yeah. Well. You could be right.' He stared vacantly beyond my head.

'You'll go there?'

'In a minute. I shan't be able to stand it, though, if they're all...all...' He shook his head.

'All sorry for you?' I asked gently.

'Yes. That sort of thing.'

'But it'll be sincere, you know. They'll really mean it. And after all...as long as it's sincere...'

'Yeah. I suppose so. Here—you didn't come looking for me?' He tilted his head. His eyes were bloodshot. 'Did you?'

There was suspicion, that I might be a chosen representative, sent to find him and return him to the group.

'No. I was looking for Geoff.'

'Oh...him. He's gone to his cottage.'

'I don't know where that is.'

He gave a sadly twisted smile. 'I'll show you.'

Already, he was sounding better. I had

216

given him something to do, a purpose to his actions and thoughts, even if very minor. He turned as we left the Glasshouse and switched off the lights, closing the door after us. But here, behind the house, we received no assistance from the terrace lamps. He muttered something, turned back, and put on the lights again.

'Those steps,' he told me, now that we were able to see them. 'Up there.'

They were a short flight of stone steps, deeply worn in the centre of the treads, leading up to a flat terrace of concrete. Beyond it, and a little to the left, I could see the crouching shadow of a building, its lights dim through heavy curtains.

'Well...thank you,' I said. 'I take it that that's his cottage?'

'It is.'

'I'm all right then, now, and thanks for your help.'

'I'll come with you.'

'Really, there's no need—'

'Something to do,' he said stolidly.

'Yes. Of course.' How could I now dismiss him, when I'd been telling him to find something to do? 'Come on, then.'

There was an old brass knocker on the door, shaped like a dolphin. It clacked like a pistol shot when I tried it. A light winked on beyond a square of inset glass, and the door opened.

'Philipa? Well...hello. And you too, Paul. Thought you'd have been in the bar. You know...'

Paul said, 'Getting stewed to the eyeballs? No. No thanks. Need all my wits.'

'Well—come along in, both of you.'

The tiny hall was just about big enough to stand in, and possibly to turn around. Geoff backed away, and we were in his kitchen.

Not much in the way of modernization had taken place. The sink was an ancient glazed pottery one, the chairs rather cranky-looking Windsors, the table a plain slab of pine, much scrubbed and battered. On it, he had spread out a map.

'I was just working out where to take you all, tomorrow,' he explained. 'Certainly, nobody will want to go anywhere near the coast. You'd agree to that? And look—I've found a rather interesting old castle marked here...' He put a finger on the spot. 'And a bit of a lake. That seems a likely place.' He turned back to face us, smiling.

'Do you really think they'll want to go out—' I began.

He didn't allow me to finish. 'If I have to drive you all into the coach with a whip.' He nodded, frowning severely. 'It's what it's all about. Painting. But this

218

time—nobody on their own. All together. For safety.'

'You're not really anticipating—'

Once more he cut me off. It was nerves, his words and actions straining for release from his forced restraint. 'And to what do I owe this visit?' Then he scanned from face to face. 'You're not a committee, I hope?'

'Paul came along to show me the way,' I explained.

'Good for him. And to what—'

'You've said that, Geoff. I've come for the keys.'

'Keys? What—'

'Oh, come on! Don't be stupid. The keys you took from the jag, after knocking out Len Farmer.'

He stared blankly at me. Then he smiled. 'Try to find 'em.'

'Oh—don't be a damned fool.'

'He said he was going to take Elise home—'

'All right. You can't prevent him, if that's what he wants to do. And if she's willing—'

'Willing! He hypnotizes her, I think. And the bloody fool can't see that he'd be landing her right into trouble, if he drags her off home. It'd look awfully bad. Now...wouldn't it?'

'Yes it would. And the man's an idiot.

But he's her father. If she agrees... No! keep your mouth shut for a minute, Geoff. And let me try to get this over to you. He can charge you with assault—on Farmer. He can charge you with theft—of the keys. No...listen, damn you. Do you think, for one minute, that a man like Harcourt could be stopped for the sake of a paltry set of keys! He could be on the phone to the nearest Jaguar agency in the morning, and they would send somebody out. It's the sort of service you get when you can afford that kind of car. And it's no good you scowling. You're only making things worse.'

'They'll pick on Elise.' His voice was rising, running out of control. 'The police. With the motive she'd got...Jennie...the painting.'

'It wasn't Jennie who slashed the painting, Geoff.' I turned. 'You tell him, Paul. Put him out of his misery.'

'What?' asked Paul, staring from one face to the other, as though not really understanding what we were talking about.

'Tell him who slashed Elise's wonderful painting. Go on. It doesn't matter any more who knows.'

'Oh yes. That. It was my wife, Geoff. Pam. She did it.'

'You can't be—'

'It was Pam,' Paul cut in flatly. 'And

220

I *know.*' There was so much personal distress in his voice that it could not be denied.

'But the point is, Geoff,' I carried on, 'that Elise thought it was Jennie. Because you told her so. Think about that. You could yourself be responsible for Jennie's death, if only incidentally. If Elise *did* kill Jennie, that is. No, no!' I put up a hand. 'It's no good getting all worked up. These are facts. Pam slashed the painting. You told Elise it had been Jennie. And Jennie died. What a pity you gave Elise such a good motive. But, you'll say, that's all irrelevant, because Elise didn't kill Jennie. You'll say you're quite convinced of that, because you can't believe that Elise would have done such a thing.'

'But...but...'

'But nothing.' I was somewhat impatient with him. 'Now you've tried to stop Harcourt from taking her home, which, as we all know, would be exactly the action of somebody who believes she's in danger of arrest. Her own father believes she's guilty, in other words, and doesn't give a damn. And he wants to protect her...take her home and surround her with a whole army of lawyers. And now...you've made it look as though you believe she's guilty, but would be safer here with you. You complete idiot, Geoff, you're making it worse. Harcourt'll stop at nothing, now. He'll see you as a threat. So give me those damned keys, and stop playing at Sir Lancelot.'

'Who?'

'Never mind. You know what I mean.' I held out my hand, palm upwards. 'The keys,' I demanded.

Reluctantly, he produced them, and handed them over. 'I'm telling you,' he said miserably, 'that he'll be taking her home.'

'I realize that. At least, he'll try. Haven't you been listening? But damn it, Geoff, she's a grown woman, past her age of majority. So she can do exactly what she likes with her own life. And what's Harcourt going to do if she simply refuses to go with him? Use violence on her? I can't see that, somehow. So why *should* she do as he says?'

He growled something that I couldn't catch. 'Pardon?'

'Her mother died when she was born, I gather from what she's said, and he's ordered her around from the time she started walking. Oh...never a blow. Nothing like that. But all the same, he terrifies her.'

'All right, all right. So what's her great big protector doing about it? Tell me. I don't see anything happening. You could have her here, living with you, and he couldn't do a thing. You could marry her, and he couldn't stop it. And...yes...yes. I know what you're trying to say. He mustn't be upset. Rubbish. It's probably the weapon he's used on her all her life. One thing or another. "You mustn't upset your father, my love...now be good." Be good! Oh...I'll bet she's had a lifetime of being good. It's called emotional blackmail, Geoff. Worse than any other sort of blackmail, because, however much you pay, you can never get free from it. I bet she's had a lifetime of blackmail. Don't you think she's paid enough? So what you've got to do is persuade her she now owes him nothing.'

He grimaced. 'Small chance of that.'

'So what d'you want to condemn her to?' I asked, losing my patience with him. 'The rest of her life devoted to looking after his welfare, and letting nothing upset him? Ah—but yes...I think I understand. He wants her to marry Len Farmer, and Farmer's the one who looks after his business interests. Oh yes...it becomes very clear. Elise's father is beginning to worry that he couldn't run his business on his own. He needs Len Farmer, and he needs Elise, or his life will be in ruins—if you believe a word he says, and all the words he doesn't say. Geoff, you'll have to do something, if you're going to save her from a miserable existence.'

And Paul said, condensing it all into one crisp sentence, 'Marry her first, and argue afterwards.'

I had forgotten he was there, and turned to him. 'Ah! The expert on married bliss!'

I was in a grand mood by this time, furious with both of them, for the way they had treated—or intended to treat—the women in their lives. Poor Paul! He had to bear the backlash of my anger at Geoff's failure to make any decisive move. 'Paul would do it, wouldn't you, Paul?'

'Do what?' He was eyeing me warily.

I gestured widely, intending to embrace the whole cottage, the whole emotional background. 'It's called common-law marriage. Everybody's doing it, these days, but they don't use any fancy terms for it. She moves in with you, Geoff. Just like that. And if her father doesn't like it, he can lump it, as they say where I was brought up.'

He gave me a soft, forgiving smile. 'It wouldn't do for Elise.'

'Then sort it out for yourself,' I told him, finally losing my temper.

Again that smile. 'If you'll be seeing the others, tell them: nine o'clock tomorrow morning, and we're off into the mountains.'

'Yes, Geoff,' I said. 'I'll let them know.'

I could hear the mock humility in my voice.

Then we left, Paul and I. Our group would be somewhat depleted in the morning. Only six of us—seven if you included Geoff himself.

'I think I could manage a drink, now,' said Paul. 'In fact, I'm dying for one. Let me buy one for you.'

'Thank you.'

'Your husband will be in the bar, d'you think?'

'Oh yes. I expect so.'

'Hmm! Pity.'

'There. You see,' I told him. 'All it needed was a bit of distraction, and you're back to your old self.'

He hesitated in his step, and at first I thought he was going to stop, to reach out with his hand and stop me too. He said, 'All what needed?' It was said suspiciously.

'Your misery. It's gone. You're picking up already.'

He stood aside for me to lead the way down the steps, and said as he followed me, 'You're being sarcastic. It doesn't become you.'

I didn't know whether he intended this as a compliment or a criticism. 'It was not intended as sarcasm,' I assured him over my shoulder.

'You were implying that I didn't feel a thing for either of them.'

'Was I? I didn't intend it so. I've told you that.'

I paused before we reached the door to the bar. It was a warm night, and the door was open, a great clatter of vocal noise coming from it.

'Either of them?' I asked, as we paused just beyond the spill of light. 'You're as good as telling me that your feelings—the ones on the warm side—were for only one of them?'

Someone must have nudged the door. Perhaps there was a draught. In any event, it began to swing shut, slicing the light across half of Paul's features. His expression was hardening, setting into a twisted smile.

'Is that the impression I gave?' he asked, a hint of amusement in his voice. 'But surely—a person can have affection for only one other human being at a time.'

It was not completely valid. I had affection for both Oliver and Harvey Remington—but in different ways.

'But *you* didn't convey that impression,' I assured him. 'You were—what's the word?—accommodating both Pam and Jennie at the same time.'

'Not really,' he said modestly. 'I loved only one. Shall we go in?'

I caught his arm. 'A minute. Just tell me, who was that, Paul?'

'Jennie, of course.'

'Why of course?'

He didn't answer that, but took my elbow in his hand—gently, even caressingly—and eased me forward, then led the way to the bar.

But I didn't need an answer. Jennie would have been more eager, and perhaps more expert than Pam in satisfying his sexual needs. Was that what he called love? Had that been the sum total of his emotional requirements?

Suddenly, I was deeply sorry for him, more sorry than I had been in respect of his loss of both women. But already he had his intentions levelled elsewhere. Me.

Oliver spotted me, and called out, 'There you are, Phil. I've got a drink for you.'

I smiled at Paul, patted his arm as a gesture of dismissal, and managed to squeeze myself into a space beside Oliver. On the far side of him was seated, and looking lost in a group not of his own social choice, Len Farmer.

I leaned across Oliver and slipped the car keys on to the table under Farmer's nose.

'With the compliments of Geoff Davies,' I told him. 'He's realized the error of his ways, and sends his apologies.'

That was not exactly the truth, but it

did provoke a weak smile, which caused a wince. 'No need to tell my boss, then,' he said. It was a concern that had worried him.

'Best left in ignorance, perhaps,' I agreed.

Paul was already passing on the message from Geoff. It was to be business as usual in the morning. I didn't detect any vast enthusiasm, but it was what they had come here for, so they might as well get on with it. Heads were nodded. Raised eyebrows were presented to me. I had to lift my voice in order to carry it over the general clatter.

'This time, Geoff says, we're going to stay together, not split up. And it's inland—in the mountains. A lake, and with an old castle.'

That seemed to ease a few minds—the staying together and the lake. A change, it is said, is as good as a rest. With all the stress and action that we had encountered, this first day, everybody could do with a relaxing tomorrow. And, it seemed, an early bed. Very soon, goodnights were being called, fingers were wiggled, and the bar began to empty a little. The German linguists and the Chinese Brush painters were untouched by our double tragedy. But as each of our group departed, I noticed, the clamour died and eyes

228

followed our departure.

There's nothing so intriguing as a good murder. Unless it's two, and that was what we had to offer.

13

Tuesday...and so much seemed to have happened in one evening and a day. We were dressed, and ready to go down to breakfast, a quarter of an hour too early.

'It's going to be a grand day,' said Oliver, who was sorting and tidying his pastels.

'It looks like it.' I opened the windows and went out on to the balcony. The town and its estuary rested clean and bright in the morning sun. From that viewpoint I could just see the corner of the gravelled area, in which the Jaguar had been parked—and now was not.

'He's done it,' I said. 'The Jag's gone.'

'Huh!' said Oliver in disgust. 'The man's a fool.'

The air was crisp at this time, the sky a cloudless blue. But I could always put in my own clouds. I like a few clouds in a landscape.

'He'll be back,' said Oliver.

I closed the windows. 'You sound certain of that.'

'Because I am. With the case the superintendent's got against Elise, I was surprised he didn't take her in for interrogation yesterday. He'd have been justified.'

'But Oliver...that would be terrible. Worse for Elise than for anybody else, of course.'

'Yes. Perhaps that's why Llewellyn held off. Well, he's held off too long, and he's lost her.'

'Not lost, surely,' I said.

'Well, perhaps not. Wrong word. Was that the breakfast bell? Mislaid temporarily, rather.'

'It *was* the bell. And—temporarily we must hope,' I said.

We went down. Our group seemed very much diminished, and, like aliens, we tried to keep together. To have become involved with either of the other groups would have entailed having to dodge questions from right and left.

'What's this?' asked Philip. 'Something was said about heading inland.'

'Yes,' added Martin. 'Nobody told us. Or perhaps we weren't listening.'

'It's a lake with an island,' I said. 'And a bit of an old castle, and probably water

230

birds, swans and the like. It sounds ideal to me.'

I had built up on the image in my mind, and all from a tiny indication on a map.

'I wonder how many of us will come back,' said Paul morosely.

Philip was quite short with him. 'Don't be an idiot. And where's Elise?' he asked. He was a little deficient in sense of humour, I decided.

'I rather think that her father's taken her home,' I told him.

Martin stared at me over his fork. 'That's surely not a good idea. In fact, it's bloody stupid.'

I smiled at him. 'Don't worry. I think we'll be seeing her again. Oh...I was forgetting to tell you...Geoff wants us to stay together, today. In one group. Just to play safe.'

'Hah!' Philip commented. He nodded his understanding.

Then we were silent until breakfast was over, and we all went along to the Glasshouse, in order to get our stuff organized.

I had expected to find Geoff waiting for us, but he wasn't there. He must have breakfasted earlier, or in his own little cottage. Then he came striding in, looking harassed. 'Ah—you're all here.' He didn't mention Elise. 'Good. Have you heard what we're going to do? It'll be a pleasant change for all of us. And productive, I hope. The coach is outside, so let's get moving.'

He hadn't said anything about the absence of Elise. Perhaps he had watched her leave. Perhaps he believed she would be back. Or even, if he had phoned Llewellyn, was certain.

The trip inland was more entrancing than I had anticipated. The rolling Welsh mountains seemed to loom all around us, the narrow roads creeping against their flanks and venturing down into deep valleys, across the fast-flowing streams and then up again to cling to the side of precipitous cliffs. Until...there it was.

We wound down towards the lake, which became more and more enticing every second, until we ran out of tarmacked surfaces, clung to our seats as the coach bucked over rudimentary paths, and finally halted a little short of the lake.

We clambered out, and stood and stared. It was beautiful, with grey purple slopes beyond, and rolling mountains behind those, with an island graced by a single tree two thirds of the way along the lake's length, and with two swans, and mountain sheep speckled across the stubble grass and the gorse of the hillside.

'Ah!' said Geoff. The rest of us simply sighed.

In practice, it was not necessary that we should remain in one tight group. We spread ourselves around, but each of us within view of all the rest. It could hardly have been otherwise in that open expanse. We were becoming paranoiac on the question of safety. And, after a little while, silence settled around us as we each concentrated on our individual masterpieces. We could, too, expect with confidence that on the next day, and Thursday no doubt, we could return here.

Of the reputed castle there was no sign. The sheep slowly drifted along from the surrounding hillsides to see what was going on, until they became a positive threat to our easels, which offered them convenient scratching surfaces and edges. But they eventually ambled away, and from then onwards they ignored our presence.

Geoff now had his task made much more simple than it had been at the bay. He could stroll from one to the other of us, and comment as required. And if he spent quite a long while gazing back the way we had wound our way down to the lake, no one commented on it. But it was unlikely that Harcourt's Jag would drift down into the valley, returning Elise to what, with the sheep all around us, could perhaps be called the fold. All the same, Geoff watched—and was disappointed.

We ate our lunches, strolling round and chatting, arguing as to the positions we might take up the next day, where the sun would be at which time, and when it might throw a splash of colour on the craggy face of the mountainside, which we were all trying to capture on our individual flat surfaces.

I had not previously thought of landscape painting as anything but a quiet and relaxing interest, but by the time we were ready to leave, with shadows now exploring the sides of the mountains and flowing into the valleys, I felt quite exhausted. Concentration, I supposed. Sitting still for so long. In any event, it afflicted all of us, judging by the awkward way the others were fumbling into the coach.

'We'll be back by seven,' said Geoff. 'Gives you time for a bath. It's been a useful and productive day, I think.'

We all agreed that it had been a good day, and as we had found time to wander round and see how the others were doing, a fair amount of congratulations were being tossed around. Modesty predominated. It could well be dangerous to express too much possessive pride. You either got your painting slashed, or your head bashed in. It was an indication of how tired I was that I should have allowed such thoughts to creep into my mind.

And it seemed that I had concentrated so intensely that I had completely forgotten to give any thought at all to Elise. I realized, from this flush of self-criticism, that she meant more to me than I had believed. She had, herself, chosen to make a friend of me, and to trust me. Now I thought of her as my own particular friend. Vastly different. Wherever she was, she would be in a state of misery. Certainly, nothing approaching enjoyment could now be engulfing her.

When we drew in and parked at the Manor the Jaguar was there again, on the gravelled parking place. So he had brought her back...but no, perhaps not. Llewellyn could have brought her back, escorted in an official police car.

'Harcourt?' I demanded. 'Where is he?'

Nobody seemed to know, and not to care, greatly. Oliver said, 'Leave it for a while, Phil. Let's get our stuff into the Glasshouse, and have a quick shower, and perhaps a pint...'

'Let's try the bar first,' I suggested. 'I'm sure that's what you want, Oliver. The rest can wait. If Harcourt's there, I want a word with him.'

'As you wish,' said Oliver equably.

So we went to the bar, which was open

but nearly empty. Those on the other courses were still struggling with their expanding abilities. I wondered what would be German for Chinese Brush Painting.

There was no sign of Len Farmer, but Harcourt was there, solitary in a corner. He was cuddling what looked like a double whisky. Leaving Oliver to attend to our own requirements, I went across and sat with Harcourt.

'Well?' I asked.

I realized, then, that he was looking terribly jaded. What had seemed like rugged health had now deserted his face, and he was left with a craggy, furrowed mask, from which his eyes stared above blue-grey pouches. He did not at once reply.

Oliver slid my Dubonnet and lemonade in front of me. I didn't take my eyes off Harcourt.

'Well?' I repeated. 'What's been happening?'

'I took her home,' he said hollowly. 'All bloody tears and protests; never shut her mouth all the way there. But I wanted to get her there, and get my solicitor on the job.'

'Let me guess,' I suggested. 'Llewellyn had already contacted your local police, and they turned up, and...'

I stopped, because he was shaking his

head miserably. 'No. Not that. *He* came, himself. Llewellyn, with that policewoman. And they simply took her away.'

I glanced at Oliver, but he merely raised his eyebrows.

'Just took her away in his car,' went on Harcourt, his voice drained of emotion, as though he was relating a nightmare. 'Said he was bringing her back here for...' He shook his head wearily. 'Inter-something.'

'Interrogation,' put in Oliver quietly. 'It's not as bad as it sounds. They have to go very carefully. Can't do any bullying or anything like that, or it invalidates the lot.'

'But...why, why, why?' He thumped the table with his now empty glass, then stared at it as though he couldn't remember how it had become empty.

'Because she had such a good motive for killing Jennie.' I had difficulty preventing myself from reaching across to clutch his hand encouragingly. 'You know about the slashed painting?'

He groaned. 'I've heard it a thousand times. Do I know! Hah!'

So I went on, 'Elise could have picked up a lump of wood anywhere. Then she would've had the means to do it. But the most important thing is that she says—said to me, anyway—that she'd gone to that place in order to use the ladies' toilet, and that she *did* go in there, and that Jennie was killed just outside, while she *was* inside. But Elise couldn't have done what she claimed she did, because that ladies' toilet is closed for alterations, and has been for weeks. No, don't interrupt. Let me say it. If she insists on saying that, then she's telling a lie, and a lie she wouldn't have told if she'd even attempted to go in there. So she hadn't tried it—in which case the police will ask her: why else would she have gone there, to a spot only yards from Jennie? What possible reason could she have had—unless it was to come on Jennie from behind? The ladies' toilet must therefore have been no more than an excuse to *go* there...and to do what? To punish Jennie for having slashed her painting to shreds, that's what.'

'You can't be saying...no...it's just not my Elise. She would never do a thing like that.' He shook his head vigorously to underline it.

'All right.' I held up my hand. 'So maybe she intended to do no more than ruin Jennie's painting. Break up her easel or something. That would verge on being excusable. Just retribution. But Jennie's head was smashed in, and she was dead. *Now* do you understand? Llewellyn's got a damned good reason for holding Elise for questioning. Particularly after the way she

238

slipped away from here. And if he doesn't get a valid explanation of that lie about the ladies' toilet, or an admission that it was a lie, then he can... What *can* he do, Oliver?'

He shrugged. 'He can stick his neck out and charge her. Or—if he doesn't think he's got enough evidence for that—he could take his case to a magistrate and apply for an extension, for further questioning. But...your solicitor...is he there with her?'

'Of course he is. What d'you think? I'm paying him enough.'

'Then he'll know how to look after her,' I said. 'Stop worrying, Mr Harcourt.'

'Hah!' he said. 'Stop worrying, she says!'

I smiled at him, encouragingly, I hoped. 'But you'll have to excuse us...'

He nodded, and Oliver and I went along to our room.

'Shower,' I said. 'I feel all gritty, after that little chat.'

'Did he upset you that much, Phil?' he asked, concern in his voice.

'Upset? Well no, not that. It's just...oh, I don't know. That man! Harcourt. He's so damned possessive! *His* Elise!'

'Well...she is.'

'It's the way he assumes she can't look after herself. You're not a woman, Oliver. You don't know what it's like. He won't

239

let her stand on her own two feet, or let
her make her own decisions. Oliver, she'd
be so much better if he was well away
from here.'

'Yes, Phil. I can see that.'

It had been his patient voice. I almost
snapped at him. 'You *don't* understand.'

'Oh—but I do. If it was you, Phil,
round at their station and being questioned
intensively, wouldn't you feel lost and
deserted if I just left you to it?'

'I could manage.'

'Yes, my love. I'm sure you could. But
you'd feel deserted if I just sat back and
said nothing. Admit it.'

'Oh...you men!'

He grinned at me. 'As I would if the
roles were reversed.'

I got up on to my toes and kissed him.
'Shower,' I said. 'Me first?'

'By all means. Ladies first.' And he
grinned.

A quarter of an hour later we stood
together at the window. Neither of us
said anything. There wasn't anything left
to say, except...

'Oliver!'

'I'm here.' He squeezed my arm to
confirm it.

'Do you realize something—it's all been
discussed, argued, disputed, and the rest,
around Jennie's death. There's been no

mention at all of Pam's. Now—isn't that strange?'

He thought about it for a moment or two, then, 'Well yes. I suppose it is, now you come to mention it. But after all, Phil, the police *have* had something to work with, on the Jennie murder. But with Pam's...well, nothing really, as far as we know. No clues, nowhere to look.'

'There's the fact that it's the same weapon.'

'So they said. But does it *tell* us anything, even if it is?'

'And that Jennie died first.'

'Well yes,' he agreed. 'Blood grouping. But that only suggests that Jennie was killed first, Pam afterwards. Apart from that, there's no direct link between the two murders. I mean—there doesn't seem to be anybody who would want to kill both of them.'

'Hmm!' I said.

'Isn't that the dinner bell?'

It was, and we went down to see what they were laying on for all of us. And this time I had a healthy appetite. Afterwards, we walked around outside, just because we were both restless, up and down the terrace, round the lawn and back, to the gates and back. We had been sitting all day, and now we were restless. I didn't want to go into the bar—it would be too noisy. We spoke very little, there not being anything left to say. Simply, as the dusk enclosed us, the mood was too restful to be disturbed.

In fact, we were so absorbed with the seclusion that it must have taken a minute or two before the fact registered with either of us that a car had drawn up on the terrace, opposite the main entrance. Someone who looked very like Llewellyn opened the rear door, and out stepped Elise.

We began to move in that direction, but not hurriedly. He was saying something urgently, his head bent close to hers. Then he got back into his car. It backed up to where it could turn, then it drove away.

I ran up the steps from the lawn, leaving Oliver to walk at his own measured pace.

'Elise!'

'Oh...Philipa! Philipa!'

We hugged each other, but she was nowhere near tears and could only laugh her pleasure.

'Was it very bad?' I asked.

'No, no. Not really. All I could tell them was what I heard and saw, which wasn't very much, as you know. But it *was* irritating when they kept asking the same questions over and over. Poor father! He must have been worried out of his mind.'

So it was 'father' now. It seemed that Elise had matured, abruptly and calmly.

'We've all been terribly worried.'

'Oh—there wasn't any need for that. After all, I hadn't done anything bad.'

And then, there was Harcourt, at the head of the steps to the front door.

'Elise!' he roared. He bounded down the steps, and hugged her and kissed her on both cheeks, and said, 'You can't know how relieved I am that you're safe, my love.'

She stepped back a pace, no doubt to observe the depths of that relief. 'Of course I'm safe, father. I've been at one of their police stations, and what could be safer than that? And they were ever so polite to me, and so patient.'

I wondered whether he had noticed that he'd been demoted to being her father rather than her daddy.

'I'm sure my man, Greatorex, looked after you, baby.'

Baby? After all, he had noticed her use of 'father,' and was trying to neutralize it.

'Oh—that stupid man!' she cried. 'Why on earth did you send him? Nothing but interruptions. "You don't need to answer that," he'd say. Why shouldn't I? There wasn't anything they asked that I couldn't answer. And he'd say, "That is a leading question." Oh...I could have killed him.

I'd have been back here an hour ago, if it hadn't been for your ninny of a solicitor and his *habeases* and his *corpuses,* whatever those silly things are. And Geoff... Where's Geoff? Geoff...'

He had to be somewhere near, because all the rest were out there now, including the office staff, to welcome home their adventuress, but he had been hanging back quietly and unobtrusively, even shyly. Now he came forward into the light from the terrace lamps, slowly and hesitantly.

'Geoff, love,' she whispered.

Then they were in each other's arms, and tears there were at last. Eventually, he held her away from him, the better to see her.

'Welcome home, my sweet.'

Home? Was that how he considered Bryngowan Manor? His home. Well...after all...it was.

'Home?' she asked.

'The cottage, love,' he explained. 'Come along. We'll brew a pot of tea, and you can tell me all about it.'

As far as they were concerned, the rest of us might not have been there.

'This place,' Geoff was saying, as the terrace lamps released their hold on them. 'The place I've found...it's way, way out in the mountains, and you're going to love it. Sheep and swans. Everybody likes it. And you'll be thrilled when you see what's been turned out...'

She wasn't saying anything, was content with his presence, his calm and matter-of-fact voice, and his arm protecting her.

'Fetch your stuff over later...'

Those were the last words I heard him saying to her.

The spectators quietly dispersed. That left Oliver and me on the terrace, with Harcourt. He seemed bewildered. After all he'd done for her, how could she have been so ungrateful? But Elise had proved to herself that she didn't need the strong arm of his considerable income to support her. Geoff's strong arm around her waist would be sufficient.

Then I was abruptly withdrawn from my romantic musings by Oliver, bringing me back heavily to earth again.

'He didn't drive away, you know,' he said.

'What? Who?'

'Our friend, Llewellyn. His car's pulled on to the gravel patch, and he's waiting there.'

'What for, I wonder?'

'Well, I should imagine to observe the result of Elise's release. Who acted how. That sort of thing.'

I shook his arm. 'Don't be so obscure, Oliver, please.'

He stopped, gripped both of my arms just above the elbows, considered what he could see of my expression in the half-light, and said, 'He's being crafty, that's my guess. He couldn't put together a solid case against Elise, so he's made a gesture and released her. But only, I'd guess, to see how this affects the murderer's actions. With Elise free, who will now become all nervous and anxious? That's what he's looking for.'

'So?' I asked cautiously. Llewellyn wasn't going to see much about people's reactions, sitting there in the car park.

'That Llewellyn's no fool,' he assured me, as though I hadn't realized that. 'He's playing it gently. He'd have known, almost at once, that Elise could not have killed Jennie. She's much too naïve to be able to hide it. But that doesn't mean she's not intelligent, Phil. And Llewellyn would recognize that. So he releases her, and tells her to keep her eyes open. Probably mentioned no names to her, I expect, just left it to her. So—who would you guess to be the person he really suspects, Phil? Go on, tell me.'

'I can't follow your tortuous mental processes, Oliver,' I protested.

'Not mine. Llewellyn's. He's thrown her back into the group—and in what direction d'you think he has pointed her?'

'You can't mean...' I stopped dead, clutching his arm. He said nothing, but waited for me to complete it. 'You can't mean Geoff? Oh...come on! Not Geoff!'

He was quite solemn about it, not a hint of a smile. 'Not my reasoning. We're talking about Llewellyn's thoughts. What he's thinking. Who she's closest to.'

'Geoff? Oh no!'

'Remember, I said it's Llewellyn's thinking that counts. And Phil, if you give it a little consideration yourself, you'll realize why. Who, down by the estuary, had the most freedom of movement of all of us? Geoff, of course. And don't tell me that Larry wouldn't know all about them, because I've realized that. But would Larry say anything that might harm Geoff? I'd lay all my cash on it: he wouldn't say a word. So that doesn't come into it. Geoff knows that area inside out, probably knows the paths through all that woodland. And who could approach anybody in the group without the slightest suspicion from them? And who didn't get round to speak to anybody about what they were doing, all morning? Geoff again. And who had a motive quite as good as his cherished Elise had—because it was the very same one? Geoff.' Then at last he was silent.

'Oliver!' I whispered. 'Not Geoff!'

'It's how Llewellyn could be seeing it.

247

And all he might be looking for now is one tiny morsel of evidence. So...as a bribe for releasing Elise...he's offered her this. One loose word, one whispered secret. Pillow talk.'

'No, no, Oliver! For pity's sake, don't even say it. Elise couldn't...wouldn't...she'd never agree to that.'

'How do you know how terrified she might have been?' he asked. 'Oh sure...she implied it had all been a pleasant and diverting little chat. Nonsense. For a young woman like our Elise, it would've been sheer hell.'

'And you're saying that they've managed to scare her into agreeing to cheat Geoff? I simply do not believe it.' I clutched at Oliver's arm. 'She might have *agreed* to do it—but she would never, never *do* it.'

'We don't know what she's prepared to do, my love. You might understand, where a man would find it difficult. Perhaps she *is* prepared to undertake such a thing, for her freedom. Perhaps I'm talking a load of nonsense. But the least we can do is to keep a sharp eye on the situation.'

'I don't believe,' I said, measuring my words, 'that Geoff could harm anything, let alone a person.'

He drew me closer and spoke quietly into my ear. 'It's Elise I'm thinking about, and how much *she* would be prepared to harm somebody. How ruthless, would you say, is our darling and delightful Elise?'

'She's not ours, Oliver.' I found I was whispering it.

'That's no answer.'

'I don't know any answer,' I said. But I said it miserably.

14

The following morning we went straight from breakfast to the Glasshouse. It was Wednesday, the weather was still fine, and I hadn't yet given due attention to Oliver's pastel efforts from the previous day. My mind was on other matters, that was the trouble.

Geoff was alone in there, tidying things that were already tidy. Pam Wilton's painting equipment was still on the counter. Perhaps Paul was reluctant to move it, as he would have been removing an essential aspect of Pam's life. Her last painting! There it was. The spray-can, which had been standing beside it, was still in the same position. I picked it up and gave it a shake, as I had before, and heard the same sound.

'Elise is coming with us, I suppose?' I asked Geoff.

He looked at me in surprise. 'Of course.' If only to keep her away from her father's influence, was what I inferred from that. 'She's gone to avail herself of one of the bathrooms in the annexe,' he told me. 'I'm afraid the facilities in the cottage are rudimentary. But I'll get something done about that.'

'Yes. I'm sure you will.'

Then, because we neither of us could think of anything to add, Oliver stepped into the gap.

'Is this Pam's last painting, Geoff?' he asked.

'It is. Good, isn't...wasn't she?'

'I'll never get to that standard,' Oliver said wistfully.

'You don't know that.' Geoff smiled, at some fond memory from the past, I guessed. 'You should've seen some of Pam's work three or four years back. You wouldn't think it was the same person's. So don't give it up, Oliver. Go on—trying and trying. It's all there, waiting to come out, and you'll find yourself developing your own particular style. Then it will all be yours. All of it.'

Oliver grunted, but looked pleased.

'I suppose,' I said, 'that Pam had barely started this, when you first saw it? She'd be the first you'd visit.'

'She's certainly taking her time.' He looked towards the door.

'You'll have to get used to that,' I told him. 'Women take more time than men.'

'There've been occasions,' said Oliver, despair in his voice, 'when I've read half of *Pride and Prejudice*, just waiting while she gets her hair right.'

It was a wicked lie. My hair never presents any problem. I kicked his ankle. It wasn't the first time he'd said it.

'Of course,' I said, refusing to be distracted, 'you started with Pam, didn't you, Geoff? On your rounds. Pam first.'

'Always do—did. Nothing I could've taught her, though.'

'So she couldn't have got far on this one, when you saw it?'

'Well...no. Though I can't understand what you're trying to get at.'

'I was only trying to get a time-scale in my mind.'

He frowned. Shook his head. 'Why?' he asked.

'Because I'm nosy. I get that from my father. If you can't understand something, he used to say, ask.'

Geoff's smile was twisted and tentative. 'Well, if you *must* know...'

'Or she goes into a decline,' put in

Oliver seriously, moving his ankle out of the way.

'If you'll let me *say* it,' Geoff said. 'She'd done no more than a basic outline. In sanguine.'

'What's that?' asked Oliver. 'I've been using a grey pencil.'

'It's your reddish brown pastel. It's what most pastellists use for sketching. Sanguine means blood.'

Oliver said, 'How very appropriate.'

Geoff ignored that. 'It was unusual for her,' he went on, musingly. 'Nothing that matters, mind you, but she usually used a grey pastel pencil for her outline sketches.'

'So when you'd watched her do that...' I let that tail away, as though it was a question. He nodded. 'Then you left her to get on with it?'

'I can't see what you're getting at, Philipa,' he complained.

'Well...if you weren't with Pam for more than a few minutes, and then you started on your rounds, why didn't you turn up at Elise's place next? We didn't get a sight of you—until we all found ourselves trying to cope with two sudden deaths.'

He looked from Oliver to me. Then back again. There was a hint of resentment in his voice when he continued, frowning at me.

'I can't see why I should explain how I do my job, Phil. If you've got any complaints, I suggest you have a word with Mr McHugh himself.'

'Oh...come on, Geoff,' said Oliver. 'Nobody's complaining.'

Geoff sighed. 'All right, say what you've got to say.'

'Philipa's only trying to get some sort of mental picture—to make sense of it all. Just because, as she said, she can't bear not to understand things. It's the time aspect, you see. A great big chunk of time before you came to see Elise and Phil and me, and we'd surely have been next, after Pam. But it was lunch time. So...and I'm surprised that the police haven't asked you this...so where the hell's all that time disappeared to? Just asking, you understand. Just asking.'

He sighed. 'I suppose I ought to have come a bit earlier to see you both, Philipa and you. I'm sorry. It's just that I've got so used to the rest of the group, and I know they don't really need any advice, and you'd got Elise with you, anyway. So I did the same as usual, and let you all get on with it. Till about lunch time—as you said. *Then* I started on my tour. *Then* I looked in on Pam again. And...and...for Chrissake, you know what I found that time. *Now* are you satisfied?'

253

It was to me he had been addressing himself, mainly. I shrugged, glanced round at Oliver, pursed my lips, and he shook his head. Leave it, Phil, leave it. That was the message. I inclined my head in agreement.

'And in the morning she managed to get all that done?' I asked, gesturing at Pam's painting.

Geoff grimaced, and said the obvious. 'There it is, if you really need proof. She must've worked like a navvy at it. There'd be a full day's work in that, usually.'

'Yes,' I agreed. 'She must.' A navvy with pastels instead of a shovel. 'And somebody walked up behind her as she was putting the finishing touches to it.'

Then the others began to trickle in, the twins, Elise, and Paul. Geoff seemed to be relieved.

'So *there* you are,' Geoff said, going forward to take Elise's arm, leaning in order to kiss her lips tenderly, as though he hadn't already done it that morning, glancing darkly at Paul.

'Right,' he said. 'Let's get all our stuff ready, shall we?' He was like a teacher, addressing a class of infants. 'It should be another good day, but the weather forecast doesn't sound too good for tomorrow.' He grimaced.

But Thursday was going to be our last day of practical painting. I now knew that we were to spend the Thursday evening—if things ran as planned—mounting our bits of art in a manner rendering them fit for display, so that on the Friday morning the other groups could come along and view the exhibition.

Then we would all flock home after lunch on Friday.

Some of Oliver's work, the previous day, was certainly good enough to mount, I thought. He had improved steadily and positively. His main problem would be the question of choice, when it came to the mounting stage.

Quietly, I was quite pleased with my own efforts. At school, my art teacher had praised my work, and, in recovering my touch with watercolours from those distant years, I was achieving results of which I was certain she would have approved. There was nothing that I need hide with shame.

Today, therefore, would in effect be a bonus day. Something perhaps a little better to be produced this time.

We had all collected our equipment together, leaving our finished work on our own sections of the long counter's surface, and we were waiting only for the sound of the coach's engine as it arrived and backed up, ready to head out to our treasured lake.

But we heard no engine, because the police car had parked short of the terrace, allowing Supt Llewellyn and WDI Perry the shortest route on foot to the Glasshouse, and the one most unobtrusive.

They stood just inside the open door. Llewellyn said, 'I'd like you to accompany me to the station, Mr Davies, if you don't mind.'

'What!' Geoff took a step forward, stopped, looked round, and asked, 'Can't you come back a bit later? We're just starting out... What *is* this, anyway?'

Llewellyn advanced on him, and put a hand to his arm.

'Geoffrey Davies,' he said, 'I am taking you under arrest for the murder of Jennifer Crane. You need not say anything, but what you do say may be taken down and used in evidence. Shall we go, sir? Quietly, please. You'll be able to contact a solicitor and—'

It was then that Elise screamed, and Oliver moved in quickly, his good arm to her waist, restraining her.

'But you can't...can't...' Geoff wanted desperately to get to Elise, but Llewellyn's grasp on his arm, seeming to be so relaxed, was in fact quite inflexible. The other side of the open door I could see two more men waiting, strangers to me and clearly police officers, to be called on if necessary.

'Now come along, sir.'

Llewellyn could have done it with more discretion, quietly and calmly. He had missed his vocation; he ought to have been an actor. But if he was aiming for effect, he certainly achieved that, Elise screaming and breaking free from Oliver's grasp, and running at Llewellyn, hammering her paltry little fists on his chest, and WDI Perry ineffectually trying to drag Elise away and give her boss a free run towards the open door. He snapped out names, and the two men came in from outside, but mistakenly assumed he had called for assistance in relation to Elise, when their superintendent had clearly intended that they should take charge of Geoff so that he would be free to restrain Elise himself.

I came up behind her, reached past her and managed to grasp her wrists. 'Elise! No, no,' I whispered in her ear. Whether or not she heard me I couldn't tell, but abruptly she whirled round and was sobbing all over me in a second.

Geoff, after one agonized glance at her, mumbled something, but he himself made no attempt to resist. If he stumbled a little at the doorway, it was because he was looking back, his eyes wild, and searching the full expanse of the Glasshouse, perhaps in a final attempt to lock into his memory what had come to be the centrepoint of his existence.

Oliver had come to my assistance. There was now no need to use force in order to control our Elise, because there was no strength left in her. It was no effort at all to lead her to one side, and with Paul rushing for a folding stool we had at least something on which she could sit, bury her face in her hands, and weep to her heart's content.

I bent over her and whispered, 'You know it will be all right, Elise. You've been there yourself—'

Instantly her head came up, and now there was anger in her eyes, dredging away all the tears. 'It's *not* the same!' she cried furiously. 'You're just being stupid, Philipa. You heard him. Arrest, he said. Not the same as for me. It'll be more than just questions, you can be sure of that. Are you even aware...have you got the faintest *idea* what it's like, you with your fancy father—what it's like just to sit there and listen to their stupid, stupid digging, and their silly questions, over and over. That's what I got, and then they sent me home. Another hour of it, and I'd have gone clear out of my mind—I can tell you that—and I'd have told them *anything*. Just for it to stop. And now they've got my dear, darling Geoff...and it's not near the same. You *heard* what the man said. Arrest. Arrest was what he said. You and your paltry, *stupid,* "It'll be all right". Of course it's not all right. What do they want to do—spoil everything for us, just when it was going...going...' She took a deep, sobbing breath. 'Do you think that my father could have slipped them a handful of notes, for a promise...a promise—that they'd ruin everything...*everything*—'

'Now, Elise—that's really the most arrant nonsense.'

I reached forward to touch her shoulder in support, but with a wild swing of her arm she swept my hand aside.

'Don't *touch* me. Don't...Don't...'

Then she was finally lost for words, choked on the last one, and before I could do anything about it she was running for the open doorway, swinging her arms as though sweeping away any suggestion of being so much as touched.

I sighed. 'Let her go. Let her go, Oliver.'

The others had been watching this numbly. Theirs was no doubt a tranquil passage through life, the high spots of which might be the production of an excellent painting or two, with no stronger emotion involved than a sigh of contentment when the end result turned out to be

259

good...good enough to attract praise from Geoff. Then the swell of pride. But this was something new, something appallingly violent. Dragged away by the police...their Geoff...and charged with murder. It was nearly beyond endurance for them.

They all looked around vaguely at each other, at Oliver, and at me. For guidance.

'Leave her in peace,' I told them. 'She knows Geoff better than any of us. Let her think about it, when she's more calm, and realize that Geoff couldn't do anything more violent than breaking a pastel in half, and that only in order to get a sharp edge.'

'All right,' said Paul. 'So what're we going to do now?'

'What?' I asked. 'It's up to you, Paul. To all of us. Oliver—you'll know all about these things. What do you say?'

'Up to me? My experience is at the other end—the police station. What the people left behind do, I haven't the faintest idea. Sit and wait, I suppose. You'll have to make your own decisions. Just stick around. And anybody who wants to do any painting—why not in here? It's supposed to be a studio, so what's the matter with painting inside it? Better than going off home, or something like that.'

'And what about you?' asked Paul. 'I bet you're itching to get off home.'

Oliver beamed at him. 'But no. I want to see an end to this. And I wouldn't be able to drag Philipa home. Isn't that so, Phil?'

'Quite correct.' But I was contemplating the fact that we wouldn't be able to *get* home, unless the work on our lane was finished.

Then, after a conference, it was recalled that Geoff was supposed to have some photographs, somewhere, from which we might work—if the worst came to the worst—and it couldn't get much worse if it really tried.

So I asked Oliver, 'Do you want to do that? Paint from photos.'

'I can't say that I want to do anything— with all this upset. Let's look for Elise.'

So we left the others to their search for Geoff's alleged photos, and went outside for a breath of fresh air.

And there she was, sitting on the bottom step of the shallow flight down to the lawn. Quietly, we walked down and sat one each side of her. She gave us each a quick glance, then resumed her distant, miserable contemplation.

'They've taken him away.' She had to clear her throat.

'Yes,' I agreed.

'Arrested him. Taken under arrest. That's serious, Phil, isn't it?' she asked, reaching a questing hand for my arm. 'Serious. Worse than when they took me.'

Oliver said, 'It'll be much the same. Questioning.'

'But there's nothing—absolutely nothing —that he's done,' she appealed. Her voice was breaking.

'The police must have something in mind,' Oliver told her. 'Something they can work on.'

'Now how,' demanded Elise, 'can they have anything? Anything new...' Her voice faded away, and she shook her head violently, brunette hair flying around. Tears still stained her face.

I said casually, 'Well that rather depends on what you told them—doesn't it, Elise?'

'What?' Her nails clawed at my arm. 'What do you mean? You can't *say* that! It's not fair—you're trying to frighten me, Philipa. And I didn't tell them a *thing.*'

I had to treat her with great delicacy. Like porcelain. I smiled to myself. Take her a bit further, and I would have her in hysterics, her glazing all crazed. And if her father discovered her in such a state, then he'd have her away from there if he had to use force. I didn't dare to imagine what would happen to her mental stability if that happened, though no doubt Harcourt had his own doctor, who could deal with such hysterical attacks: a shot of some supposedly mild tranquillizer. And she would finish up as a useless, curled-up lump of misery.

'Suppose you tell me just what you told the superintendent,' I suggested to her. 'I might spot something that you said—unthinkingly, of course—which could have led him to arrest Geoff.'

She shook her head in rejection of this, then buried her face in her hands. I watched until her shoulders ceased to shake, then I whispered, 'We'd at least be doing something to help Geoff. Between us, Elise.'

I had no doubt that Elise would have said anything at all to please Llewellyn, and hasten her own release. She would not realize it, but one ill-chosen word could explode a keg of incriminating facts, some of them involving Geoff.

'Yes,' she agreed wistfully. The desire to help Geoff would be overpowering. 'Let's do that.'

'Very well.' I was trying to keep my tone light, not making a challenge out of it. 'So we'll assume that Mr Llewellyn began by asking you about your visit to the ladies' toilet, the one just behind the yew hedge, beyond which Jennie was sitting and painting.'

I was being very careful and very precise.

'Yes,' Elise whispered. 'That's how it started off.'

'You told him, did you, that you went inside?'

'Yes, yes. I've said that to you a hundred times.'

'Never mind what you've told me, Elise. I'm asking you now about what you told the superintendent. Which was that you not only went inside, but also availed yourself of the facilities?'

I couldn't have put it more delicately than that, I thought.

'I *did* say that,' she declared, almost in triumph.

'You said that to the superintendent?'

'Oh no...no. Of *course* not. It was to the lady detective. I didn't know they had lady detectives, but apparently—'

'All right, Elise. They do. And this one's called Woman Detective Inspector Perry.'

'Yes,' she said. 'That's the one.'

'All right.' I sighed. 'It doesn't really matter. The point is—did they believe you?'

'Oh no.' On this point she seemed quite confident.

'Elise,' I said, 'you're talking as though it doesn't matter what they thought. And it really does matter, you know.'

'I have told you what they thought.' She

was now spacing her words heavily. 'Isn't that enough?'

'Yes. Yes, Elise, of course,' I said quickly, aware that I could lose her confidence with one wrong word, one suspect tone of voice, one expression of doubt. 'So they clearly thought you were lying. Did they actually say so?'

She tried to laugh lightly about it, but her voice was unsteady.

'They called me a first-class liar. Dyed in the wool. They said I'd got a good reason for going to where Jennie was working, because they knew all about the painting I'd had slashed, and that I'd found out that Jennie had done that, and they said they knew I'd *really* gone across the bridge, and up that cobbled bit, to have it out with her. Have it out! What a funny saying. He meant: have a go at her. Oh, you needn't worry, I knew exactly what he was getting at. But I've got no patience at all for that stupid nonsense. All right! So somebody had slashed my painting, and Geoff had found out for me that it was Jennie. You can believe me, but I was looking for the chance to tell Jennie a few things. Some words. But words, Phillie. Not *hitting* her. Not with anything. And not at *that* time, anyway. But perhaps...'

She stopped abruptly, bit her lower lip, then turned up her hands and stared at them, as though they had betrayed her by resorting to violence when she wasn't looking.

'Perhaps what, Elise?'

'Scribbling my fingers all over her new painting. Ruin *hers,* d'you see?'

'Yes. I see. A good idea. But you didn't do that?'

'I didn't even see her.'

I shook my head. 'But you said you did see her, Elise. Afterwards. When the woman found her, and ran off...'

'Yes. *Then* I saw her. A peep. But I didn't get to see her when she...when I could've told her what I thought about her, and her painting was already spoilt, because the easel was knocked over and the painting was on the ground, and...' She clamped a hand over her lips.

'Words,' I said. 'Sticks and stones.'

'Pardon?'

'What we used to say when I was very young, Elise. Sticks and stones may break my bones, but words will never hurt me.'

'Oh,' she said. 'I've never heard that one. It's not true, anyway. Words...words...they can be terrible.'

'It depends, perhaps, on who says them,' I offered, just to keep her going.

'Well...*he* said them. That Llewellyn person. He kept saying them.'

'What words did he keep saying, Elise?'

She didn't at first reply, but stared ahead, her mind with the cobbled walkway and the bridge, but nevertheless observing her surroundings.

'The weather's going to break. Look what it's like over the bay,' she said emptily.

I looked. Heavy grey clouds hung in the west, and the horizon was no longer visible. She was trying to distract me.

'What words, Elise?' I persisted.

'He called me...' Her voice was hushed, almost in wonder. 'Called me a liar. A born liar. A blatant liar. With his face right close up to mine. Sneering. Said he knew I was lying. Knew it. But I wasn't, Phillie. Really, I wasn't.'

'He meant what you'd told him about the ladies' toilet,' I explained. 'Isn't that so, Oliver?' I asked, because he'd been silent for too long.

'Undoubtedly,' he agreed heavily. 'Because it's closed. So he would assume that the rest was lies, too, when you'd said you went in there, Elise.'

'But I did. I *did!*'

Oh dear. Tears again in a minute, I thought. So...ask her for details.

'And did you *hear* anything, Elise? Could you hear anything from inside there?' I wanted to tie her down to a valid picture.

'Oh yes.' She nodded violently, her hair falling over her face. She swept it back. 'I could hear quite clearly. The windows at the side were open, you see.'

This was the first mention of windows that she'd made.

'Windows, Elise?'

'You know. High up in the wall. Small windows, opening out like letterbox flaps.'

This was very graphic. I glanced at Oliver, and he smiled thinly. It was not something that she could have invented, and it carried with it a convincing verisimilitude. I wondered why she had not mentioned the windows before. But probably she would not appreciate their significance.

'Yes. I know what you mean,' I assured her. 'So you were able to hear *something* out there?'

'Not much. But I did. Something.'

'Such as what?'

'Oh—somebody running. All the way across the bridge. Running—and those planks, they rattle, you know. Running, and then up the cobbles and past the Ladies, and then...' She stopped, her eyes vague. She was probing her memory.

'Then, Elise?'

'Then—after a minute—running back.'

'Back across the bridge?'

'Yes.'

'And that was all?'

'All there was.'

'You're certain, Elise?'

'Haven't I said?'

Then she tossed her head, stuck out her lower lip, and looked sulky.

'And you told that to Llewellyn?' I ventured.

'Oh yes—but he didn't believe a word of it.'

Yet—it was circumstantial. If the place hadn't been closed, it would have been acceptable.

It seemed for one moment that she had detected my scepticism, and that she was on the verge of tears again.

'But the superintendent wouldn't have left it at that, Elise,' I said quickly. 'There must have been more that you told him.'

'Well...yes.' Now she seemed uncertain.

'Then tell *us*, Elise.' Still she was requiring a little pressure before she parted with her confidences. She had learned that it is dangerous to confide anything to anybody in whom she could not completely trust. I found this a little dispiriting.

'Tell us what else he asked, Elise,' I persisted, though gently. 'He couldn't have spent all the time he had you there, just asking you one question. Over and over.'

'Oh—of *course* not.'

'So...what?'

'He started *telling* me things, instead of asking. He *did* explain that. He said it might be quicker.'

'That sounds reasonable. Go on, Elise.'

'And he was forever turning to that woman of his...' She paused.

I was amused by this description of their professional relationship.

'And talking,' Elise went on stubbornly. 'To each other—as though what *they* were saying was the truth. Then glancing at me every now and then and saying, "Isn't that so, Miss Harcourt?" And if I said no or yes, it didn't seem to matter a toss. They'd just smile at me and say, "Oh, but you tell lies, Miss Harcourt." And shake their heads.'

She stared at me with huge, hurt eyes. They had not pressured her, they had not bullied her or trapped her into dangerous admissions. They had coerced her into agreeing with what they believed to be the truth, on the simple principle of pretending to accept that everything she said on her own initiative had to be lies.

Artless Elise would never have been able to oppose that. She would not realize that the only way to combat it would have been deliberately to tell lies, until it all became ridiculous nonsense. Because she could not tell lies—except for that central one. She had not used that ladies' toilet, argue as she might.

'What you should have done, Elise,' I told her, trying the idea on her, 'was to tell deliberate lies. Pile them on, until they became farcical.'

She clutched at my arm. 'Oh...but I did.' And she giggled.

'Real, genuine, all-along-the-line lies?' I asked challengingly.

She nodded with extreme gravity.

'Such as?' But I was feeling very depressed.

'Oh...' She shrugged. 'Pretended I *had* seen somebody. It was what he wanted, because he kept asking that. So I said I *had*.' Her eyes were huge. I nodded agreement, though my spirits were sinking.

'Go on,' I ventured. Elise's lies would be apt to carry more weight than her truths.

'I said I'd seen somebody—a man. Somebody in slacks, anyway. And running away, then disappearing under the trees. This was when I came out, you see. Standing outside. And—silly me—I said I thought it might've been Geoff. Though why he'd be running, I don't know. And—'

'What?' I cut in sharply.

'Because *he*'d suggested that, and it was just the most ridiculous thing to suppose, so I agreed. Telling a lie, d'you see.

271

Because, of course, it couldn't have been Geoff. Couldn't. Because he hadn't been to see *us*—now, had he! And he'd do his tour of all of us in order. Pam first, then me (and you and Oliver, of course, Philipa) and then Philip and Martin...oh, you know what I mean. But Geoff hadn't *been,* so I reckoned it couldn't have been Geoff I saw the other side of the bridge...' She drew in a deep breath. 'So that was why I told him a lie, and said it could've been.' She hesitated and looked thoughtful. 'And of course, I suppose—really it could.'

'Even though you made it up to entertain Mr Llewellyn?' I took her nod to be agreement, and tried to smile at Oliver. His eyes looked blank and empty.

'You *did* see somebody, though?' I asked. 'Somebody who was more real?'

'Oh yes.'

'This was before or after you went into the Ladies?' I was virtually conceding the possibility that she *had* been inside. She didn't even blink.

Her eyes were wide with innocence. 'Oh...before. Somebody different. Not Geoff,' she clarified. 'When I'd nearly got there, crossing the bridge. Going away from me, you see. Didn't I tell you that? Well, I *did* see somebody, walking away up the cobbles—towards the market-place.'

'Away from you?'

'Of course. If it'd been towards me, we'd have met, wouldn't we?' she demanded with crushing logic.

'Yes, I understand that, Elise,' I said. 'But that was before you'd even reached the Ladies?'

'Oh yes.'

'So it'd got nothing at all to do with the person you heard running?'

'Oh no. Because *that* was after I was inside.'

'Yes, Elise. I see what you mean.'

I glanced at Oliver. His face was expressionless, his raised eyebrows indicating his thoughts. He nodded for me to carry on.

'I don't understand you, Elise,' I told her gently. 'You said—somebody, when you were just arriving, was walking away from you up the cobbles and towards the market-place. Did you recognize *that* person?'

She shrugged, pouting. 'It was somebody. A man I thought. Divided legs, you see, though these days... And I couldn't see very well, of course.'

'Why of course?'

'Well...oh, you are slow, Phillie...the sun was right in my eyes.'

I conjured up a mental image of relative locations. Yes—it had been about midday, and Elise would have been looking south.

That sounded valid.

'In any event,' she said, 'I'd never have recognized whoever it was, sun or no sun.'

'Why not?'

'Well...' she said, sighing as though she couldn't for the life of her understand my failure to grasp it. 'I hadn't got my contacts in, that's why.'

'Contacts?' I looked at Oliver. He lifted his shoulders. Then I understood. 'Contact lenses?'

She nodded. 'I'm short-sighted. Not many people know. I don't spread it around. And I'm not getting along with them at all well.' She made a gesture of annoyance. 'So I suppose it'll have to be specs, after all. I *did* promise my optician I'd give his contacts a try. But it's no good. I just don't like them. So I'd taken them out, as it was only a matter of walking to the Ladies, and I knew the way with my eyes shut.'

'Eyes shut,' I murmured.

'So—whoever it was I saw, it could've been Geoff, as much—'

'Wait,' I cut in. 'Hold on a minute, Elise. We were talking about the person you saw ahead of you, walking up the cobbled slope.'

'Oh...were we?' she asked politely. 'I thought—the other person, and I suppose *that* one really could have been Geoff, as much as anybody else. But I told that Llewellyn person it was, just to satisfy him, and he looked at that woman, and smirked.'

'You could see *him* clearly enough, then?'

'Mr Llewellyn?' she asked. 'Oh yes, quite clearly. Close to, you see. I'm short-sighted. Didn't I tell you that? I mean, I can see *you* well enough, Phillie. And Oliver.'

'So you're not wearing them now?'

'No. Just for distance. Driving, and things like that. And painting. But if I can see the scene nice and sharp, they make the actual painting a bit blurred. Oh—it *is* annoying.'

Oliver cleared his throat. 'I understand there are bi-focals.'

'Yes, I know,' she said eagerly. 'I'm going to try those next. When I get home.'

'So you *were* really telling him lies?' Oliver asked. 'Telling Llewellyn you'd seen Geoff...it was a lie, because it could have been anybody.'

'Oh yes. And it *was* fun. He obviously didn't understand. I suppose they don't have to be too bright to become policemen. It livened them up no end, though. But they didn't seem to be able to decide if I was telling fibs—or not. So it was all a bit of a giggle.'

'And were you?' asked Oliver. 'Or not?'

'Oh! What? Oh, I see what you mean.' She put a hand on his arm. 'Well...I'll never know, now, will I! It was *somebody,* anyway.'

'But Elise,' I said quickly, because she was becoming far too intimate with my Oliver, 'if you saw this person, not clearly, but as a person, when you were coming out of the Ladies, and that person was leaving rapidly the other side of the bridge...' I paused in order to confirm that I still had her attention. 'But,' I went on, 'did you see that same person when you were arriving—ahead of you on the bridge?'

'I couldn't possibly have told if it was the same person. You don't listen, Philipa. I hadn't got my contacts in.'

'Yes. But you did see a person, ahead of you. Going up the cobbled walkway?'

'Yes. That's so.'

'Did *that* person look as though they'd just come round from Jennie's site, or just come across the bridge? You'd have seen this person ahead of you.'

'I don't know! You keep asking me the same things. As bad as that Llewellyn person, you are. I hadn't got my contacts in, and the sun was in my eyes—and anyway, I was watching my feet. That close, I can see well enough.'

'Your feet...'

'In case I tripped. Those planks aren't at all level, Philipa. And there're some loose. You want to watch your footing.'

'I'll be careful. But did you—from size or shape, skirt or slacks—think you knew *that* person?'

'Not really.'

'Who did it look like? Not Geoff— surely!' I prayed desperately that she would say no.

'Oh no,' she said positively, and I sighed. 'Baggy slacks,' she added. 'Geoff never wears baggy slacks.'

'Could it have been somebody we know?'

'It could have been anybody, anybody at all.'

'But tell me—was this one of your deliberate lies, Elise, thought up just to entertain Llewellyn? When in fact you saw nothing.'

'No, no. It wasn't a lie. I *did* see somebody, and divided legs, you know. But everybody wears slacks these days. Oh...you know what I mean.'

With a little effort, I did. 'Baggy ones,' I muttered. But I had to drain every possibility. 'Elise,' I said, 'women walk differently from men. So—from that—could you say whether it was a man or a woman?'

She frowned in determined concentration. 'I'd say...a woman. But Philipa—I told you—the sun was in my eyes.'

'Not one of ours?' I persisted. 'Our women.'

'Well...no. Not Jennie, I'm sure of that—the way she always swung her hips. Blatant, I always thought. Oh...' She put a hand to her lips. 'Shouldn't speak ill of the dead.'

'But you didn't call out—on the chance...'

'Definitely not. Because if it had been a stranger—how embarrassing!'

'You're not speaking ill of the dead, Elise,' I said, desperately trying to keep her on the one subject. 'We were talking about the person, possibly a woman, who was walking away from you up the cobbled slope.'

I thought that ought to tie her mind to one subject for a moment.

'I was speaking ill of the dead, Philipa. And not Jennie. Pam.'

'Pam?' Why on earth did she allow her mind to flit around like a butterfly? 'We were not talking about Pam Wilton, Elise. We were talking about the person who was walking away from you—'

'Yes, I know! I know, Philipa. But I didn't like Pam, either.'

'Oh!' I didn't dare to glance at Oliver now. 'We were talking about the person walking away—'

'I *know*, Philipa. But I thought we'd

finished with that. I didn't know who it was, and I don't know now. And I did not like Pam.' She nodded her determination not to be distracted from that.

I sighed. 'And why not, Elise?'

'Well...' she said. 'I mean to say...she couldn't have been a very good wife to Paul, if he had to resort—is that right, resort?'

'In this context, it will do,' I assured her.

'Yes. Well. If she'd driven Paul to resort to a blatant creature like Jennie Crane, who was no better than she ought to have been, then Pam couldn't have been much of a wife. Now could she!'

No better than she ought to have been. It was a phrase I had often heard, but had never clearly understood. But I knew that Elise meant that Jennie had been no better than a common tart, though she would never dream of saying that out loud.

'So,' I said, 'if you didn't wish to meet this person—who might have turned his or her head, and who could have been Pam or anybody—what did you do?'

'Oh...' She shrugged. 'The obvious. You *are* slow, Philipa. That was when I popped into the Ladies.'

'Ah!' I said. I'd asked for that one. 'And you said all this to Superintendent Llewellyn?'

'Oh yes.'

'Just as you've told Oliver and me?'

'Oh yes, it's quite true.'

'But you said you'd decided to tell him lies, Elise. Now you say it's true.'

'Ah...yes.' She laid a hand on my arm, signifying a confidence. 'Yes, Philipa. I'm telling you exactly what I told *him*. So I am telling the truth.'

'You are, in effect, giving a true account of the bundle of lies you told Mr Llewellyn?'

'If you care to put it like that,' she told me, pouting.

'Oh, I do,' I assured her.

And it was now crystal clear why Llewellyn had brought her back.

15

Abruptly, she said, 'I mustn't stop here, chatting to you, Philipa. There's so much to do, and I've got to get the place all clean and tidy for when Geoff gets back.'

'Can you get in?' I asked.

'Oh yes.' She patted the little breast pocket of her striped shirt. 'I've got my own key.'

'Ah!' I said. 'So you've found something to keep you busy.'

She sprang to her feet. 'You never said a truer word, Philipa. You should *see* what it's like. Men just don't understand how to look after themselves.'

'Don't I know it, my dear,' I said, and Oliver's reaction was to send her on her way with a pat on her behind. She was off like a startled rabbit.

'You *do* know how to liven up the ladies, Oliver,' I said, not really meaning it as a compliment.

'I had quite a reputation for it in my younger days.'

'Hmm!' I said dubiously.

Silently, we then sat and watched the heavy clouds creeping towards us over the bay. A sudden, cool breeze fluttered the trees facing us, and I said, 'It'll be raining in a minute.'

'Then we'd better get inside.'

But he made no move to do so. 'There was one thing out of all she said that sounded true, Phil,' he said quietly.

'Oh? You spotted something?'

'Well—yes. She saw somebody walking away from her, up to the market-place. A woman, if it *was* somebody, and she didn't simply make it up, as a good lie to offer to Llewellyn. A woman, who couldn't have been related to our group, because there

281

were only four of you, Phil—you, Elise, Pam, and Jennie of course. But around that time Jennie was being killed. And the person whom Elise saw couldn't have been Pam, because at that time, or a little after that, Pam herself was killed, nearly a mile away.'

'But you don't know that,' I protested. 'No precise times.'

'No...we don't know that.' He was stubbornly digging his teeth into a theory he must have been working out.

'But Oliver, you don't have to make too much out of that person walking up the cobbled way, because the odds are it was simply a local resident in this town. You're concerning yourself over the fact that Elise, whether she intended it or not, implied that it was Pam. Something she recognized about how that person was walking...or something like that.'

'All right. But look at the time-scale, Phil. That person—whoever she might have been—must (if we're going to eliminate our lot) have been an ordinary local, who'd simply been round there to see how Jennie was coming along with her painting. Geoff said that sort of thing happened. And she was clearly not in a panic, as she would've been if she'd just found Jennie dead. So—Jennie alive then. Next, Elise inside the Ladies. She *hears* things. Somebody coming running, then running back. Doesn't that sound like the time of the murder? Because, when Elise came out, if we accept, for the sake of argument, that Elise did go inside the toilet, somebody else found Jennie dead, and went running up into the town and raised the alarm. See how tight it is.'

'I see what you're getting at.'

'And the police say that Pam and Jennie were killed with the same weapon. Then that means that somebody moved very fast. The alarm raised—the weapon removed. It really must have been removed by the person who'd just killed Jennie with it. The running person that Elise heard. Heard coming, heard leaving—and actually saw disappearing into the distance, in the general direction of where we were all working. And that person then killed Pam.'

I was silent. Something didn't sound right. Then I got it.

'But Oliver...just imagine how that would be. This person of yours, running over the bridge with a chunk of wood in his hand—and Jennie, whose view couldn't be better from her site, didn't even notice, didn't pay attention, didn't spot that chunk of wood, and it wasn't small, you know. Not like a knife would have been. No...it doesn't sound right. It would have had to be done by somebody she either knew and trusted, carrying nothing, or somebody who was able to sneak up on her without Jennie being alerted.'

'Hmm!' he said.

'You don't like that?'

'I don't like the bit about the running. Clearly, Elise heard that. She can't have made it up, as a complicated lie. Not Elise. I've got a feeling that the murderer would've had to creep up behind Jennie. Creep.'

'We'd better get back inside,' I suggested.

So we turned to go, but my mind wasn't on it, and I nearly tripped myself on the steps. Oliver steadied me with a hand on my arm.

'You're not thinking about what you're doing, Phil. What is it that's worrying you?'

'Oh, you know. Elise. What she said. She had the impression that it was Pam, walking away...'

'Oh heavens, stop worrying about it, Phil.'

'Yes, but...could it have been Pam, Oliver?'

'How *could* she, Phil? Damn it, I've got a bit of experience in pastels now, and I'd be willing to swear that Pam just couldn't have finished that painting

284

of hers—and it *was* finished, Phil, and spray-fixed—and she was actually touching up her highlights when she died. She just could not have done all that—and it's a really detailed painting, Phil, which would take ages to get right...she couldn't have done it *and* found time for a trek all the way to Jennie's site—nearly a mile—Phil, and all the way back. No...I'd be willing to wager anything that she never lifted her behind from that stool, all morning, from the time Geoff saw her doing that basic outline in sanguine.'

'Yes. Geoff did say that. Sanguine. *Is* that the word, Oliver?'

'It is. The pastels have got little paper sleeves on them, with the names of the colours. I've got my own sanguine, if I want to use it.'

'All right, Oliver, you've made your point.'

We still hadn't made much progress up the steps. There was suddenly the shushing sound of heavy rain on trees, the wind carrying the sound to us a little ahead of the rain. We ran across the terrace and round the corner to the Glasshouse, just as the first heavy drops reached us.

They were there, those remnants of our group still active. But frankly, there was no life in them. Misery and boredom seemed to have a firm grip, and lunch—as a possible diversion—seemed ages away. The rain was suddenly thundering on the roof.

'Did you find Geoff's photos?' I asked, addressing the remains of our group.

Blank faces confronted me. Men can be so useless, unless they're given something to do. Philip and Martin looked glumly at each other. At their individual homes, with their wives, they would no doubt have shown a little initiative. Paul...well, Paul was completely bereft. At times like this, when the repressive circumstances seem to assail them so forcefully, it is the highly emotional of us who are the most forcefully stricken. If the sex drive can be classed as emotion, then Paul had every excuse to present to us an undermined and defeated character.

As he did.

'I've got some playing cards in my car,' said Martin, but with no enthusiasm in his voice. 'We could make up a four for bridge, if anybody's interested.'

Nobody seemed to be interested. I began to hunt through the drawers in the long counter, on which our properties were still lying around uselessly. I found the Stanley knife, which Geoff had thought to be the one used to slash Elise's painting. I found boxes of pencils and erasers. And I found a whole drawer full of Geoff's photos.

They hadn't searched with any noticeable enthusiasm.

Geoff had spoken quite casually about them, as though he had no pride in their production. It would not be an art to him. But to me, after a quick flick through them, it seemed that he had been over-modest.

They were eight by tens, and clearly, being an artist himself, he had concentrated on producing pictures that were in themselves artistic. All were landscapes. All were simply crying out to be presented in acrylics, watercolours or pastels. And there were hundreds of them.

'Will you just take a look at these!' I said, spreading some of them out on a spare section of the surface.

They clustered around, suddenly animated. Soft whistles were made, sighs were sighed, and enthusiasm blossomed.

'If I could only capture that reflected light!'

'Will you look at that glow on the side of the barn!'

'If I could only get that effect of drifting mist!'

And in ten minutes we had all made a choice of photos we would like to use, and there were no arguments. Easels were rigged, drawing boards were perched, paper and canvas boards were waved in the air, and it was only the fact that we had to put on the lights that reminded us that a storm was raging outside. The rain pounded on the glass roof, but nobody had need of a voice. We became totally absorbed.

When the bell went for lunch we barely heard it, although by that time the storm had abated to some extent.

'Anybody for lunch?' I asked, and there were sundry groans of rejection. Nobody had thought to supply us with sandwiches. It would have seemed ridiculous to consider that we were far removed into a distant countryside. Yet that was the situation. We were there, each in our own specific landscape.

Oliver, using pastels, could leave his work at any time. Paul and Martin, working with acrylics, needed only to wash their brushes. The other twin, Philip, and myself were using watercolours, and needed to choose the correct moment to lift the brush, and leave the rest till afterwards.

Thus, those from the other courses preceded us, though Oliver returned in five minutes or so with the big umbrella from the car. With this, he first escorted me to the emergency entrance to the bar, then he returned for Philip.

Left, therefore, in the bar for a few moments on my own, I had time to collect my thoughts together. For well over an hour I had given not one thought either to Geoff or to Elise. And then, in the shadowed gloom of a far corner, I saw that Harcourt was waiting. Alone. His head clerk had perhaps gone ahead to the dining room.

'Isn't she with you?' Harcourt asked. Although there was still a certain amount of authority in his voice, there was also a hint of uncertainty. I couldn't imagine him, in this mood, giving instructions to juggle the odds. Indeed, he seemed to have left his business empire to look after itself, or had sent Len Farmer back to the operational centre. It would have become clear, even to Harcourt, that control of Elise's future was no longer in his clumsy hands.

I couldn't be unkind to him; he seemed bereft.

'I don't think she'll be coming in to lunch,' I told him. 'She's tidying Geoff's place for him, while he's safely shut away and unable to protest. I'm sure she'll get herself something...'

I expected him to say that he would go and root her out. But no. Wrong guess.

'If I knew where the blasted cottage was, I'd go and join her,' he said.

At that moment Oliver returned with Philip, who shook himself like a dog.

Oliver's a big man, and there wouldn't have been much spare cover for Philip.

I said, 'Oliver, do you know where Geoff's cottage is?'

'I think so.'

'Then I wonder if...' I gestured towards Harcourt, on his feet now and looking decidedly deflated.

'Sure,' said Oliver. 'The rain's easing a bit. Come along, Mr Harcourt. She'll be glad to see you, I'm sure.'

Harcourt seemed less certain that he would receive a welcome. All the same, he seized on the opportunity, and they left together. There was even less space for each of them under the umbrella, both being big men.

'I'll keep you a place, Oliver,' I called after him.

He slid in beside me, five minutes later. My neighbour the other side wished to speak only in German, so we hadn't progressed very far.

'Well?' I asked him.

A young lady placed his plate in front of him. Lamb cutlets. He said, 'She welcomed him as the lady of the house receiving the vicar for coffee and biscuits. Only, for the vicar, she wouldn't, I should hope, throw her arms around his neck.'

'Ah,' I said. 'Yes.' It seemed satisfactory.

'When I left,' he said,' he was offering

to get her the finest defence barrister in the country. For Geoff.'

'I hope Geoff's not going to need one. Not if I can help it.'

He was helping himself to vegetables. I now understood what I had been told three days before—go easy on the lunches, because there's dinner later.

'You've been getting ideas,' he said, his lack of approval very apparent.

'Well—we *must* do what we can for him.'

'Which is next to nothing. Aren't you hungry, Phil?'

'Not very. What were you saying—about Geoff?'

'Well...who had a good motive? Geoff. Because of Elise's slashed painting. Not much of a motive—secondhand—but it's still there.'

'Ah yes.' I waved a tiny potato on the end of my fork. 'But if, as the police believe, the same person killed Jennie *and* Pam, then the murderer couldn't have been working on *that* motive. Two people didn't slash the canvas, Oliver. Pam did.'

'Then perhaps he, or she—the murderer —wasn't certain, and played safe by killing both.'

'Now you can't possibly...' I stopped, realizing that he was ribbing me. 'So all right. Forget all about motives. Look at it from the point of opportunity. Geoff had a roving commission, you might say. He was the one, the only one, who could risk being seen moving around.'

'Yes,' he agreed. 'But all the rest of us could've done a bit of roaming, if we chose to use the cover of the trees. Or even—and I bet you haven't thought of this, Phil—it would've been possible to walk the full length from the furthest site—where Pam was—nearly to Jennie's site, by keeping along the bottom of the cliff. Six to ten feet or more of sand, and the tide right out. It would be possible. Ah...' He stared down at what had appeared in place of his empty plate. 'Fruit salad and ice cream. Lovely.'

We finished that. Coffee appeared. Oliver sat back, replete.

'I think it's stopped raining,' he said, turning to look out of one of the windows.

'What does it matter?'

'Maybe the sun'll come out again.'

'We'll be working in the Glasshouse,' I reminded him.

'Shall we?'

'What else is there?'

He shrugged. Around us, the dining room was emptying.

'Let's go and look at the weather,' he suggested.

It was only gradually penetrating my

conscious mind that we—the art students —were now really on our own. Certainly, we had found something to do, but somehow, without Geoff there, it seemed a purposeless exercise. Simply something to fill in time—until dinner.

We were out on the terrace again. The storm clouds had disappeared behind the inland mountains, and the sun was tentatively urging the remaining clouds to follow. We strolled back and forth. The Jaguar was nowhere in sight, so my guess that Harcourt had sent Len Farmer back to hold the fort seemed valid. Nothing, I was now convinced, would remove Harcourt from the vicinity, until Elise's situation had been stabilized.

My mind back on Elise, I said, 'You can't get round the fact that Elise lied.'

'She admitted that.'

'Yes, yes. Lied to Llewellyn. She said that. Even claimed it.'

'But that,' said Oliver severely, 'he would understand, and treat with more than a bit of suspicion. It's the big lie he's got his mind on.'

'In what way?'

'Don't you mean—with what objective?'

'You're getting me all mixed up now, Oliver. Are you implying that he genuinely suspects Elise?'

He shrugged, then stood very still, feet

apart, hands plunged into his trouser pockets, and stared down towards the village.

'She said she deliberately lied to him, so that he couldn't know what was true and what was not,' he summarized. 'So...all right. But *she* had the direct motive. *She* went all that way, she said to use the ladies' toilet there. It's not very convincing, is it, Phil? And *she* was there at about the correct time to fit in with Jennie's death. And she's stubbornly insisted that she went inside the Ladies. Of *course* he suspects Elise. Of Jennie's murder, anyway. Forget about Pam's death for now. God knows what thoughts he's got on that. But I'm certain he's picked Elise for Jennie's killing. And Geoff's arrest...I wonder if he's actually made a charge. That's the point. What I think is that he's simply putting pressure on Elise. He thinks she'll walk in on him and confess, if he does no more than lie low and wait.'

I couldn't think what to say to that. Then, suddenly, I did.

'Can he *do* that? Oliver, that's...it's cruel.'

'All is fair in love and law.' He gave a short bark of laughter, as though he'd surprised himself with that witticism.

'Seriously,' I said severely. 'Can he *do* that?'

'Well...having arrested Geoff, he'll have to get him in front of a magistrate, and convince him he's got a case. If he expects to hold him, that is. Then, perhaps, he'll get Geoff remanded in custody.'

'And Elise?'

He shrugged. 'He hopes she'll walk into his office and confess. As I've already said.'

'You're heartless, Oliver.'

'Am I, my love?'

He stopped, and took my shoulders, one in each hand, though I knew it hurt him to raise his right arm that high. 'Am I, love?'

'You must have made a really rotten policeman, I know that much.'

He grinned, leaned forward, kissed me on the nose, and said, 'They had to shoot me to get rid of me.'

'Their loss, my gain,' I assured him. 'Let's go and see what they're doing in the Glasshouse.'

They were there, but not working. When we arrived, Donald McHugh, exercising his authority as principal, was putting them in the picture, as he put it. I thought it was a deliberate play on words, but nobody smiled.

'I was just explaining,' he said to us, 'that if anyone wishes, in the prevailing circumstances, to go home, because we've lost a tutor—only temporarily, one hopes —we would be pleased to refund your fees. And I *do* apologize...' He looked round. I had the impression that he'd grown a year or two older in the past couple of days. 'Apologize for all this upset,' he completed his sentence.

But strangely, nobody now seemed to want to leave. A fresh optimism prevailed, 'Oh no,' they murmured. 'Most positively no,' I said, for Oliver and me. Not to leave Elise and Geoff in such trouble.

Which was all very well, but for the life of me I couldn't think of anything that would get Geoff out of trouble, apart from being able to produce the real murderer, and to wave evidence to prove it beneath Llewellyn's nose. And I had not the slightest idea how to go about it. Neither Oliver nor I could think of anything useful to add.

And still it rained.

Enthusiasm for painting from Geoff's photographs was waning rapidly, and boredom was beginning to overcome us.

Mr McHugh, shaking his head, quietly left us.

'Anybody heard a weather report?' asked Oliver.

Nobody had. Outside, the weather provided its own report—that it would continue to rain as long as it felt like it.

Suggestions were made that we might slip in with the Chinese Brush painters, to see what went on there, but that idea drifted past without implementation.

I said, 'Let's go and phone Harvey.'

'Why would we want to do that?' Oliver asked.

'To see how they're getting on with our lane, Oliver.'

'You're not thinking of clearing out of here and leaving them to it?' Oliver asked.

'No, no.'

'I didn't think it sounded like you, Phil.'

In any event, we did call Harvey, from the phone in the bar, and caught him at his office.

'Phillie!' he said. 'Enjoying yourself, I hope.'

'Well, not exactly, Harvey. There's trouble here. Two deaths, and both of them murders.'

Oliver was standing at my right elbow, as usual, with me holding the phone clear of my head.

'Why is it, Philipa,' Harvey asked, 'that wherever you go, there's trouble?'

'Perhaps there's a jinx on me. But Harvey, that isn't why we're calling. We may be coming home early, so I'm just checking on the progress of our lane. Our drive, as it will be.'

There was silence.

'Harvey?'

'It's just that I can't give you a positive answer, Philipa. I drove past there this morning—you know that I come into town from that direction, I'm sure.'

'Of course, Harvey. Say it...please!'

'Well...I couldn't see *what* was going on. The lane was packed with that strange-shaped machinery they use. As far as the eye could see.'

'All right, Harvey. Thank you,' I said. 'I'll call you again tomorrow.'

'Yes. You do that, Philipa. And enjoy the rest of your stay.'

'Thank you.' Enjoy!

I hung up. Oliver said it meant nothing. 'One minute they're there, the next gone.' He shrugged. He could be very philosophical, when he felt like it.

'But d'you see, Oliver—do you see? We may have to go home earlier than we expected. And if we can't even get to our own cottage...'

'Let's not tackle problems we might not encounter, Phil. Eh? There're problems here, though not ours, I must admit. They belong to Geoff and and Elise. But—'

'All right! All right!' I cut in. 'I *know* how it is. But what the devil can we *do*. I just can't see anything to tackle. Can you?'

'No. I can't, Phil. But we might—just—drop on something. It's Wednesday afternoon. And we're not due to leave until after lunch on Friday. And there's no point in thinking that we might *have* to go home before then, just because the weather's turned out to be rotten.'

'Oh—I suppose you're right. So we just sit around and pray for inspiration?'

'Something like that.'

But in the event, that afternoon, we did no different from what we had been doing in the morning; we painted from photographs.

But the life had gone from it. Geoff was not there, to comment, to criticize, to praise. There was no sign of Elise, who was no doubt having a grand time tidying the cottage. When he returned home he would probably demand to be returned to his comparatively friendly cell.

Yet it was no joke, as Oliver explained, when Paul, restless and unable to concentrate on his acrylics, came over to where we were working, and asked what was going to happen to Geoff—unless a miracle occurred.

Of course, the others had to know, the twins, and the principal, McHugh, who had wandered in restlessly, naturally concerned about Geoff's welfare, and only marginally in ours. Then Harcourt was there, having been ejected from the cottage, no doubt, and being accused of getting underfoot.

We made a small group around Oliver, who'd been asked to clarify the situation.

'Llewellyn will probably have made a charge by now,' he told them. 'No doubt he'll charge Geoff with only Jennie's death, at this stage. He's got a motive—or at least some sort of a motive—for that. Which has to be that Geoff could have killed Jennie on Elise's behalf. I know, I know,' he said, holding up his hand. 'It sounds way out. Killed Jennie as Elise's protector, sort of. But...' He looked round their tense faces. 'You're all thinking the same as I am—that it's terribly weak, as a motive. It must be rather rare—killing somebody as a favour to somebody else. Very weak. And as far as Pam Wilton's death is concerned—well, Geoff could have no possible motive for that, as far as I can see.'

He paused. In the silence, the rain seemed to pound even more heavily on the glass roof.

'But...' Oliver went on. 'And you may not know this, but there's no legal requirement for the prosecution—that's Llewellyn at this stage—to produce a motive. Adduce, they'd say in a law court. Just the facts of the matter, that's what he'd have to put to the magistrate. And those would have to be that Geoff had had a free run of the area involved, and couldn't be challenged wherever he'd gone, and that there's a sighting, which is rather doubtful, of Geoff in the vicinity of Jennie's painting site. Oh yes, I know it would be part of Geoff's job, but it would've been out of his normal schedule, if he *was* there, and apparently for no specific reason. He hadn't visited Elise and my wife and myself, or Paul, or the twins. At this stage, all Llewellyn would be requesting would be a remand, to give him time to get a case together. Remember, he did say he was going to get formal statements from us all—and he hasn't done that, yet. Now, perhaps, he will...once he's got Geoff remanded.'

'I'll put up the bail,' said Harcourt flatly.

So he had now realized that his darling's happiness rested on Geoff, so he offered all he had to offer. But Oliver shook his head.

'He'll ask for remand in custody,' he said. 'Two murders, don't forget, though how Llewellyn hopes to connect Geoff with Pam's death, I can't imagine. In fact, the motive for Pam's killing is as vague as Jennie's. So...I can't see that we'll have Geoff back with us for a while.'

'You mean...' Martin spoke up. 'In prison?' And he shuddered.

'A remand centre.'

'Isn't that the same?' Philip demanded.

'Well...no. But from inside, it'd seem exactly like one.'

There was silence, broken at last by Paul.

'I just can't imagine Geoff killing anybody. I just can't.'

'The magistrate,' said Oliver, 'doesn't have to use imagination. In any event, imagination would be a distinct drawback in his occupation.'

'So what can we do to help him?' demanded Paul. 'We ought to be doing something.'

'Might I make a suggestion,' said McHugh. 'You said something, Oliver, about Mr Llewellyn still needing to take formal statements from everybody. Perhaps it would help if a few inaccuracies—shall we call them—should ease their way in. Yes? They don't have to be sworn, do they?'

'Well...no.' Oliver beamed one of his best smiles. 'No they don't, and no to the suggestion as well. It would be immediately obvious, if we told lies, and it would be treated as a deliberate action to impede the course of justice—and we would *all* finish up in a remand centre.'

'Do you mean we can't do *anything* to help Geoff?' asked Paul, a hint of anger in his voice.

'Only by stating the exact truth, as you all recall it, because—and you never know—when everything's put together, all the statements, something could arise that shows Geoff couldn't have done it. Done either of the killings. Times, sightings, situations. You never know.'

But it made nobody happy, and very soon the group broke up, to go their individual ways.

16

It was still raining in a desultory fashion, but we decided, being restless, once more to go for a walk. So we retrieved our waterproof outfits from the car boot (having no wish to take umbrellas), our slickers, waterproof over-trousers, walking shoes and waterproof hats. It promised to be a rather warm walk.

Without consultation, we turned away from the town, its river, and the bay. Uphill into the slopes behind the Manor we headed, but the problem seemed to chase after us, in fact to go ahead.

'So what do we do if the lane's not finished when we get home?' I asked.

'Get a room in a hotel, and sue for

the cost.'

'Sue the council! Hah! A likely possibility, that is. We'd finish up owing them.'

'Then we sue Harvey,' Oliver suggested. 'It was all his doing.'

'Oh yes! What a splendid idea. Wouldn't he be furious!'

'We could even ask him to act for us.'

'Against himself?' I asked.

'Yes.'

We paused while we built on it. A good laugh never does anybody any harm. Leaning over a five-barred gate we had come across, we looked down on the Manor and beyond it to the town. The sky was now clear. I was beginning to feel very warm, inside all the waterproofing.

'It's going to be a clear evening,' Oliver decided. 'Phil—I might even get the chance of doing the picture—the river and the town and the bay.'

'Yes.' I glanced at him. 'You must.'

'Hmm!' He was silent for a minute or two, then, 'She could have been lying to us, you know.'

'What?' He had caught my mind in a different environment.

'Elise. What she told us. A pack of deliberate lies.'

I thought about it. I couldn't completely agree. 'The bit about the windows open, like letterbox flaps...now, *that* sounded real and true.'

He turned to me, grinning. 'She could have seen them from outside. At the side, she said, and she would be facing the side of the building as she walked across the bridge.'

'Oh, come on, Oliver. If she'd killed Jennie...heavens, she'd have been in no condition to notice details like windows.'

'An artist's eye?' he asked. 'It would record itself—remember what Paul said about having a long visual memory. She produced it from her memory as a colourful detail to assist the lie: that she was inside the Ladies when Jennie died. And we know she couldn't have been.'

'Let's get back,' I said.

'If you wish. I want to polish my pastels, anyway.'

'Polish?'

'A joke, love. Against myself. My old trousers are covered with pastel dust.'

'Hmm!' I said, and we turned to walk back slowly to the Manor. The sun now welcomed us. The clouds had drifted inland, behind us, and our slickers were now dry, so that we could put them away in the boot straight away.

The rest was boredom, and painting now held no charm. There was nothing to do. The bar was open, but almost empty. None of the remaining few of our group was present. We sat and talked and drank, Oliver and I, and dinner seemed an eternity distant. We had hit a low ebb, when all that was left to do was to eat and drink.

But later, after dinner, Oliver stood at our open window, and watched the lowering sun over the bay.

'We forgot to see if Geoff's got any black pastel paper in his store cupboard,' he said. So it was lucky that the weather hadn't been quite right, the previous evenings.

'Geoff said he had,' I assured him, but on no concrete basis.

'Did he? I don't remember. Let's go and have a look, shall we?'

It was something to do. So we went.

The lights were on. It wasn't really dark enough to justify lights, but we said nothing, walking in on Paul, who was standing with his back to us and staring at the long counter at the far end.

'Found something to do?' I called out.

I seemed to have startled him. He whirled round. 'Philipa! you frightened me to death. I was just wondering whether to pack Pam's stuff, and take it home.' He shrugged. 'Hell—I don't want it. It'd only remind me...' He stopped, and ran his palms down his face. 'Would you like to have her pastels, Oliver?'

'Well...no, Paul, thank you. I appreciate

the offer—but really, I've already got all I'll ever need. Thanks, all the same. But Geoff might like to have them.'

Paul shrugged, tried to smile, and turned back to his contemplation of the counter.

'Ah hell,' he said. 'It can wait.'

Then he whipped round, almost ran past us, and left the door swinging behind him.

I stood for a minute, staring after him. Then Oliver said, 'Let's look in the cupboards. Black pastel paper, love.'

'Yes...yes.'

We looked round, and we found some. Oliver took out of the cupboard four sheets, twelve by eighteen. 'We'll have to find out who we've got to pay for this,' he said.

'Yes, Oliver. Yes.'

But I was speaking absentmindedly. I was staring at Paul's own collection on the counter. Amongst it was the number three round sable brush that I had last seen at his painting site, when I'd retrieved it from where he had thrown it to the ground. I had popped it into his water bottle to keep the paint moist. It was still there. I picked it out again, but the paint had been allowed to set solid. A good sable ruined.

Strange, that was. Instinct—even allowing for his personal distress—should have prompted Paul to clean out the paint properly when he'd got it back here. But he had done nothing to it, although he seemed to have washed his other brushes. Too much on his mind, no doubt.

'Phil?' said Oliver.

'Coming...coming.'

We put off the lights behind us and turned to leave—but hesitated outside the door. The car that I was beginning to know as Llewellyn's was running along the terrace, and stopped just beyond us. We paused. We waited.

Llewellyn, seeing and recognizing us, approached and asked, 'We need to speak to Paul Wilton. Can you point us in the correct direction?'

'Not Paul! Surely?' I said.

He smiled tightly. I got the impression that he was very close to exhaustion. 'It's just a matter of formal identification,' he assured us, using his matter-of-fact voice. 'He's the ideal one—he knew both the women.' He lifted his shoulders in a tired shrug.

There was no denying the logic in it. But Paul would not enjoy a trip to the morgue.

'Try the bar,' I suggested. 'You know...'

'Yes. I'm getting to know my way around.'

Now he and his WDI headed in that

general direction, and in a minute or two returned with a violently protesting Paul.

'It's all right—all right,' Llewellyn was saying encouragingly. 'Just identification. For the inquests.'

'I don't want to see—'

Llewellyn completely ignored this. 'In the back with me,' WDI Perry suggested. 'That's right, sir. It'll be over in no time at all, and we'll bring you back straight away.'

That time-schedule depended on how far they had to travel to the morgue, on which point we had no knowledge at all. The car turned and drove away, with Paul actively protesting, still.

'Very soon,' I said, 'he'll have the lot of us there, or in his office.'

'Hmm! At least it'd be something to do.'

'You'd feel at home in a morgue, would you, Oliver?' I asked.

'I've been in morgues. Not exactly like home, Phil. Very much more cold.'

I didn't like to think about it. 'One thing about it, Oliver,' I reminded him. 'You've got your black pastel paper, all ready. So you can always go and stand at the window and wait for everything to come right. The setting sun, any clouds, the street lights—you just wait. Now...won't that be exciting, Oliver?'

He grunted, but nevertheless we went to our room. We waited. Oliver did preliminary sketches—to get his eye in, as he put it. Eventually, dinner intervened. Afterwards, we went back to our room. Hopefully.

But Oliver's hopes were dashed once again. Street lights came on, the tide was a little past its highest level, and reflections were superb. Until a dirty black cloud swept in and dropped a curtain of rain on the whole scene, then raced inland to sweep down on the Manor, and Oliver cursed the weather, the location, his pastels, his trousers—the lot.

Then, when it was clear that he wasn't going to get anywhere with it, we sought out the only refuge—the bar.

Paul had returned, and looked jaded. The twins were quietly drinking the evening away—and Elise was sitting in a corner with her father, and with a man I hadn't seen before.

Harcourt raised a hand and snapped his fingers at us. Very bad manners, I thought. 'Here they are now,' he said to the stranger. 'Can we have a word, Philipa? And with you, Oliver, please.'

'Certainly.' I smiled at him. It was now obvious that the newcomer was Harcourt's solicitor, who had not impressed Elise at all, I recalled.

I had guessed correctly. Harcourt said, with a certain amount of pride, 'This is my solicitor. Rupert Greatorex. These people, Rupert, seem to understand what's going on.' He tried for a self-deprecating laugh. 'Which is more than I do.'

We accepted this as a compliment, though Harcourt's smile had been somewhat cynical. Greatorex got to his feet and shook hands.

'My husband,' I said, 'is an ex-policeman. CID. And I know quite a bit about what goes on. Do you think you can help Geoff, Mr Greatorex?'

'That remains to be seen. I can try. I'm meeting Llewellyn, with the magistrate, in the morning. He'll be asking for a remand in custody. I shall, of course, oppose that. But I'd hope to secure something better than a remand on bail. I want to destroy the case against Geoffrey Davies completely.'

'I'll get 'em in,' said Harcourt, trying to be useful. Apparently, nothing could be discussed in a serious manner unless we all had drinks to inspire us. So there was a short wait while he arranged that.

At this time in the evening I would have expected the bar to be packed with the Chinese Brush painters and the German language enthusiasts. But no. No sign of any of them. There had perhaps been a communal agreement to leave us in peace for a while. Or maybe there was something gripping going on in the television room.

'So,' I said. 'What can you do for Geoff, Mr Greatorex?'

He smiled. He was one of those men who seem to be solid through and through, bone and muscle and personality. If he stated anything, you would be taking a great risk by questioning it.

'Motive,' he said, nodding sagely. 'That's going to be the central issue in my argument. As you'll probably know, Llewellyn isn't required by law to adduce a motive, though of course it's always a useful lever. But I don't think he will try it. What he's got is very weak, and Llewellyn knows it. You know what I'm talking about, I'm sure. That Geoff Davies would kill both women because one of them *might* have slashed Elise's painting. Tcha! Ridiculous!'

'I don't think you're quite correct, there,' I put in politely.

'What?' He frowned heavily at my interruption.

I smiled. 'There's been no suggestion that Geoff could have killed both Pam Wilton and Jennie Crane. That *anybody* did that, in fact. The weakness in any case against Geoff is that he should have killed Jennie Crane on behalf of Elise, you might say. If so, it would be a very unusual motive for murder—killing somebody as a favour, you could describe it.'

'That,' said Greatorex heavily, 'is what I'm trying to say. That Geoffrey Davies did have a very weak motive for killing Jennie Crane. There has been no suggestion yet that Llewellyn is thinking of a charge of murder in respect of Mrs Pam Wilton. And it's that weakness in motive that I shall challenge. And I shall make a central point out of it. Means—yes. Davies would certainly have been able to acquire a length of wood—as would anybody else. Opportunity? Of course. But Llewellyn wouldn't be able to build a case on that, because everyone of the group had freedom of movement, so all of you had the opportunity.'

'Except for Elise,' I said. 'She was with Oliver and me. Apart from...' I deliberately left that hanging, to see whether he was aware of all the facts.

Greatorex glared at me. 'We are talking, here, about Geoffrey Davies, not about Elise Harcourt.'

'But I think I'm getting to know Llewellyn,' I assured him. 'He's very subtle. And I think he'll be thinking, suggesting, and leading you towards Elise—and *her* opportunity.'

'People don't *lead* me, young lady.' His

face was now carved into sharp angles, his eyes narrowed, the knuckles white around the glass that was now, so suddenly, empty.

'Of course not,' I said soothingly. 'You'll introduce the subject of motive, I've no doubt, because Llewellyn wouldn't wish to—not when he's talking about Geoff, that is. Because—for Geoff—it *is* so terribly weak. Kill somebody in order to please Elise! As you said yourself, it's a bit far out.'

'Now you just listen to me—'

'Let her say it,' Oliver put in. So quietly, he suggested this, but there was a warning tone in his voice. I touched his arm. A thank-you.

Greatorex glared, seemed about to burst into violent and extended protest, then abruptly he sat back, a faintly condescending smile on his lips. Then he nodded his permission. Let the woman make a fool of herself.

'And once the motive of the slashed painting was introduced,' I continued, 'Lewellyn would take it up, and he would pick it to pieces, and he'd ask you whether you were implying that, although that motive wasn't really valid, when applied to Geoff, it wasn't very appropriate when applied to Elise. And he would point out that Elise herself had

314

a perfect opportunity to kill Jennie, because she was, at the specific time, within yards of her. And I'd expect him to remind you that this opportunity was engineered by Elise. No...damn it...let me say this. It wasn't, in fact, Jennie Crane who slashed the painting, it was Pam Wilton. And her husband, Paul Wilton, could verify that fact, and might already have done so to Llewellyn, which would—'

'Now listen here...'

It was his warning, bullying tone that annoyed me. 'No!' I shot back at him. *'You* listen. This matters. I've met Llewellyn more often than you have. I know him better. I know exactly what he's aiming at—what he's got in mind. And that's a set-up in which they did it together, Elise and Geoff. No, Elise, you just sit there and say nothing. I'm talking now on your behalf, and Geoff's. And I'm convinced, Mr Greatorex, that if you tackle this in the way you're proposing, you'll be playing right into Llewellyn's hands. And he'll hold both of them, Elise and Geoff, on a conspiracy to murder charge.'

Greatorex thumped the table. His face was flushed and his eyes were wild.

'Never...never in my life...I'll not have it! I'm not going to listen to anything you've got to say. People who are ignorant of the operation of law and the courts—'

'Very well.' I smiled at him. I smiled at everybody. 'Do it as you wish. But I'm going to bed. Coming, Oliver?'

But Oliver was already standing behind me, ready to draw back my chair. I got to my feet, smiled all around, and said, 'Goodnight, all. See you tomorrow.'

17

I was sure that Oliver would have liked to continue the discussion with Greatorex, and that he had a few points to take up that I had missed. But he caught my eye, and we left him to retrieve his standing and authority with the man who paid his fees. In any event, there was just a chance that the sky would have cleared.

But it hadn't. For quite a while Oliver stood by that window, but, if anything, the situation became more and more impossible. So, although it was a little early for us, we retired to bed.

When we went in to breakfast in the morning, I had a brief look round. There was just a possibility that Llewellyn had returned Geoff to us, without Greatorex's persuasion. But there was no sign of him, and he was not breakfasting in his cottage with Elise, because there she was at a far table—and no Geoff.

She saw us and waved, but there was no space at her table and we had to search elsewhere for two seats together, and found ourselves sitting with the twins, one each side of them.

'I hear he's coming to do it today,' said Martin gloomily.

I glanced at him. There seemed to be something wrong with his moustache. If he'd trimmed it that morning, he'd done a very poor job. It seemed to be a little twisted.

'To do what?' I asked.

'Take all those witness statements he was talking about.'

'Ah yes.' I'd rather forgotten that. 'It'll be something to do.'

But he seemed more concerned than the simple taking of statements justified.

'We'd like to show you something,' he said, sounding miserable. 'Philip and me.'

'Oh...what's that?'

He shook his head. 'Better to show you.'

I didn't press him. There seemed no point. 'Where?' I asked.

'In the Glasshouse.'

Then he devoted his full attention to his breakfast.

Oliver and I strolled on the terrace until

317

the twins appeared, both looking rather downcast.

'What *is* this?' I asked, but they were stubbornly unresponsive.

Fortunately, and as I had expected, we were the only ones to show any interest in the Glasshouse. Martin led the way, directly to the counter at the far end.

All our individual piles of equipment were still where the police officers had left them, apart from the minor disarrangement caused by the upsurge of painting from photos, the day before. The equipment belonging to Jennie, and also that of Pam, were the only ones untouched.

It was to Jennie's that the twins steered us.

Martin seemed to have been elected as spokesman for them. He stood with his back to the counter, smiled a little emptily, and said, 'You know about the trick Jennie tried on us?'

'Oh yes.'

I glanced at Oliver. We had not seriously considered the motive the twins shared for a basic dislike of Jennie. The incident had seemed so paltry, that Jennie would have sought to upset their personal relationship with that telling remark: 'You were wonderful last night, darling.' They had been able to deal with that quite simply, and I'd had the impression that they'd forgotten about it, or at least no longer been concerned about it. But it now seemed that they had been more seriously disturbed than I had thought.

And now it appeared that the method used to disconcert them had been seen as an insult, one which they still deeply resented.

'Well...' Martin sighed. 'We decided to give her a bit back. She deserved it, you'll admit.'

'Indeed she did,' I agreed. But I was beginning to feel disturbed.

'Anyway...we worked something out, ready for when we got here. Philip and me. Two things, really. One of them was related to being twins—which was what she'd tried to use against us.'

'Just retribution,' murmured Oliver. But he too sounded unhappy about what we might be about to hear.

'Yes.' Martin gave a twisted smile at his brother. 'And I was the one who made the sacrifice.'

I glanced at Oliver. He shrugged, pouting. Then Martin reached up, and peeled off his moustache.

'Oh...no!' I said, though whether in mourning for the discarded moustache, or in protest at the deceit, I wasn't myself certain.

'But look at these, first,' said Philip eagerly.

He was referring to the paintings on the counter—Jennie's work, that fatal morning. I didn't suppose that anybody had interfered with them since they'd been placed there, but now, spreading things out a little, I saw that Jennie had worked hard—and fast. There were eight partly finished paintings of the estuary, with the tide out, and from what she had done I was able to confirm my guess—she had used a sandy-coloured wash to replace the black of the slime. The paper used for these was even thicker than I had been using, and with a different surface. Possibly Canson 400, 1 thought, and there was something strange—wrong—about each one of them, I puzzled over this for a few moments. Then I saw what it was.

On each of them, where paint had been applied as a flat wash (and with acrylics, Jennie would probably have started with basic washes) there was visible, in letters two inches high, these lighter than the washes, the word BITCH, or I AM A BITCH, or, in one instance, ROTTEN BITCH. Each painting effort was ruined in this way.

'But how...Oliver, look. How...'

He smiled. He had worked it out.

'We came in here,' said Philip. 'Late on the first night—Sunday—and we painted the letters on all her blank sheets, with oil. It rejects the water paints, such as acrylics, you see. We experimented at home. In my house—or rather, in my workshop. Three-in-One oil was the most effective, but when it dried—or soaked in, rather—you could just detect it, which we didn't want, because then she might have spotted the trick before she even started. In the end we settled for WD40 oil. So that's what we used. It comes in a spray-can, but you just spray some into a saucer. A number four brush for the lettering—you get the idea?'

I drew in a deep breath. Oliver said, 'Very ingenious.'

'And she'd see the words coming up on the paper, as she painted,' Martin said, 'where the oil rejected it, and she'd have no spare paper, and she'd waste the whole morning getting some fresh paper. Oh...it was beautiful.'

'You watched her reactions?' I asked. They wouldn't have been able to resist that.

'Oh yes. Of course.' Martin nodded, and his moustache, insecure, fell off. 'We watched from behind the yew hedge.' He had managed to catch it.

'Giggling?'

'Trying not to.'

'And...the moustache?' I asked Martin.

'The real one was sacrificed in the cause of art.' He pursed his lips. 'We thought we ought to use the fact that we're twins against her—as she'd tried to use it against us. So I sacrificed my moustache—and Marie will bawl me out when I get back.' He grimaced.

'It'll grow again,' I said comfortingly.

'Yes. It'll grow.'

'So...' said Philip, sighing, 'we went along there—'

'You were there?' I demanded.

'Yes,' said Philip seriously. 'Martin told you that. We went along to watch her face when she got going, then we paraded round and round her, both of us with false moustaches, sometimes on, sometimes off, and laughed our heads off at her language when she tried to get going with her painting.'

'Wait, wait!' I cut in. 'Have you told any of this to Llewellyn?'

'Him? Lord...no. It was just for a laugh, and I can't imagine *him* laughing.'

'Then you'll have to. You must tell him.'

They looked at each other, eyebrows raised. 'If you think so.'

'If you don't I'll have to.'

They nodded miserably.

'And this was...right at the start?' I asked.

'Oh yes,' said Philip. 'We gave her a quarter of an hour to get going, then we went along to see how she was getting on.'

'And...'

'Well...' Philip spread his hands. 'She was cussing away, and we had a good laugh, and did the moustache trick on her, then we went back to our own painting.'

'Hmm!' I glanced at Oliver, and he inclined his head.

I had been idly turning over the paintings Jennie had worked on. Two were completed, and with no defects. 'But she *did* manage to get some more watercolour paper.'

'Yes.' Philip nodded. 'She came along to where we were and handed out a good cussing, so we gave her some of our paper. Only fair.'

'Yes. Only fair.' I glanced at Oliver. 'And you didn't go there again? To Jennie's site, I mean.'

'Well...yes. About lunch time. Wasn't it, Martin?'

'About then. A bit before.'

'And everything was normal?'

'Normal?' Philip glanced at his brother. 'I suppose so. She was working, and didn't notice us.'

'Nobody else about?'

'Well...no. Did you see anybody, Martin?'

Martin shook his head, then changed his mind and nodded. 'Only Elise. She was coming towards us, when we were part way back. She didn't see us. We were under the trees.'

So Martin and Philip wouldn't have much to tell Llewellyn. Nevertheless, I instructed them:'Tell everything to Llewellyn. Everything. Every detail. It's what he'll expect.'

Martin grimaced. 'Everything?'

'Indeed. The lot.'

Grumbling to each other, they wandered away. It occurred to me, from what I'd just heard, that Llewellyn might have gained quite a fair amount of information from the painting equipment spread along that counter, yet he hadn't thought of that. I hadn't, either. But I had now lost the opportunity, because Llewellyn arrived, along with his inspector, and a somewhat jaded Paul, and I discovered he had selected the Glasshouse as the centre for his interviews. Long, deep and searching, they would be, I expected.

The thought did cross my mind that it would be a good moment to choose in order to acquaint him with the possible significance of the equipment displayed, but he forestalled that intention by telling me to clear off. Therefore, I left him to realize that he would find no comfortable armchairs in the Glasshouse.

But he had that aspect covered, having brought a team of constables, who were now bringing in several upright chairs, and opening out one or two of the folding, green-baize-topped tables. The indications were that we were in for a concentrated day of intensive interrogation.

And so it became. We were called in one by one, so that Oliver and I were interviewed separately, and as the day wore on, and facts revealed by one of our group involved the actions and movements of others of us, some interviews had to be made a second time. Even a third.

The weather continued to be unsettled. At one stage Llewellyn made a phone call, points having arisen that required Geoff's confirmation or his contradiction, and Geoff was returned to us. This was done in such a casual manner that Geoff's arrival, in a police car, was almost unnoticed, and only by the signal of a scream of delight from Elise were we alerted. And, whilst we all flocked around Geoff, Llewellyn barely raised his head.

The day wore on, and though (when

my own time for interview and signing of my statement came along) I tried to put across the possible importance of what the bundles of equipment might reveal, if carefully examined, this was dismissed with a sad smile.

They all left before dinner-time, having received free lunches and perhaps not having the nerve to commandeer free dinners as well. Now that the painting equipment was available to me, I decided that immediately after dinner a check on it all would be attended to.

There was a strained atmosphere in the dining room that evening. No doubt all our group were reviewing in their minds what they had told Llewellyn, and what they regretted. I was aching to get a free run in the Glasshouse as soon as dinner was over.

But... 'Let's phone Harvey,' said Oliver, as we walked out.

This aspect I had forgotten—our lane! And we would have to call him at home. I checked on his phone number in my diary, and we went down to the bar. At this time it was empty, except for Paul, sitting moodily in a corner.

I got through straight away. 'Harvey! It's...'

'I know, Phillie,' he said, and I heard what might have been a sigh. 'I've been expecting you to call.'

'And?'

'Information right up-to-date,' he said blithely. 'I drove past this evening—kept late at the office, you know—and there was one of those portable barriers across the entrance...'

He left that hanging, for effect, I supposed.

'And?' I demanded, a little sharply perhaps.

'It said: Closed. Roadworks In Progress.'

Very nearly, I screamed. Not a habit of mine. I took a deep breath. 'Harvey...' I whispered, overdoing the self-control.

He laughed. I would have killed him, if it could have been done over the phone.

'It's all right, Phillie. Don't get all worked up. The sign was only very light, so I lifted it out of the way, and drove up to your cottage. And the work's completed. Finished. And a splendid job they've made of it.'

'But you said...the barrier.'

'Oh, you know what they're like. Always forget something. They'd simply forgotten to remove their sign.'

'Forgotten...' I whispered. 'Oh Harvey, you lovely, lovely man.'

'What...'

'Thank you, Harvey. Goodbye,' I said, and hung up. Then I turned to look at Oliver, checking he had heard every word.

'Philipa!' he said softly. 'The Ladies "closed" sign! For heaven's sake! I'll go and get the keys.'

Then he ran for the hall stairs, leaving me whispering to myself, 'Simply forgotten to remove the sign. Simply!'

I was standing beside the car when Oliver ran from the door and down the steps. He threw the keys ahead of him, so that I'd unlocked the doors before he reached the car. We tumbled in—and to hell with the seat belts. It wasn't far. Down the slope to the right turn at the river, and along to the footbridge...

We dived out, leaving the doors swinging, and Elise had been quite correct about the footing across the bridge. It was tricky, running across. Oliver had a hand to my arm, his feet being bigger and thus more secure.

The sun was now setting over the bay, but there was enough light left for the sign still to be readable. Closed for Alteration.

'Shall I?' I asked quietly.

'We can't just stare at it.'

So I put a hand to the door, and it swung open smoothly. I was inside a normal and operative ladies' convenience, with the side windows open like letterbox flaps.

But I wasn't inside for long. Looking up into Oliver's smiling face, I said, 'So Elise told the truth.'

'It does rather seem so,' he agreed.

'And so—'

'I don't know, love,' he admitted. 'We'll have to—'

'But don't you see! It means that when she spoke about somebody running to here over the bridge, going round to Jennie's site, then running back over the bridge...that was true. And it means that when she said she saw somebody walking away, and up to the market-place, she *did* see such a person...'

'Yes, Phil,' he said gravely. 'And when she said it was possibly Pam, or rather when she wouldn't commit herself but obviously thought it was Pam...then she did see such a person.'

'But the sun was in her eyes, and she wasn't wearing her contacts,' I reminded him, playing devil's advocate.

'But Pam,' he said, 'and I'll swear to this, just couldn't have painted and finished such a very good painting as she had—and reached the stage of spray-fixing it, and retouching the highlights, which we know she was doing because of the white pastel pencil in her fingers...' He took a deep breath. 'That was a day's work, Phil. By working very hard she *could* have completed it in a morning. But not...not, Phil, if she took time out to walk all the way here—and I'm sure it couldn't have been Pam running whom Elise heard, because *that* person only stayed a second... Oh hell, what was I saying?'

'You were saying,' I told him, helping things along, 'that all we've found out doesn't tell us who killed Jennie and who killed Pam.'

He shrugged, and managed a smile. 'Maybe it will, when we've taken a good look at that painting. Neither of us got more than a glance at it. Well...I *did* look, but only a quick glance.'

'Come on, then.'

Oliver's larger feet allowed him to get ahead of me over the bridge. He headed for the driver's seat.

'I'll drive,' I said.

'No, Phil. The mood you're in, you'd have us off the road.'

'But don't you see...'

'Yes, Phil. Yes, I see. But there's no panic rush.'

And, annoyingly, he drove even more carefully than he usually does. Perhaps his mind, like mine, was too involved with trying to make sense out of what we'd discovered.

In the event, a little more speed might have saved a lot of trouble. He drove sedately up to the terrace, and I shouted, 'Stop, Oliver. Stop!'

His eyes had been searching ahead for the parking space we had vacated, but I had been directing my attention to the Glasshouse.

'There's a fire,' I shouted at him.

But now he had seen it, and he braked to an abrupt halt. Inside the Glasshouse there was the red and yellow fluttering that means fire. The door swung open as I tried desperately to see more, and a shadow darted away. I ran. The huge surface of glass facing me was reflecting the setting sun, providing its own red glare, but that was stable. The fluttering red inside could have been nothing else but a fire.

Oliver beat me by two yards. He flung the door wide and ran inside, directly to the source of the fire, which was at the far end and dangerously close to the counter. I flicked on the lights, whipped up one of the fire extinguishers always standing inside the doorway, and shouted:

'No, Oliver! Let me.'

This was because he was heading straight for the source of the fire, and clearly intended to stamp it out. Dangerous.

'Let me *see* it, Oliver!'

He moved to one side. It was, I now

saw, centred on, or rather inside, one of the green metal wastebins. Oliver kicked it over and it rolled away from the counter in a wide curve, towards the centre of the floor.

'No, Phil!' he shouted, as I levelled the fire extinguisher, trying to remember how they worked.

The fire was scattering itself out of the wastebin as it rolled. Oliver pounced in with his big feet. It was all paper, torn paper and crumpled-up paper. Painting paper. Discarded efforts. He stamped and jumped on it, until the flames died under his weight. I stood the extinguisher on the floor. It was not going to be needed. Then we stood and watched it smouldering itself to extinction, only tiny plumes of smoke rising now. I was aware that we were no longer alone.

They were all there, Geoff and our group, the twins, Paul, Elise. All that were left. And Llewellyn was standing in the doorway, watching. He had brought Geoff home, to see what happened next. Well...this fire was next.

'What the devil's going on here?' he demanded, concerned that it might have some effect on his investigation.

I smiled at him. 'I think somebody's tried to destroy the evidence,' I told him, though I had not the faintest idea how this

332

could be evidence of anything.

'What evidence?' There was now an edge to his voice, a controlled anger with himself, that he should not have realized that there could be evidence sufficiently important that it needed to be destroyed. He was a very tired man. I felt that, had he not occupied the Glasshouse for a good part of the day, this evidence might have been revealed earlier. Or destroyed earlier.

'Somebody,' I said, 'has torn up a pastel painting, and then tried to burn it. You can see that it *was* a pastel painting. Doesn't that show it's important?'

'So how...' He gestured angrily.

'So we try to put it together again,' I suggested. 'Like a jigsaw puzzle. Sellotape it together. Geoff—is there any Sellotape?'

'Of course.' He crossed to one of the drawers. 'Here.'

I caught it. 'Good,' I said. 'So let's see what we've got here. What's so important that it had to be destroyed?'

And they all gathered around, to discover what the devil I was talking about, which I wasn't certain myself, until I noticed that Pam's painting was no longer with her equipment on the counter.

At least, I now knew what I was attempting to reconstruct.

18

It was easy enough to say that we would tape it back together, but the torn painting, clearly a pastel from the cream colour of the back of the paper, had not been the total contents of the wastebin. Many other torn-up and therefore unsatisfactory painting efforts had been thrown into the wastebin, several screwed up into balls. And all had, in one way or another, been scorched, even completely destroyed.

'We'll have to be careful,' I said, crouching down and delicately picking out the cream bits, trying to prevent them from falling apart. One at a time, I placed them on a clear section of the counter, face up.

Lots of edges were curled and scorched, but I decided that there was enough left of each portion to allow reconstruction, allowing space for the blackened and curled edges.

'Geoff,' I said softly. He came to my side. Llewellyn also drew closer. He had no idea of what I intended to do, or what I was thinking, but he didn't demand to know. He would soon see for himself.

'Would you say that this was Pam's painting?' I asked Geoff.

He had previously seen it lying on top of Pam's equipment, and it wasn't there now, so he wasn't straining the truth when he said, 'Yes. That's Pam's style, right enough.'

'All right. So we'll try putting it back together,' I said.

'But why?' he asked, scratching his chin.

'I don't know, Geoff. But if it was so important that it needed to be destroyed, then it's important that we should reconstruct it.'

Llewellyn said, 'I'm not sure I can waste time—'

'Then don't,' I cut in. 'Leave it to us.'

He grimaced. 'If it doesn't take too long...'

But it was already clear that it was going to be a lengthy and difficult job. As much as half an inch around some of the edges were black and crumbling, and there were no convenient shapes to fit together, like a jigsaw puzzle. But gradually the general body of it was growing. We knew that blue had to be the sky, and therefore to the right and the top, and that banks of green were the trees to Pam's left. There were sixteen pieces, each about four inches square.

Around me, there was a general muttering of incomprehension. Then at last

I had it, at least a recognizable picture, though with charred gaps of as much as half an inch here and there. But then I found that Sellotape would not grip to the pastel surface of the paper, even though the painting had clearly been spray-fixed.

'Would you say that this is Pam's painting, Geoff?' I asked.

He was hesitant, wary of committing himself to a decision on too little evidence. 'Well...I'd say it was her work, but whether it was Monday's painting, I couldn't say. You'll realize, Philipa, that all her stuff was much alike. I mean, everybody liked their own places to paint from, so everybody always got much the same picture. But the burning's really messed it about.'

'So let's turn all the pieces over, and see if the tape'll stick to the back.'

Llewellyn said, impatiently, 'But is there any *point*? It could take ages.'

'I don't know whether there's any point,' I told him patiently. 'But if it was worth going to the trouble of destroying it, then it's worth trying to put it together again.' How many times did I have to say it?

Turning each portion carefully was easy enough, but now I had no guides as to the gaps due to the burning. Nevertheless, it grew, until I became aware that the back of the paper was not completely blank.

'Geoff—what do you make of this? It's

beginning to look like an outline sketch.'

He was now leaning against my shoulder. I could hear his breathing. 'But it can't be,' he whispered.

'Can't it, Geoff?' I asked.

He breathed out slowly. Now his interest was involved. 'Finish it, Philipa. Finish it.'

When I eventually had it taped together, though it was only vaguely accurate, I pointed to what both Geoff and I had noticed. It was definitely an outline sketch of the scene, and it had been done with a sanguine pastel. The reddish-brown colour was unmistakable.

'Didn't you say that Pam usually did her sketches in grey pastel,' I asked, 'but this time she used sanguine?'

'Yes,' said Geoff, 'that's so.' So very quietly, that was, that I barely heard it.

'So this was one of Pam's outline sketches, but it had to have been done on Monday?' I asked. *'This* Monday. The day she died.'

'Well...yes,' agreed Geoff, though with indecision in his voice. 'It must be.'

'But the actual painting's on the other side.'

'It is,' he agreed.

I glanced sideways at him. He was frowning heavily. Then I reached past him for Pam's painting board. It was a sheet of hardboard, with a dog-clip on the top edge.

'And when you last saw this outline sketch,' I persisted, 'it was clipped to the board?'

'Well...yes.'

Llewellyn hadn't gone away, as I'd thought, but was now at my other shoulder, aware that I had something positive on my mind.

'I wish I could see...what're you getting at?' he asked.

'I'm getting at the fact that after Geoff saw Pam draw this outline sketch—in sanguine—and had left her, she must have unclipped the sheet of paper and turned it over. But not because she was unsatisfied with the outline sketch she'd just made. That wouldn't be of great concern to her. No. Because, I'm suggesting, she already had this finished painting on the other side. A spray-fixed one. And all she needed to do to it was liven up the highlights—and there she would be, with a whole day's work displayed—or a very quickly completed half day's work...and the whole operation would have needed no more than two minutes.'

'Needed?' asked Llewellyn softly. 'Are you saying it was deliberately planned?'

'That's what I'm saying. What else could it be? She wouldn't *need* to use the back

338

of a sheet she'd already painted on. In fact, the surface on the back wouldn't be ideal. It was done on purpose. This painting was actually one from a previous painting course. She's probably got a dozen or so—and all done from the same site. Isn't that so, Paul? You'd know. And what she must have been rigging was an alibi. With that painting clipped to her board, she could afford the time to be away from her easel for two hours or more, and nobody would know. Geoff had already been to see her starting off—with that sketch in sanguine—so she wouldn't expect him to be around to see her again until later in the afternoon.' I turned to see where Paul was. '*Did* she bring any of her previous paintings with her, Paul?' I asked him.

In a dead voice he said, 'She'd got at least eight. Always kept 'em together. I know that much. But there's nothing to show that that's one of them. She *could* have done that in a morning. Could have. It's possible.'

'It's actually impossible, Paul. Think about it. This painting's been spray-fixed. Oliver can tell you that, because he touched it with his finger—that time when we first found her. But she hadn't got her spray-can with her. And that—though she couldn't have realized it—was a mistake.

She knew she wouldn't need it, so she left it behind. One mistake—and the whole thing, otherwise, was so carefully planned. She *ought* to have had the spray-can with her, just to add the final touch to the deception.'

Llewellyn said, 'Some of this is a mystery to me. You'll have to give it to me in detail...'

'Later, Mr Llewellyn,' I promised. 'I'll give you a condensed course on art, with special reference to pastel work. Oliver knows it all. But I was saying... The spray-can should have been with her, but she left it behind. Didn't need it, you see. All she was concentrating on was the fact that she would eventually be found at her easel with a finished and sprayed painting—which Geoff would agree—if she needed his agreement on the point. It was all intended to show that she couldn't have found the time to make the trip through the trees and the town, to Jennie's site, with the intention of killing her.'

Somebody drew in a deep hissing breath.

'And you're saying?' asked Llewellyn, cutting in and ruining my train of thought.

I sighed. 'I'm saying that Pam had just about had enough of Jennie Crane and her affair with Paul here, especially when she heard that Jennie was pregnant. That was what pushed her over the edge, to the sticking point,' I said grimly, recalling our little chat. 'And I believe that's what she must have done, gone through the trees to the traffic bridge, then through the town. She could have counted on being able to find some sort of weapon, in all that woodland, and to teach Jennie a lesson she wasn't going to forget. Because Jennie, dead, wasn't going to remember or forget anything...' Then I seemed to lose my voice, and could only put a hand to my mouth.

'Phillie!' said Oliver softly, having detected the bitter tone in my voice, because nothing would persuade me that Jennie, whatever her faults, had deserved sudden death.

'We have no evidence that Pam Wilton was anywhere near Jennie Crane's painting site,' said Llewellyn stiffly.

'You've got Elise's evidence, from the sighting she got of somebody walking away up that cobbled lane and into the market-place. She hadn't got her contact lenses in, and the sun was in her eyes, so she wouldn't commit herself, but it was clear to me that she'd had the impression it was Pam Wilton. But nobody took that seriously, because everybody assumed that Pam could not have moved from her own site.'

'I *did* think it was Pam,' burst out Elise.

'The shape. She'd got big hips, and those baggy trousers of hers... But nobody would listen.'

Llewellyn sighed. He had listened, but he hadn't believed.

'Yes, Elise,' I assured her. 'We believe you. But you see, Mr Llewellyn, nobody believed that Elise had gone inside that ladies' convenience, because the sign said it was closed. In fact, it was not closed. I've checked that myself—half an hour ago—and it was open, but with the closed sign still there on the door. Elise was telling the truth. Always has. What she heard from inside the toilet was somebody running towards her across the bridge and round to where poor Jennie was already lying dead, then immediately back again, when it was obvious she was. And what she saw, from outside, was a man running away from the far side of the bridge, and if you prompt her a little, she may even say that when she saw him, he was carrying that stump of wood...' I turned to her.

'Oh I did!' she cried. 'Now you mention it.'

Which—though she would not have realized this—destroyed it as evidence, because it had been prompted.

'Somebody,' said Llewellyn, somewhat wearily, 'running away with the stump of wood that subsequently was used to kill Pam Wilton?'

I felt tired. Tired of it, of the mental effort to put it all together. I sighed.

'I suppose so.'

'Who?' he demanded.

'Well...the way I see it...it really does seem that it would have been somebody who had actually witnessed the killing of Jennie.'

'Witnessed?' Llewellyn asked, using a brooding voice.

'The only one who could have seen it happen,' I reminded him, 'is Paul. I think I'm right, there. And Paul was witnessing the killing, by his own wife, of the one woman he was genuinely in love with. Or so he told me. And he'd had about as much as he could stand of Pam. You can't blame her, because she was driven to desperation by his affair with Jennie. And Paul, seeing her kill his beloved Jennie...well, what *would* he do? Exactly what Elise heard—pounding feet across the bridge, then going round to the actual site, where Jennie was lying dead—that would be Paul going to confirm the reality of what might have seemed to be a nightmare, and confirming it at one glance, then grabbing up the stake of wood and running back. All of this, Elise heard.'

'Oh, I did! I did!' cried out Elise,

slapping her palms together.

'And Paul,' I said, 'probably ran himself to exhaustion in order to avenge Jennie's death, as soon as possible. I don't know the route he took, but he must have kept under the edge of the trees, because Geoff didn't see anything of a running man. And in the meantime, Pam, hurrying back to her painting site, would nevertheless use the route she'd chosen to get there, which was through the town, through the woodland, and back to her site well beyond where the coach was standing.'

'You can *prove* all this?' asked Llewellyn wearily.

'Not prove. No. It's just putting facts together, so the details could be a bit shaky. But I've no doubt that a bit of interrogation will just about confirm what I'm saying. The odds are that Paul got to Pam's site before she did. So he would have to wait for her, hidden in the trees. And wait for her to take her seat again. Then he killed her in exactly the same way as Pam had killed Jennie. And he would perhaps have never been suspected, if it hadn't been for the spray-can.'

'What's this about the spray-can?' demanded Llewellyn. 'I keep hearing about it. You said that Mrs Wilton hadn't taken it to her site—a mistake on her part.'

I was suddenly feeling very tired, and

couldn't help sighing. It seemed so very obvious to me. But nevertheless I explained it.

'Yes,' I agreed. 'A mistake on Pam's part. And Paul realized this. The spray-can ought to have been found on the site, so when all her stuff got back here, brought by your very careful and efficient officers, Mr Llewellyn...'

'Are you trying to be sarcastic?' demanded Llewellyn.

'By no means,' I assured him. 'They did a very good job. Pam's stuff neatly laid out on the counter—but without a spray-can. And, as I said, there had to be a spray-can, and Paul fetched it from their room and put it where it ought to have been—with her painting equipment. Now it looked just as Pam had planned that it should—that she'd painted that picture in one morning—which in itself, Oliver assures me, would have been quite an effort, *and* sprayed it.'

I smiled at him. He raised his eyebrows, and nodded.

'You can understand Paul's reasoning in this,' I told Llewellyn, who clearly didn't. So I told him. 'Paul wouldn't want any suspicion of Pam being responsible for Jennie's death, so the spray-can had to be there. Any suspicion of Pam would, he thought, point to a motive on his part to kill her. In blind fury, perhaps, but not so blind that he failed to see that point. So—he had to go along with what Pam had planned—her alibi.'

I turned to face him. His face was drained of blood, but his eyes were bloodshot. The completely blank expression he offered to me was brought about by the fact that his mind was scrambling for a way out.

'There's not an atom of proof in any of it,' he said flatly, even with contempt. 'What Pam must have done—yes. I'd go along with that. She hated Jennie bitterly. But you can't involve me in it. I was painting. All the time. Damn it, I was still working when you came to tell me that Pam was dead. When the superintendent and you, Philipa, came to tell me about her. I was painting, so how could I—'

'But you were not painting, Paul, that's the point.'

I went across to the counter, to Paul's equipment. The black-handled brush was still there, in the water bottle in which I had put it, in order to save it setting hard. The police had been so very careful, not even spilling the water. I picked out the brush. I indicated its stiffness, the red acrylic paint having set solid in the sable hairs. It had almost become a lethal weapon.

'This is the brush you had in your fingers when we found you, Paul, still apparently painting. Red paint. That would be from when you painted Jennie in, perhaps. It doesn't matter. When you were told that Pam was dead, Paul, you threw this to the ground in anger. But I'm a tidy person, Paul. I'm sorry—I can't help it. And I saw it was a quite expensive sable. So I picked it up and popped it into your water bottle, so that the paint wouldn't set. That bottle.' I pointed. 'I'm surprised that you didn't clean it, when your stuff came back here. But perhaps you didn't think about that. It didn't occur to you that if you'd really been painting when Mr Llewellyn and I walked in on you, the brush would have been soft. I can't blame you—there must have been so many other thoughts charging around in your brain. But there it is. Hard. If you had been painting with it, the paint would have been soft at that stage. So what had you been doing, Paul? Just sitting there and holding the brush, waiting for somebody to come along and tell you Pam was dead?'

He moved a pace, angrily, and Oliver growled in his throat.

'If so,' I went on, 'you held it for too long. You weren't painting, you were posing—as a painter absorbed in his work.'

Then he broke free of the group. I

thought for one moment that he was going for my throat—I saw that intention in his eyes. But he did no more than thrust a shoulder into mine, as he made a break for the door, nearly spinning me off my feet.

Oliver turned to follow him, but Llewellyn snapped, 'No!' And when Oliver poised himself on one foot, he added, 'It's all right. I've got two men waiting by his car. I'd come along in order to arrest him, anyway. But thank you for the detailed evidence, Mrs Simpson. Thank you.'

Later that evening, with the sun just below the horizon but still reaching up to inflame the scattered clouds, Oliver stood by the window, with only the bedside light on in order to allow him to choose his colours, and he at last captured the magic of the town lights, the estuary, and the red snake of river. Our friend, Tom Carter at Penley, framed it for us, and it now hangs in pride above our old fireplace. From time to time I stand in front of it, and remember...remember...

The publishers hope that this book has given you enjoyable reading. Large Print Books are especially designed to be as easy to see and hold as possible. If you wish a complete list of our books, please ask at your local library or write directly to Magna Large Print Books, Long Preston, North Yorkshire, BD23 4ND, England.

This Large Print Book for the Partially sighted, who cannot read normal print, is published under the auspices of

THE ULVERSCROFT FOUNDATION

THE ULVERSCROFT FOUNDATION

. . . we hope that you have enjoyed this Large Print Book. Please think for a moment about those people who have worse eyesight problems than you . . . and are unable to even read or enjoy Large Print, without great difficulty.

You can help them by sending a donation, large or small to:

**The Ulverscroft Foundation,
1, The Green, Bradgate Road,
Anstey, Leicestershire, LE7 7FU,
England.**
or request a copy of our brochure for more details.

The Foundation will use all your help to assist those people who are handicapped by various sight problems and need special attention.

Thank you very much for your help.